Stirred with Love

D1579816

Stirred with Love

MEL SHERRATT writing as
MARCIE STEELE

bookouture

Published by Bookouture

An imprint of StoryFire Ltd.
23 Sussex Road, Ickenham, UB10 8PN
United Kingdom

www.bookouture.com

ISBN: 978-1-910751-39-8

ACKNOWLEDGEMENTS

Writing as Mel Sherratt, I am well known for my crime thrillers and psychological suspense novels, where drama meets crime. But all my books are steeped in emotion, and that is the main theme throughout all my writing. I've written under the pen name of Marcie Steele for quite some time now, so when I had the opportunity to work with Bookouture, I snapped it up.

Thanks to my agent, Madeleine Milburn, for listening to me wittering on for the past twelve months about how much I really wanted to write another Marcie novel. Thanks too, to Oliver Rhodes for taking me on board. Having a professional team behind me is incredibly important and I struck lucky in lots of ways. I've known Keshini Naidoo and Kim Nash for many years and getting the chance to work with them has been incredible. Two excellent women who I am proud to call friends as well as colleagues.

Thanks to my coffee mates – Alison Niebieszczanski, Talli Roland and Sharon Sant. For always being there for me, whether it is listening to me chattering on excitedly, or giving me a shoulder to lean on, or just for coffee and cake – that's what friends are for. Thank you to my many readers who give me tremendous online encouragement. Also thanks to the Bookouture authors who have taken me under their wing, especially Angie Marsons and Caroline Mitchell (even though I am on the pink rather than the dark side.)

Finally, thanks to my fella, Chris who continues to support me and never fails me with his generosity and understanding. Only writers know how difficult it is to live with a writer... You are my rock, Chris. I'm so blessed to have you by my side.

CHAPTER ONE

'Don't you think it's the perfect way out for you?'

Kate Bradshaw glanced up at her friend with a puzzled expression. Louise Chatfield wasn't laughing. In fact, she wasn't even smiling. She seemed to be deadly serious.

Kate handed back the newspaper that she'd been given to read. 'I couldn't do that.' She shook her head. 'I want to leave Nick, not Brentside.'

'But you won't leave Nick, will you? So the other alternative is to leave Brentside – so that you won't be watching the main door like you are now in case he walks in and spoils your appetite.'

Kate hadn't realised she'd been that obvious and looked away guiltily.

Although there were an abundance of empty tables in the window area of Charley's Wine Bar, she'd chosen one further back where they wouldn't be seen from outside. Her husband, Nick, only worked two streets away. They'd often meet for lunch, but in recent months it was usually to try and patch things up from the night before. Today, she didn't want to be spotted by him at all.

Wearily, she opened her handbag, searched around until she found her mirror and flicked open the cover. Almost at once, she wished she hadn't bothered. Underneath the bright make-up, her blue eyes had lost their sparkle and her lips couldn't manage a pout. Her skin was flaky around her nose and she had a cluster of stress spots on her chin. She flicked the mirror shut again with a snap.

'Are you sure you're okay?' Louise asked.

Kate nodded. She continued to stare through the window, her eyes locked onto a couple in their mid-thirties talking animatedly as they walked hand in hand.

Louise followed her gaze before speaking again. 'You've got to leave him,' she said.

'You've been telling me that for months.'

'And I'll keep on telling you. Spare yourself the misery. He's not worth it. What were you arguing over this time? You never did tell me.'

Kate shrugged. The truth was, nowadays the slightest thing caused her and Nick to disagree.

'It's bullying tactics, if you ask me,' Louise continued. 'You know you can always crash at our place for a few nights?'

Kate gave Louise what she thought was a convincing smile, knowing full well that they'd known each other far too long for her not to see right through it.

'Brentside is my home,' she said, answering Louise's earlier question. 'Why should I leave?'

'Oh, like you have everything to live for here?' Louise scoffed. She pushed a blonde fringe away from her eyes. 'It's only forty minutes by train.'

'But a waitress, Lou?' Kate raised her eyebrows. 'I don't know the first thing about working in a café.'

'Don't be daft. I bet they'll want management types too.' Louise scanned the advert again, following the words with her index finger. She tapped it twice. 'It says here that help is needed to set up the business. You'd be good at that. And there are rooms provided so you don't even have to worry about finding somewhere to live. Anyway, who said anything about a café? It could be a restaurant. Or a wine bar, like this one.'

Kate scanned the room quickly before picking up her cappuccino. Even midweek, it was busy. Although she loved lunch breaks at Charley's because of its friendly atmosphere and its bright flip-back-in-time-to-the-seventies décor, she wasn't sure she'd want to work somewhere similar.

'I can't leave a permanent position,' she said moments later. 'It's not as easy nowadays to stay in work. And I know my job is hard at times, but it's challenging. And it pays well, with a company pension.'

'Jeez, Kate!' Louise waved to catch the waiter's attention as he stood in the middle of the room, holding a plate of food in each hand. 'You sound like you're sixty-two not thirty-two. What's that got to do with anything?'

Kate thought for a moment before she replied. 'I'd probably have to learn the ropes and somehow I can't see myself doing what he's doing,' she said, gesturing to the waiter. 'Besides, you know I don't give up that easily. I don't want to be a divorcee and I'm not about to leave Nick, so shut up and eat.'

'Will you stop beating yourself up over nothing!' Louise tutted, shaking her head in frustration. 'Just because your parents divorced and you found it traumatic as a child to live through, it doesn't mean that you should be chained to Nick for the rest of your life.'

'Yes, but…'

Louise threw Kate a steely look.

Kate sighed. She bit into her sandwich instead of arguing the point but it was hard for her to switch off.

Her parents' divorce when she was nine had affected her deeply, so when she'd married Nick, she'd been convinced she'd found her soul mate, and that they would be together forever. Kate had put a lot of work into their relationship, knowing that she didn't want to end up the same way as her mum and dad.

Yet for months now, as she'd sat crying on her own after Nick had stormed out following another bitter exchange of words, she'd been working out if she could afford to pay the bills on her salary alone. The feeling of coming home to an empty house that wouldn't be invaded by World War Three at least twice a week was extremely tempting.

But despite her watery threats to herself, Kate knew she didn't have the courage to go it alone. And if she was truthful, she was more frightened of that than of staying with Nick.

Covertly, she eyed the young couple at the next table. They were hunched forward sharing a menu, their heads barely an inch apart. The boy whispered something to the girl, who giggled, before moving nearer for a kiss. Kate lowered her eyes, embarrassed by her interest in something so intimate.

Louise folded over the newspaper so that she could see the advert in full before tucking into her food.

'Would you like to be a waiter/waitress with a difference? Do you have the imagination and flair to help me set up a new business in Somerley and contend with the competition out there? Would you like a room of your own and money in your pocket in exchange for enthusiasm and pride in your work? If so, pick up the phone. Excellent prospects for the right people.'

Kate wondered just exactly what being a waitress with a difference entailed. The room and the money parts sounded very appealing, especially at the moment, and she always took pride in her work. She looked over it again. Yes, she was definitely self-motivated and energetic. As far as skill required, she had got the lot.

'Where's Somerley?' she asked Louise, reaching over to pinch a chip from her plate.

'It's in Hedworth. About forty miles away.' Louise sniggered as Kate dropped it when her fingers began to burn. 'Let me look at it again.'

Kate passed the newspaper back to her. 'It says there are excellent prospects for the right people.'

Louise nodded. 'Surely it's got to be better than Brentside?'

Inwardly, Kate disagreed. She could think of far worse places to be raised and a thousand reasons why she shouldn't leave. And, she *did* like her job. After years of not knowing what she wanted to do – or indeed, what she was good at – trawling around from one office junior position to another, just before she'd met Nick she'd landed a job as a research assistant for Brentside Housing Association. Three years later, a project officer called Yvonne had decided to try her luck in Spain and Kate had been earmarked for her post. The role entailed writing reports for senior management, creating procedural documents for tenants to adhere to and working with residents' focus groups to ensure that they were complied with. A stickler for routine, forward planning and evaluating, Kate fitted into it naturally.

'So,' said Louise, interrupting Kate's thoughts and making her visibly jump. 'What do you think?'

'About what?'

'The *advert*. Is it Brentside or beyond?'

'Oh, I don't know.' Kate shrugged.

'Come off it. I can hear your brain whirring from here. You're actually giving it some thought, aren't you?'

Kate shook her head in amusement. 'Listen here, Miss Entrepreneur!' she teased, wagging a finger. 'Don't think I haven't worked out what you're up to. You've wanted my job for ages, you cheeky cat!'

Yet, as they tucked into their lunch, Kate thought about the advert again. Now, if she could leave all her problems behind, and not have to worry about anything but the future, then she would definitely be up for it.

If only life were that simple.

While Kate Bradshaw spent her lunch hour worrying about the state of her marriage, Chloe Ward was in no rush to start her day. Even though it was lunchtime, she'd only been out of bed for an hour. She sat in the kitchen, head resting on the table, willing herself to wake up.

There was a noise behind her and her brother, Ben, came into the kitchen.

'You haven't skived off another class?' he questioned as he threw down his car keys next to her.

'Mmmphwa,' was all Chloe could reply.

Moments later, he slid a mug over in her direction, moved a mass of her red curls away from her ear and shouted loudly. 'Coffee!'

'Frigging hell, Ben!' Chloe flinched. She lifted her head and promptly put it back down again.

'You young ones are always trying to burn the candle at both ends,' Ben mocked as he retrieved a cardboard box jammed with papers and folders from its hiding place in the larder unit. 'When I was eighteen, I never got into that much of a state.'

'You're only five years older than me.' Chloe lifted her throbbing head again, this time resting her chin in the crook of her hands. 'And it seems you've conveniently forgotten about last Friday night.'

'Unplanned nights are always the best,' Ben had to agree. 'But now I'm working, I can't afford the time to party often. You'll understand when you have to get a job.'

'Speaking of which – why are you home from work?'

'I can't find a document I need. I thought it was in the office but I've looked everywhere, so I was wondering if I'd left it here.'

Chloe glanced at her brother as he opened first one folder, then another. Full of the morning sun, their dad would say. Taller than her by a couple of inches, unless she was wearing heels, Ben had inherited the Ward stick insect profile, as well as blond hair from his father. It was cut short and spiky to hide the fact that it was receding rapidly. Since graduating from university, he'd been a trainee solicitor at MacDonald, Furbur & Co. Chloe still felt proud when she saw how smart he looked in collar, tie and tailored trousers instead of his usual jeans and trainers.

Pulling a face at him as he emptied the contents of the box onto the table, Chloe took her coffee through into the conservatory and relaxed back into the wicker settee, her eyes vaguely wandering over the garden. The late spring weather looked promising as the sun shone brightly – too brightly for her – through the remainder of a few wispy clouds. With a flick of her wrist, she closed the vertical blind nearest to her and laid back on the settee. Thankfully, her dad was away on a conference today – at least *he* wouldn't be able to catch her bunking off.

'Here.' Ben handed her a ham sandwich. 'I've made enough for two.'

'Why can't I just stay at home all day and party all night?' Chloe questioned as he sat down next to her, pushing her feet out of the way before he squashed them. 'I don't want to work.'

Ben turned to face her, eyebrows raised questioningly. 'You mean stay at home all by yourself? You'd go mad with no one to talk to, Miss Chatterbox.'

Chloe grinned. Never one to create an awkward silence, this character trait had gotten her into many scrapes; with the teachers at sixth form always asking her to be quiet.

'I'll have to do something, I suppose, or I'll die of boredom,' she said. 'After uni, I could get a part-time job. Maybe even travel.'

'Dad won't like that.' Ben shook his head. 'Remember how hard I had to work on him so that he'd let me go to Spain? He wants to see what he gets for his money when you pass your finals.'

'But you took a year out!'

'Yes, but men are entitled to go off for their last taste of freedom because they have at least forty years of solid slog ahead of them. Women only have to work a few years before they start a family.'

'That's so sexist!' Chloe retorted. 'And I might not want to have any children. Therefore I'm entitled to take a year out because I'll have nearly fifty years of solid slog ahead of me. Women have to work longer before they retire.'

'You'll never win that argument.' Ben shielded his eyes as the sun moved around the room. 'Dad won't let you take a year out because he knows you'll never go back. He's fought to keep you there for the past two years.'

'Fought is a very good choice of word,' Chloe nodded, recalling the times when their father had arrived home from work early to find her lounging in her pyjamas when she should have been attending a class – a bit like today really.

Suddenly, Ben raised a piece of paper in the air. 'Found it!' He gulped down the remains of his coffee and stood up. Before heading out of the room, he threw a newspaper into her lap.

'Maybe – because I know you won't be bothering with school today – you should check the situations vacant column. There's bound to be a job cleaning toilets. Just your level.'

Once Ben had left, and the house became quiet again, Chloe couldn't help but envy her brother. Ben had aspired to be a solicitor since he'd left school, but Chloe hadn't got a clue what she wanted to do in life, although she knew working in an office wouldn't be her style. It would be far too quiet and she wouldn't want to complete boring paperwork all the time. She would die of boredom after a week or so. But, apart from that? Nothing.

She relaxed back in the settee again. If her dad had anything to do with things, she would be off to university in October anyway. He'd been badgering her for ages to make up her mind what she wanted to do. So, best to get on with it.

Once her exams were out of the way.

CHAPTER TWO

Kate's fifteen minute drive from work was a nightmare that evening but, finally, after calling at the supermarket and battling her way around the busy aisles, she was home.

'Hey, Rosie!' Kate plonked her shopping bags onto the kitchen worktop so that she could greet the mound of excitement at her feet. She bent to ruffle the greying beard under the Jack Russell's chin. 'Come on then, girl. Let's grab your lead and have a quick stroll around the block. I'm dying for a coffee.'

After Rosie was walked and fed, Kate dropped down onto the leather two-seater and flicked her feet up to the side. When she and Nick had moved into their house six years ago, the kitchen had been the size of a small box room but knocking through into the equally small dining room had cleverly combined the two into a large airy space. Fitted out with beech shaker units and cream worktops, they had been planning to fit French doors on the outer wall next year to bring in even more light.

The phone rang as she was reaching for her first sip of coffee. It was Nick.

'Hi, you've only just caught me,' she told him. 'I had a detour home and then I had to queue for ages in the supermarket. What do you fancy for supper? I have steak or chicken in –'

'I'm sorry, Kate. I have to work late.'

'Oh, Nick! You promised to be early tonight!'

'I know, but I might be about to clinch a deal on the Matthews' cottage and you know how much commission I'd receive. I'll make it up to you at the weekend.'

'I won't be here,' she reminded him. 'It's Stacey's hen party.' Stacey was an old school friend of Kate's and Kate had been looking forward to the weekend for some time.

'Can we discuss this later?' Nick broke into her thoughts. 'I'll have to go to football training straight from here. I'll be home around ten. Bye.'

Getting to her feet with a huge sigh, Kate pulled out a box from the freezer, ripped open the packaging and began to pierce the plastic covering with more force than was really necessary.

How could he do this to her again, she seethed, after all he'd promised? Nick had always kept himself fit by playing football on a Sunday morning but recently he'd taken to staying on after the match for lunch with the lads and then going out in the evening to analyse their game, as well as training for the next one during the week.

And *he* had the audacity to moan at her when *she* wanted to go out on the odd occasion?

Kate tossed the ready meal into the microwave, slammed the door shut and punched in the allotted time. Pouring herself a large glass of wine, she switched on the evening news and slouched down into the settee.

Dinner for one it was then.

Later that same evening, Chloe was in her bedroom, trying desperately to get into gear for today's bout of revision. Just for a moment, she imagined what it would be like if she didn't have A level exams to sit in three weeks. Last September, as her second year in sixth form was about to start, she was supposed to have sent out applications for university places but, intentionally, she hadn't got round to it in time. Her dad had been furious, but until she knew what she wanted to do, she couldn't see the point of more time in a classroom. Ever since, though, he'd been badgering her to think about what to do once she knew her grades.

She stretched her arms above her head while her eyes vaguely wandered over the garden, the view far more appealing than the textbooks spread out in front of her. On the desk, her mobile phone beeped and, unable to resist the lure of a message, she picked it up. But it was only from Christian, her man of three dates.

Well, hardly a man at all, Chloe sighed, that was the problem. Although they were the same age, Christian seemed so juvenile. Chloe wanted a man with a car who could take her out to places, not a student with a Saturday job in Carphone Warehouse. Her friend, Manda, always went on at her about Chloe's lack of interest in boys her own age. But then again, Manda hadn't had to grow up as quickly as Chloe.

Chloe had been seven when her mum, Christine, was killed. The family were on their way home from a wedding when a newly qualified driver flew around a blind bend, hurtling toward them at sixty miles an hour. On the wrong side of the road, he'd hit the passenger side with a tremendous thud. Because she'd been strapped up in the back of the car with Ben, the two of them had both escaped serious injury, while their father, Graham, had pulled his neck, strained his lower back muscles and broken his left arm. But Christine was trapped in the car, unconscious. Chloe could still clearly remember sitting in the back of the ambulance whilst the firemen worked to free her. Ben, at twelve too big to sit on his dad's lap, sat on it anyway.

Eventually the paramedics had insisted that the three of them should go on ahead to the hospital so that they could get checked out. It had taken another hour until they'd finally freed Christine from the indistinguishable mound of metal. Unfortunately, she'd taken the brunt of the impact and, although the medical staff who treated her had refused to give up for what seemed like ages, she was pronounced dead at the hospital. The young slip of a boy who crashed into them had been driving his father's new car. He received a six-month suspended jail sentence and a small fine. They received a life sentence of grief and unfulfilled opportunities.

All things considered, Graham had brought them up well. Chloe really admired him for what he'd done.

It must have been hard for him to put his children first when he was suffering so much pain. She knew it was his manners and calm attitude that had made her into the strong redhead she was today. Her hair, with its natural spiral curls, was forever being swept up from her face in a way her dad often told her reminded him of her mum. Her eyes were the same shade of green, her stature tall and thin like her father and brother. Yet, although he was the best dad possible, Chloe still wished she had a mum to share her dreams with. Even after all these years she regularly woke up, the images of that night still vivid.

The mobile phone beeped again as another message arrived. Not bothering to open it, Chloe pushed the phone across her desk and reached for her books once more. Four more weeks and it would all be over. At least then she would be able to relax and take it easy for a while.

Reluctantly, she turned the pages but her mind kept wandering back to the advertisement she'd read earlier. Someone was after waitresses to work in nearly Somerley. Chloe fancied doing something different over the summer. She stared through the window while her mind worked its way through the finer details. She imagined the café in Somerley to be a favourite meeting place – and a place where she could make some money of her own. It might not be too boring, just enough to keep her interest until the university term started. And she was sure she could sell the idea of a summer job to her dad, Mr Workaholic.

But, let's not get *too* carried away, Chloe reminded herself. How many times had she heard her friends complain about the menial work they did for a pittance of a wage? So was a job waiting on tables really what she wanted to do, even if it wasn't going to be forever?

Chloe checked her watch: seven thirty. There might not be anyone there but she could leave a message if there was an answer machine, and at least it would make her sound keen by phoning the night before. Never one to let the grass grow under her feet, she reached for her mobile with eagerness this time.

Lily Mortimer checked over her list and made a few changes before swapping the notepad in her hand for a mug of hot chocolate. Only then did she contemplate what she was about to do. Making decisions again was one thing, but re-opening the café?

She moved her tiny frame to get comfortable on the chair, becoming more sensitive to the gloominess around her. The room she sat in needed much more than a lick of paint to brighten it up. Once, it had been bursting with life. Twelve tables, full of chattering customers all enjoying her homemade cakes and Bernard's thick sliced toast. Lily could clearly picture him dashing around, clearing the debris and complaining about the weather, making customers smile with anecdotes of his time working on the railways.

It had been tough for her to see how illness had dragged him down during the last few years of his life.

Only three months had passed since his death in February and Lily could still feel his presence. When she woke up, the first thing she thought of was Bernard. During the day she could sense him watching over her. When she went to bed, she rubbed her hand across his pillow. She knew he was there, watching her every move as she closed her eyes, having endured another long day without him.

Would he be proud of what she was about to do, or annoyed with her for meddling? Lily knew what a huge risk it was. What would happen if her plan failed? What if she couldn't make things work on her own, without Bernard beside her? So many places in Somerley sold food now. Even the newsagent around the corner made sandwiches. Maybe that had been the reason why Lil's Pantry had dwindled over the past few years?

No, Lily told herself as she took a sip of her drink. The business had dwindled because Bernard had been dying. It had been left to die with him. But new blood would change that.

She knew it seemed a strange plan, but what did the future hold for her? Time spent alone was the last thing she needed. Re-opening the café would be her way of dealing with Bernard's death. Instead of sitting around feeling sorry for herself, Lily would be *doing* something.

She popped out two aspirins from their silver packaging, hoping to alleviate her aches and pains. Then she picked up the notepad again, smiling fondly. Bernard used to laugh at how many things she would write down. 'You're always making lists,' he'd tease her. But she couldn't deal with not being prepared for every eventuality, plus she'd found it amusing to make him shake his head by adding something else to it.

Worryingly, it was her body letting her down now and she knew before long she wouldn't be able to prepare for every eventuality. But she didn't want to dwell on that right now.

Where was she? Ah, yes, interview questions.

CHAPTER THREE

Nick hadn't arrived home that night until quarter to eleven. By that time, Kate's frustration had turned to blind rage and her accusation of him not wanting to come home had started them arguing.

They'd ended the day sleeping back to back.

Things didn't seem any better the following morning. In the icy atmosphere of their bedroom, Kate lay in bed while Nick dressed for work. Hearing Rosie pattering about downstairs, she whistled when Nick opened the door out onto the landing. He frowned as the dog dashed past his feet.

'Don't let her jump onto the bed,' he chastised.

Kate waited until she heard him go downstairs, then patted the duvet defiantly. Rosie jumped up without a moment's hesitation.

'Good morning, my lovely.' Kate ruffled the dog's fur under her chin. At least Rosie was always pleased to see her.

Eight years ago, Rosie had been abandoned in one of the properties owned by Kate's employers. The tenants had made a run for it without leaving a forwarding address. Rosie and her three brothers had been left behind too. When the housing officer brought them to the office to await the arrival of the dog warden, Rosie had won Kate over as soon as she'd picked her up.

Rosie licked Kate's hand a couple of times before promptly curling up in a ball to doze off again.

Kate gently tugged at her collar. 'Not this morning, I'm afraid. Places to go and people to see.'

Dressed and showered thirty minutes later, Kate drew back the curtains and noticed that Nick's car was still in the driveway. Her shoulders dropped: great, that was all she needed this morning, his miserable face putting her off her cereal. Carefully, she arranged the heavy muslin into two perfect arches and then made her way downstairs to face him.

Nick was sitting at the table when she walked into the kitchen. He met her eyes for a moment before turning away to continue his drink.

Well, sod you, thought Kate. She flicked on the kettle, grabbed a mug from the rack and raised the volume on the radio.

Rosie headed straight for her bowl. Kate spotted the morning's newspaper folded over on the table and reached across for it.

'I want that,' said Nick.

'Oh, it does speak then,' Kate replied coldly.

Nick didn't acknowledge her. Instead, he snatched the paper from out of her grasp.

'But I want to flick through it before you go to work,' she protested.

'I'm going in a minute.'

'I'll only be a minute.'

Nick slammed down his mug, the contents dripping over his clean shirt. Kate hid a smirk as he tried to brush them off with his hand.

'Why do you always have to wind me up, Kate?'

'Oh, take the blasted newspaper if it makes you feel better!'

'Don't be so pathetic.'

'Don't be so childish then.'

'You're the one who's childish.'

'*Me?* You're the one who thinks he's still sixteen. Going out playing football, drinking with your mates and leaving me here of an evening. If I weren't so sure, I'd think you're trying to tell me that you'd rather be single again.'

'Oh, here we go again.'

'Single, with no responsibilities.' Kate popped two rounds of bread into the toaster and deliberately kept her back to him. 'That's what you really want, isn't it?'

Nick stood up, shoved the newspaper inside his briefcase and clicked the lid shut. Much to Kate's annoyance, he then switched off the radio. She stared at him until he lifted his eyes to meet hers, his look dark and menacing. But she refused to be warned off.

'I'm right, aren't I?' she asked.

'Maybe, but not for the reasons you've given.' He paused before continuing. 'You make me feel like you don't want to be around me anymore.'

Kate kept her eyes locked on his, for fear of giving her innermost secrets away. *Could* he read her mind?

'You only make an effort when you're going out with your friends.'

'No, I don't!' she cried, insulted by its very meaning. 'You know I never leave the house without mascara and lipstick. And I always try to look –'

'I meant making an effort for me.'

'That's laughable, when you're hardly at home for me to make an effort for.'

Nick raised his hands in the air. 'See what I mean? You're going to twist everything I've said now to your advantage. That's so fucking selfish.'

He walked past her as if to leave the room, but Kate stopped him with a hand on his arm. In the moment she took to catch a breath, her eyes skimmed over every familiar characteristic of his face: the small chip in his front tooth that used to make him look sweet and innocent, indigo eyes that used to bewitch her, the lips that she used to love to nibble. Kate could see herself beginning to despise him. The scowl on his face did nothing to deter her and she carried on regardless.

'If you really want to know what's wrong in Kate's world, I'm tired of all this arguing,' she admitted. 'I'm tired of coming home to an empty house. I'm tired of finding things to do to occupy my time. Our sex life has become so infrequent that it reminds me of a scheduled trip to the dentist. I'm fed up of you never finding time for me when you find time for your friends –'

'That's because you'd rather moan at me and –'

'Don't try and change the subject!' Rosie flinched and jumped into her basket. Kate lowered her voice before continuing. 'You know I hardly go out, and I get that we need to spend time apart, but I'm not prepared to wait in for you most evenings while you're out enjoying yourself. I'm too independent for that and I'm not going to apologise for it. It's what attracted you to me in the first instance.'

Nick faltered. 'You know that's not what I meant. I –'

Kate moved away. 'I want to spend more time with you but sometimes I feel like I don't know you anymore. I want us to have fun *together*, like we used to, going out for the day, lunching, enjoying each other's company. And if that's not what you want anymore, then I'm…'

Kate stared directly at him. The thud, thud of her heart and the uncontrollable shaking of her hands made her recognise that with the mention of a few choice words she would blow her cover and burst into tears. She couldn't give him the upper hand. Quickly, she chose a few words of her own.

'Then I'm leaving.'

* * *

Just before eleven that morning, Chloe steered her car into the lane which would take her towards Somerley. Her foot slammed on the brake as the traffic lights worked against her, but at least it gave her time to check the slip of paper on which she had drawn an array of arrows and circles. 11, Church Square was where she was heading, if she could only get off this ridiculously large traffic island.

Chloe had been surprised to feel excitement begin to bubble up inside her about five miles from her destination. Before she'd started out, she'd done some research on the internet and found out that the northern city of Hedworth was made up of four towns, Somerley being one of its most industrial areas and Hedworth the largest at the centre. It was famous for its transport museum built in the late eighties, but Chloe hadn't wanted to know anything regarding its history. She'd quickly clicked onto the link that would inform her of Hedworth's nightlife and had been pleasantly surprised to find that the city had a population of 165,000, four colleges of further education, a university, five decent night clubs and a four star rating when it came to a night out in its many pubs and wine bars. Perfect.

She drove on and factories and warehouses began to be replaced by neat rows of pre-war semi-detached houses. A sharp left, and another, and a final right gave her a tiny glimpse of Church Square up ahead. Once she'd parked, she hurried back out into the open space. There was a church to her left, scaffolding erected around its walls. In the centre of the square was a huge oak tree, obviously taking centre-stage long before the block-paving and wrought iron fencing had been added. A triangle section of grass decorated each corner, with four wooden benches underneath the shade of the branches.

She ran her eyes along the row of properties across the square. Number eleven was the only one with double-fronted access, two half-glass panelled doors at its middle, and set back from the pavement. Either side of the doors, there were two windows. To her left, the spacious bay window had a low wall beneath it. The wall on the right side a few bricks higher, almost level with the panel in the doors, had a straight pane of glass above it.

Confused, Chloe looked down at the paper in her hand and back up again. It seemed to be the right place but the closed sign wasn't the only unwelcoming sight. Swirls of orange and yellow framed each of the windows, café-style nets hung forlornly in front. As she drew closer, Chloe became conscious that it wasn't closed for lunch. It was closed for the day, the week. Maybe it hadn't been open for weeks – or months.

She crossed the road and stole a peek through the window to the right of the doorway. The large room was dark, as if somehow forgotten. The furniture looked old and drab, chairs stacked precariously on top of tables.

'Hello, you must be Chloe.'

Chloe stepped back from the window and looked down to see someone standing at her side. It took her by surprise. She hadn't expected anyone so old. The woman was small and thin, wearing a navy skirt and matching jacket. Her mouth curved into a smile, the clear blue of her eyes looking out of place inside the creases of her skin. Her grey hair was cut short with roller curls in an elegant style.

As Chloe smiled at her, the woman held out a wrinkled hand, the nails decorated a similar colour to her lipstick.

'I'm Lily,' she said. 'Why don't you come in? It's not as bad as it seems.'

As Lily went into the building, Chloe wondered what she had let herself in for. She hoped she hadn't driven all the way there for nothing. Still, although it was hardly the buzzy place she had dreamt about, she might as well go in and see what it had to offer.

CHAPTER FOUR

'I don't know how you've put up with him for so long,' said Louise, fighting her way through the busy wine bar to a quiet corner she'd spotted. She put down two glasses and a bottle of wine before hoisting herself onto a tubular bar stool. 'I'd have left him a long time ago.'

'I'm sure you would.' Kate glanced at Louise as she climbed onto the stool beside her. 'But you know me, Lou. I'm gutless.' She turned away before she could add anything else. Talking about Nick was the last thing she wanted to do. Since their latest argument the other morning, they'd been tip-toeing around each other. So far she'd texted him twice but he hadn't bothered to reply.

It seemed a little strange being in one of Brentside's local wine bars yet apparently being away for the weekend. Kate couldn't get her head around the logic but Stacey, so engrossed with her wedding, had decided that she didn't want to be far away in case anything went wrong on the weekend before her big day. So Stacey had booked them all into the Grand Hotel, smack in the middle of the town, and ordered them to attend a girlie shopping spree tomorrow as well as today, including a boozy Sunday lunch. It certainly beat waiting for Nick to get home from football training.

They'd only been in Liberties Bar for half an hour, yet the hen was slightly inebriated to say the least. About a dozen girls had turned up, all congregated noisily around the bar in the middle of the room.

Seeing Stacey in a white dress, tiny veil and an L-plate attached to her chest had reminded Kate of her own hen party. She'd bought a new dress for the occasion and absolutely refused to parade around in silly bridal things. But six women had forced her into the ladies' and pulled it off regardless. A few minutes later she'd emerged, looking even more ridiculous than Stacey. Kate had been mortified and had taken no part in the dressing up of Stacey on her big night out with the girls.

'What's with the long face?' Shelley, the bride's sister enquired as she sidled over to them, hoisting up her multi-coloured boob tube as she did so. 'You look like a cat's just peed in your handbag.'

Kate smiled, wondering where Shelley had picked up that phrase. 'I'm fine, really,' she replied.

'She's having man troubles,' said Louise.

'Don't tell me you're not happy with that bloke of yours!' Shelley looked on in disbelief. 'I'll do you a swap for my Darren any day.'

'Looks aren't everything,' said Kate.

'But he's gorgeous,' Shelley slurred. She swayed dangerously towards Kate, stopping so close to her face she nearly collided with her nose. 'Your Nick, I mean. Not my Darren.' She snorted like a pig.

Kate turned her head away from the stench of alcohol as Louise made a circling motion next to her temple.

'Who's gorgeous?' Stacey asked, as she finally got to them and steadied herself on the table.

Shelley pointed at Kate. 'Her Nick.'

'Who? Oh, yeah, I remember him.' Stacey stared through half-closed eyes. 'He reminds me of a movie hero – someone handsome who could sweep me off my feet.'

Nick reminded Kate of a movie hero all right, but she was thinking more along the lines of *Nightmare on Elm Street* rather than *Notting Hill*. Still, Stacey had a point. Nick did look after himself. He always had a hint of stubble, with dark artfully mussed up hair. His dress style was smart casual, suiting his medium build and, even though she hated how he'd started to scowl at her recently, he did have the most amazing eyes.

'Do you mind,' she said with mock indignation. 'That's my husband you're talking about.'

'He *is* good-looking, though.' Stacey lunged forward, someone pushing her from behind as they moved past their group.

'You're getting married next weekend. You're *supposed* to have eyes for no other man.'

'Yes, but you know what they say about a last fling. Do you think you can loan him out for the night?'

Kate raised her eyebrows. 'It's a good job I'm not the jealous type.'

'At least he gives you some attention.' Shelley leaned forward and helped herself to their wine. 'That's more than my Darren gives me. I've only been married for two years and already he treats me like a sister. You're really lucky.'

Kate watched Shelley knock back her drink, slam down her glass and totter back to the bar. Before long, she'd thrown herself into the arms of some poor bloke who'd had the misfortune to look her way.

'Isn't it funny what people on the outside see?' Kate turned back to Louise again. 'I don't think I'm lucky.'

'No, you're just married to an arsehole.'

'I still love him, Lou. It's just…'

As tears welled up in her eyes, Louise touched Kate's arm. 'I know. It's just not fun at the moment.'

Kate sniffed and formed a weak smile. She wondered if she should change her drink, go for the pass-out zone to dull the pain. She skimmed her eyes around the room, full from wall to wall with people enjoying themselves. It made her realise that she had two choices about how the night could end.

'Hey?' she nudged Louise's elbow, 'you know that bouncer you mentioned at Macey's? Do you think you can swing free entry for all of us?'

'But, why a *waitress*?' said Graham. 'You'll always have a job in my office. You know I'd pay better than a small café.'

'Of course I know that.' Chloe tried to dazzle her dad with a smile. Catching the last rays of sunshine on Sunday afternoon, she linked her arm casually through his as they walked around the garden.

Home for the Ward family for the past ten years had been a new build, four-bedroom house, part of a development on the outskirts of Penlingham. As she'd grown up, Chloe had realised that Graham had chosen it because it held memories for no one and didn't require any work doing to it before they moved in. With two young children to look after, he'd needed somewhere for them to feel safe and secure.

It was one of the reasons why she wanted her dad's approval about moving to Somerley for the summer. Very often she felt envious of her friends, like Manda. Pleasing only one parent was hard work sometimes: she couldn't use persuasion tactics. The only negotiator she had was Ben. There was no way she'd get Maddy to do her dirty work.

Maddy was her father's partner and had been with Graham for three years, moving in shortly after her divorce came through last summer. She was in her early forties, with long,

blonde hair that fell way below her shoulders and a toned figure that wouldn't have looked out of place on someone in their
late twenties. Her outlook on life suited her style of clothing –
young, yet sensible. Subtle, yet sexy.

Even so, Chloe wasn't certain that she was right for her dad.
She wasn't convinced that the reason for that was that she still
felt loyalty towards her mum's memory, as her friend Manda
would often say. It was much simpler than that – she just didn't
like Maddy.

'I like the idea of being there from the start,' she continued.
'And I want to stand on my own two feet.'

'But you'll be doing that in October when you go to university. Surely you can stay at home until then?'

'Are you trying to say that you'll miss me?'

Chloe turned her head towards his and raised her hand to
shield her eyes as she focused on his face, practically a mirror image of Ben's. Graham looked younger than his fifty-one
years, his clear skin showing minimal lines, and what hair he
had remaining cropped close to his head. The same emerald
green eyes always stared back at her, and at weekends his tall,
thin build would more often than not be swinging a club at his
golf club. Chloe had always been proud to show him off to her
friends, even when Manda had called him a 'last chance trendy.'

'You've got to be kidding! What could I possibly miss about
you?' he said. 'The times you've forgotten your key and it's been
four thirty in the morning? The times you've said you'll pay me
back when you earn a decent salary? The times –'

'You *will* miss me!' Chloe deposited a kiss on his cheek and
opened the gate that led them back towards the house. Anticipation fizzed up inside her again as she thought of summer away
from home, money that she'd earn herself.

'It's not that far away, Dad,' she added. 'And even though Somerley looks like a small place, Hedworth's only a couple of miles away and that promises much more. There'll be new people to meet and new places to visit.'

'You're going there to work though, remember?'

Chloe nodded, remembering her interview. At first she'd looked around the drab room in dismay, but after a while, she'd warmed to the place as much as she had to Lily. Soon after, she was imagining how it would look if it was given a bit of colour. Maybe cream or white walls, so that it was much lighter. One thing it did need was comfier seats, she recalled, aching after sitting still for almost half an hour.

'I think it needs a lot of work to get it good enough to open again,' she admitted.

Graham nodded. 'What's your new boss like?'

'She seems really nice, although I think she's too old to open a new business.'

'Chloe, you think *I'm* old.'

'Oh, she's much older than you.'

Graham pulled her in close and gave her shoulder a gentle squeeze. Chloe loved it when he did that – it made her feel loved and protected. She smiled, pleased to realise that he would miss her. The house would be much quieter without her music blaring out at every opportunity. And she'd be the first one to admit that her clothes and footwear were spread untidily throughout the house. She'd miss him too, and her brother.

'I will miss you,' Graham broke into her thoughts as if reading her mind. He kissed the top of her head. 'You might be a pain in the proverbial, but you'll always be my baby girl.'

* * *

Late Sunday evening, dropping numerous glossy carrier bags as she attempted to wave goodbye to Louise, Kate shrugged her colossal handbag from her shoulder and retrieved her keys.

'Nick?' she cried as she pushed open the door, but the unmistakable sound of Rosie racing along the narrow hallway was the only thing to greet her. 'Oh, hello, girl. Have you missed me? Ow. Get off my legs, Rosie.' She laughed. 'Let me in!'

Kate dashed through to the kitchen and set everything down in a heap on the floor, shooed Rosie out of the back door for a wee and flicked on the kettle, then the radio.

One by one, she undid the pearly buttons on her coat. Then she went back through to the hall to admire it in the full-length mirror. Scarlet and cream swirls adorned its three-quarter-length style. She stuffed her hands deep inside its pockets and, swinging her arms out to the side, twirled around in a circle to admire every possible angle.

Kate still couldn't believe she'd been bold enough to buy it this morning. Usually she'd go for a classic, hard-wearing design – something that would never age in the fashion market – but the coat had caught her eye as she'd waited for Louise to try on one of many outfits. It had been priced up at a small fortune; however she'd managed to get it for half of its original price in the sale. She reached inside and fingered the label she hadn't yet had the heart to remove and laughed with glee as she saw the price slashed from absolutely ridiculous to more than a possibility.

Peering closer, she ran a finger underneath her eyes to rub off the remains of her smudged, black mascara.

Most of her make-up had disappeared over the day and the dark shade of her bobbed hair contrasted harshly with her now pale lips and complexion. She grinned at her reflection. It had been great fun to go shopping with a bunch of girls. She hadn't laughed so much in ages, especially when they'd nearly been thrown out of Debenhams for being too noisy. Hen party or no hen party, Shelley shouldn't have pulled down the trousers on one of the shop dummies.

With Rosie hell bent on rummaging through her carrier bags, Kate reached for a biscuit and began to empty her overnight case. The eight thirty news told of doom and gloom just as her stomach gave out a sorrowful groan. How she regretted not taking Stacey up on the offer to include her in their takeaway order. Instead, she'd opted to come home – to an empty house.

She wondered what time Nick would be back, at the same time wishing that he'd made the effort to wait in for her, especially after they'd had words the other night. But deep down, she'd known he wouldn't be here. She'd left two messages today as well as yesterday and he hadn't replied to any.

It was only after she returned from taking Rosie for a quick walk that she noticed the red light flashing on the answer machine. She frowned. Had she overlooked that from before or had she just missed the call while she was out? She pressed the play button.

'Erm, hi, Kate, it's Nick. I know there isn't an easy way to say this. I… when you get home, Kate, I won't be there. I've packed up my things and moved out.'

Kate looked up quickly from the leaflet she'd plucked from the post piled at the side of the telephone.

'We've both known that things haven't been right between us for some time, but I always thought we could work through our differences. The thing is, Kate. I can't live like we have for the past few months. I… oh fuck, Kate. I'll never be able to find the right words. I suppose there aren't any really. I'll be in touch later. Erm… bye.'

Kate pressed the play button again. And again. Every time Nick spoke, the tears in her eyes stung that little bit more. She stared at her reflection in the mirror above the fireplace and held onto the marble shelf for support. She watched as the colour drained rapidly from her face. Her image blurred over, his voice faded out and she fell to the floor in a heap.

'No.' Her hand went to her mouth as tears poured down her face. Please God, there must be some mistake. She shook her head as if doing so would rid her of the truth. He's joking. There's no way he'd *leave* me.

But he'd just said that he'd packed his things and…

Kate hauled herself to her feet and took the stairs three at a time. Checking the bathroom, she saw that his toothbrush had gone. She opened the cabinet to reveal empty spaces where he kept his toiletries hidden. Slamming the door shut, she sprinted through to their bedroom. It certainly seemed the same but when she flung open his wardrobe door, the empty coat hangers banged and rattled against each other.

There wasn't even an odd sock hanging around in any of the drawers.

In the spare room, she caught her breath as she registered that his prized record collection was no longer there. When Kate had first visited Nick's flat, she couldn't believe how many vinyl records he owned. They'd spent nights poring over favourite hits that brought teenage memories flooding back – fooled around to many a good tune right here on this carpet since they'd bought this house together. And she'd never been short of ideas for presents. All she'd had to do was log on to the internet and she could come up with something interesting for him to meticulously place in alphabetical order somewhere on the rows and rows of shelves that now stood bare.

She ran downstairs, into the living room. She scanned the room searching for… searching for… where was the note? He must have left one. Her eyes searched desperately but there wasn't even that. While her back was turned, Nick had left everything they'd built together over the past ten years. He'd left the house that she so desperately loved every inch of. He'd left the belongings they'd saved hard for. Worse than that, she realised, all the time she'd been trying on her stupid coat, she'd been oblivious to the fact that he'd left her without an explanation. He didn't even have the courage to face her with a goodbye.

Despair seeping in for the second time, Kate picked up the phone and pressed number one speed dial.

Not sure if the ringing she could hear was coming from the receiver or her ears, she prayed that Nick had left his mobile on.

It was switched off.

CHAPTER FIVE

The luminous dial on the clock radio read six thirty-three. Through the early morning shadows, Kate stared into the empty space beside her. Where Nick should have been, the sheets were cool as she rolled over and stretched her arm across to his side of the bed. She ran her fingers up and down, trying to sense his presence. Her arm longed to reach out and drape itself around his waist. Her legs felt the need to be entwined with his. Her whole body lurched forward to nestle into his back.

She grabbed his pillow, drew up her knees but squeezing shut her eyes only brought his image to the forefront of her mind. She threw back the duvet and pulled on her dressing gown. Fresh tears formed as she tried to get one last wipe out of a corner of soggy tissue.

The slightest move of her head knocked her off balance. She'd been crying all night, the pain so intense.

She reached into the bathroom cabinet for painkillers and moved aside a deodorant canister. Suddenly, her fingers clasped greedily around a half empty bottle of Nick's aftershave that she must have missed last night in her hurry. More tears burnt the back of her eyes as taking even the tiniest of sniffs took her back to evenings at the pub, of nights cuddled up together. It smelt of sex, of Indian takeaways, of fooling around.

As much as it reminded her of nights in on the settee, nights out to the cinema, it also reminded her of the many recent arguments, making up as she cried on his shoulder. In a fit of anger, she tipped the contents into the sink.

Until yesterday, she'd pushed away the thought that their relationship was coming to an end. She would rather think that they could make it work again than admit defeat. But now that Nick had shown it wasn't possible – their marriage really was over – she didn't know whether to be upset or relieved.

She dragged herself downstairs and let Rosie out into the back garden. The kitchen was a mess. The cooker propped up the shopping bags she'd had so much fun filling yesterday, discarded contents spilling out over the floor. Crumpled tissues littered the table. After being unable to contact Nick last night, Kate had rung Louise. She'd been back with her within half an hour and had stayed until after midnight, trying to comfort her.

Rain lashed at the window, reflecting her mood as it bounced noisily off the sill. Through swollen lids as she waited for the kettle to boil, she stared out over the garden. They'd spent a small fortune on it last April and some of the many plants and shrubs were beginning to grow again. Nick had covered half of the space with decking, then scattered geraniums and petunias around the border of the lawn to add a touch of colour. She remembered how, on the first night it was finished they'd sat on the wooden bench in the glow of their newly fitted garden lanterns, drinking hot chocolate as a toast to their success. Now he'd spoiled that memory – erased it clear, leaving her with a sordid reminder of how things had changed.

Endless questions scrambled for attention in her mind as she sunk into the settee and pulled her knees up to her chest.

How long had Nick planned this?

Why hadn't he talked to her first?

Where did he go last night? He couldn't stay with his parents. They'd go berserk if they found out what he'd done. Well, at least she hoped they would. She'd always got on well with them. No, he couldn't be with them.

What about Mark? But he was married to Sharon, and Kate had become close to her through the years. She'd never let him stay.

What about Steve? He'd worked with Nick for a long time. But hadn't his wife recently had a baby?

No, that would be out of the question. Nick wouldn't want to intrude.

She pulled her dressing gown tighter around her body for comfort as paranoia began to creep in. Had he really been working late all those nights? For all she knew, he could have another woman tucked away for reference whenever he fancied a quickie. Perhaps he wanted more than a mere fumble over the photocopier. A swift blowjob in the men's toilets. Perhaps he felt like a long drawn out session with her now.

The tears fell again as she tortured herself with images of Nick with another woman. Maybe they hadn't had much fun recently, but the thought of him licking the inside of another woman's thigh was beyond Kate's comprehension. Still it played over and over in her mind. She didn't want to think about her competition but she couldn't stop herself either.

More to the point, she asked herself constantly, why had he gone without an explanation? Surely of all people, he knew how devastating it would be for her, after her traumatic childhood.

Kate could clearly recall the day her father had left, as if it were yesterday. It had followed her ninth birthday. Her parents had thrown her a party, inviting all the children in the street that had been home for her since she was born. Lots of her school friends had come too and she'd had a great afternoon. Little did she know that was the last time she'd see them all together.

A few months later, their home had been sold and Kate and her mum moved to Brentside to stay with Nana and Granddad Morton until they found somewhere more permanent. Her father promised to come and see her as soon as he had settled into his new job and the flat that came with it. Joseph Portman became a pub landlord. Not in a pleasant pub, but a backstreet dive, full of the scum of the earth. It took Kate some years to realise just how well he had fitted in.

At first, he kept to his word and Kate was picked up early every Sunday morning. Most of the time she'd been made to stay upstairs in the huge flat of endless, empty rooms with whichever child was spending the Sunday with their father while they propped up the bar downstairs. Sometimes, she liked whoever it was she had to befriend at short notice. Other times, she hated it and would then get shouted at for being sulky.

And she missed her own friends too. Although it was only a few miles away, moving to Nana and Granddad's house meant that Kate had to change schools. It had been such a traumatic experience for her, no matter how her mum said she would get over it and make new friends. She hadn't. She was nine years old. Real friendships had already been formed years earlier. She became the odd one out, her confidence suffered for it and she began to withdraw.

Her weekend trips to her father continued until her mum intervened a year later, saying that she didn't want her daughter sitting in the smoky, drunken atmosphere of a public house all day. Or had it been sitting in the smoky, drunken atmosphere of her father? Kate could never quite remember.

After a couple of years living in a rented maisonette, Kate's mum married Trevor and they moved into his house. Kate hadn't seen her father since then. She'd been thirteen. Sometimes she wondered why she hadn't visited him again, when she was older.

But most of the time, she realised it was because the sense of abandonment had remained with her to this day.

What was it other people – more fortunate people – always advised you to do? Rid yourself of your demons, forgive and move on?

It was happening all over again, wasn't it? First her dad and now her husband. Was she destined never to have anyone stay with her, and love her unconditionally? Was she not good to be around?

Once more she had been abandoned. And, once more, she realised that it was still as painful as when it had happened the first time.

Rosie trotted in from the garden, shook the rain from her fur in dramatic style and jumped up beside her. Not caring about her wet feet, Kate pulled her close and buried her face in her fur.

'Oh, Rosie,' she sobbed. 'What am I going to do without him?'

'You're doing *what*?' Through thick-rimmed glasses, Irene Porter proceeded to cross-examine Lily as if she'd grown another head.

Lily and her friend, Irene, had taken the bus into Hedworth just as they did every Monday morning and were enjoying a pensioner 'tea and scone' deal in the station's café before paying a few bills. Over the months since Bernard had died, the café had become a regular spot of theirs. They loved nothing more than sharing gossip while someone else waited on their needs for a change.

'I'm opening up the café again,' Lily repeated. 'But this time, it's going to be a coffee shop.'

'But… but I think it's a ridiculous notion,' Irene finally spoke out when she realised that Lily was actually being serious.

She pulled in her chair as an elderly man tried to push his way through it. 'Why would you want to start up all over again? And, at your time of life? You're an old woman. You should be taking things easy now.'

Lily looked around the busy room, seeing how the three women behind the counter had trouble keeping up with their orders but went about it in a methodical fashion. She very nearly lost her nerve to say what was on her mind, but then put down her cup as she turned back to her friend.

'I have a funny feeling that Bernard wants me to do it.'

'That's even *more* ridiculous. Will you listen to yourself! Besides, Bernard wanted you to close the café down.'

Lily lifted her cup. 'Maybe he thought that was what I wanted. Oh, I don't know. I can't explain myself. It's just this feeling I have.'

Irene stabbed her knife into a square of butter and spread a thick dollop over her scone. 'Like I said, I still think it's ridiculous.'

As she watched her friend polish off her elevenses, Lily felt a huge sadness engulf her. She hadn't thought for one moment that Irene would understand, but she'd still wanted to tell her. But couldn't she say anything other than *ridiculous*?

Irene had been the first person Lily had met when she'd moved to Somerley with Bernard in 1965. Lily loved playing bingo, so when Bernard spotted a poster on the church notice board advertising it for every Thursday night, she'd nervously decided to try it out. Irene had pulled her slight frame along the seating opposite her, plonked her checked grocery bag down with an exaggerated sigh and, oblivious to Lily's anxiety, had introduced herself and told her life story within the next ten minutes. That night, they'd shared their winnings and a loyal friendship had begun.

Bernard had got along well with Irene, even more so with her husband, Albert, and they both had lots of fond memories of the four of them doing one mad thing or another. Sometimes it was all the two of them talked about. They could go on about the old days for hours, relaxing under the shade of the oak tree, strolling around the nearby park, or sitting in one another's kitchens as they baked cakes together. Neither of them realised the benefits of what they were doing, they were just so used to doing it. No one knew their husbands like they did.

Albert had been the first one to go. He'd died three years ago now. Bernard had been as distraught as Irene. He'd been a pallbearer at his funeral and had asked to say a few words in his honour. Lily could clearly remember how he had written a long speech, full of praise for his friend. But on the day, he only managed a few words before his emotions got the better of him. It broke her heart to see her husband standing in his Sunday best, with tears pouring down his face. She'd gone to join him on the pulpit, stood by his side and took hold of his hand before reading out the remainder of the tribute. It was the least she could do.

Irene's cup clattering on her saucer again brought Lily out of her memories and back to the present day. She glanced at her friend over the rim of her cup. Irene had had the same pair of glasses perched on the end of her rather large nose for as long as Lily could remember. If she looked closely, she could just about make out the browns of Irene's eyes through the thick lenses and folds of skin. But Irene's hair was her crowning glory. It had stayed thick and lustrous over the years, and although Irene had grown old gracefully by leaving the blonde dye alone in her fifties, she had kept the chin length bob that suited her round face.

Irene smiled at Lily, her top false teeth almost popping out in the process. Lily's annoyance instantly mellowed. Irene was a good friend and she knew it would have been harder to cope with Bernard's death without her. Perhaps Lily was expecting too much from her to believe that she needed to do this.

'Come on.' Lily returned the smile. 'How about I pay for these, we do our errands and then go and see what's on at the Odeon this afternoon?'

Irene emptied the last dregs of her tea before setting down her cup noisily again. 'What a terrific idea.'

In the silence of the house, Kate jumped considerably at the sound of the telephone ringing. She scrambled to pick it up.

'Nick? NICK!'

'I'm here.'

Kate held the handset close, as if somehow he'd be nearer to her that way. 'Where are you?' she asked.

'I'm… just leaving work for the day.'

Kate stalled for a moment. *Work*? He'd managed to go into work after he'd ripped her heart out?

'Why?' Her voice lost the fight to control her grief and the rehearsed speech she'd planned disappeared. 'Why have you left?'

'It wasn't working. I've been thinking –'

'But –'

'I can't make it right, Kate.'

'I just want to know,' she sobbed.

'Please don't cry. I –'

'Tell me why then.'

Nick paused to collect his thoughts. 'There were lots of reasons, I suppose.'

'We could start afresh?'

'No, we –'

'But it's not too late! I'm willing to try again. I know a lot of it was my fault but I can change. Please give me another chance.'

'There isn't any –'

'And how could you leave like that? After all I've gone through as a child. You just walked away, without saying goodbye, without explaining why.'

'I… I thought it would be better that way.'

'Better for you, no doubt. Where are you staying?' Painful though it was, Kate had to know.

'With a friend.'

'Of the female kind?'

A sigh of exasperation. 'I can't speak to you now. I'll call you later in the week, when we've both had time to think about things.'

'NICK!' Kate screamed as the line went dead, only then understanding that the conversation hadn't gone as well as she'd hoped. 'Nick! Don't go! You bastard!'

Kate stared at the phone for some time, finally beginning to realise that her worst nightmare was coming true.

Nick was gone, and he wasn't coming back.

CHAPTER SIX

'Three exams down, three to go! Thank God it's Friday!' Chloe handed a can of Coke to her best friend, Manda. They pushed their way through the student room and found an empty table at the back. Chloe threw down her bag and grabbed the nearest seat.

'I'm going to be so bored without you all summer,' Manda sighed, turning towards her.

'I know,' said Chloe. 'I can't believe I'm leaving.' She tore open a bag of crisps and offered them to her friend before taking a fleeting look around the room that had been their sanctuary for the past two years. As more and more students crammed in as their exams finished, it was hard to see the colour of the walls with their array of brightly coloured posters, harder yet to see the worn out, stained-to-death carpet. Between Chloe and Manda, they must have had a crush on every lad who'd come through the doors. It was sad to think it would all be over soon.

She cast her mind back to her interview in Somerley. She'd been so nervous but Lily Mortimer had done her best to put her at ease.

'I know what you're thinking,' she'd said as she'd switched on a lamp. 'Everyone I've interviewed has had that same look on their face. What I want to see is if it's still there when you leave.'

Chloe's eyes roamed around the room before Lily came back with a pot of tea, taking in the nasty shade of yellow woodwork and worn black and white floor tiles. The blue Formica topped tables, piled high in front of one window, reminded her of the diner in Grease where Frankie Vaughan sang 'Beauty School Dropout' to Frenchie and she could vouch that the wooden chair she sat on took her back to her junior school days.

Chloe had blushed when Lily caught her looking round with disdain, but Lily had won her over. She'd put her at ease and gradually she had settled down into a good interview.

Anticipation bubbled up inside Chloe again as she thought of summer away from home. Her own room, money that she'd earned herself. Even though Somerley was a small place, Hedworth was only a couple of miles away, so there would be new people to meet and new pubs to frequent.

'I still can't believe I got the job,' admitted Chloe. 'I put my foot in it so many times!'

Manda helped herself to another crisp and began to suck off the cheese and onion flavouring. 'I think you'll be back before the end of the first month,' she said. 'You've never done a day's hard graft in your life.'

'That's because I've only ever worked for my dad.'

'And you've never been able to make a decent cup of coffee since I've known you.'

'I'll have people helping me.' Chloe removed her feet from a stool as someone gestured to see if it was free. 'Besides, it'll be out of a machine. What harm can I do?'

'And you don't know the meaning of the word money yet,' Manda argued. 'You'll be broke before the end of your first week.'

Chloe grinned. 'No, I won't. My beloved dad has agreed to extend my allowance over summer.'

'Jeez, you're such a spoilt brat.'

'Jeez, I'm going to miss you.'

Manda slapped Chloe jokingly on the thigh. They'd talked about their friendship, knowing that once they were apart everything would change. Manda was taking a course in media and had a place at their local university. Chloe had tried hard to persuade Manda to come along with her to Somerley and waitress but she had hit a brick wall every time. 'Why would I swap my dreary bar job collecting glasses for one waiting on tables?' Manda had scoffed. Besides, Chloe knew she wouldn't leave Callum behind.

Callum and Christian arrived.

'How did you do?' Chloe heard Callum say to Manda. She watched him kiss Manda passionately, feeling awkward.

'I finished way before the end of the time limit,' Manda told him when they came up for air. 'Which means that either I'm so brainy I got it all right, or I'm stupid and have written a load of bollocks.'

'Well, I'm with you on the second one,' said Chloe. She deliberately put a foot back on the remaining spare stool to ensure Christian had to sit next to Callum at the opposite end of the seating. The flush rising up his cheeks made it obvious he knew she was being off with him.

'Top up, girls?' Callum offered. Christian followed him to the vending machine.

'You've gone off him, haven't you?' Manda said as soon as they were out of range.

'He's boring me,' Chloe admitted. Guiltily, she treated Christian to a smile as he turned back. He was cute, with a mass of curly blond hair and he did look fit in his jeans and long sleeved T-shirt but…

'He's so immature,' she added. 'We've got nothing in common. All he wants to talk about is cars and Manchester United. You know the only thing that interests me about football is the guys' bums in their tight shorts, and I can hardly talk about that with him now, can I?'

'God, Chloe, you're impossible! What you really mean is that he's good enough to shag but not to hold long and meaningful conversations with?'

'Yeah, you got it.' Apparently Manda hadn't believed Chloe the other night when she'd said she didn't want to sleep with Christian.

'Besides, what's the use of keeping it going? There'll be talent galore to check out once I get to Somerley. I'll have to start with a clean slate then, won't I?'

As Manda rolled her eyes, Chloe knew she wouldn't understand how excited she felt. Chloe had grown up with most of the people she saw every day. It would be great to meet some new friends, do something different. And it wasn't for long, so if she didn't like it, she could come back. What had she got to lose?

She couldn't wait.

Searching through the bottom drawer of her wardrobe, in a last-ditch attempt to find what she was after, Kate tipped its contents out onto the bed until she finally found the delicate underwear Nick had bought for her last year. Tenderly, she fingered the deep purple lace as the memories came flooding back. Only last year, Nick had tried to make amends after yet another explosive row by booking them into a hotel in York. But the weekend away had seemed forced somehow. Instead of using the time to make love and fool around, get together as a couple again, Nick had been far more concerned about playing with his phone.

Tears formed at the corner of Kate's eyes but she refused to let them fall. Get a grip, Kate, she told herself sharply. Now is not the time to wallow in self-pity. Now is the time to start a killer beauty regime and put plan A into action. Before she could recall anything else that was likely to upset her further, she ran back to the bathroom, shimmied out of her dressing gown and submerged herself beneath the hot water.

An hour later, moisturised, de-fuzzed and smelling exquisite, Kate checked the gold watch that Nick had surprised her with on their first wedding anniversary for the umpteenth time that night. Her hair was clipped up, just as he liked it. She wore a long, woollen plum skirt with a sheer black blouse, barely concealing the underwear she'd been looking for. Knowing she was at her best was her only defence. After five days of going through every emotion known to her, Nick was coming to see her.

Most of the days since Sunday evening had passed by in a blur. After Nick's phone call on Monday, she'd rehearsed everything she was going to say to him but he hadn't called back for three days, by which time she'd convinced herself she wasn't going to hear from him ever again.

Time had dragged all week as she'd wondered what he was doing during every minute of the day or night. She'd sat in the warm sunshine of the garden, until she couldn't bear to see what they had created looking so bright and colourful without him by her side. She'd searched in the loft to see if he'd left an old jumper or shirt that she could wear, but all she'd found was an old yellow teddy bear. She'd hardly eaten a thing and was talked out with Louise. Finally, after umpteen text messages, he'd agreed to come around tonight.

Hearing his car pull into the driveway, Kate's stomach flipped over. Quickly, she uncorked the bottle and poured the wine.

'Kate?'

'In the kitchen.'

Before she could panic any more, Nick filled most of the doorway. His appearance gave away how he was feeling: shoulders sagging, shirt creased and crumpled, one flap hanging out disobediently, messy hair crumpled beyond styling.

As he stood there looking as uncomfortable as she felt, Kate was reminded just how much she'd missed him. Missed those eyes that now gave away how tired he was, the nervous way he drew a hand through his hair. Missed the way a few hairs popped above his shirt collar where he'd loosened his tie due to the late hour. Missed…

Oh, god, Kate realised. She missed everything about him. Anxiously, she turned away and blinked back the tears threatening to spill.

As soon as she spotted Nick, Rosie ran across the room. Nick swept her up easily into his arms. 'Hello girl,' he murmured into her fur.

'I've made some pasta,' said Kate.

'I'm not really hungry.'

'Please?'

'Just a little, then.'

Moments later, Kate sat down opposite him at the table. She'd left the television on purposely in the background, but the quiet that descended between them made her feel troubled.

'How's work?' she asked.

'Hectic. You?'

'I haven't been in this week. I couldn't face it.' Unintentionally, she giggled.

Nick swallowed his food before raising concerned eyes to meet hers. 'You've got to move on, Kate.'

'I haven't accepted what's happened yet, never mind begun to deal with it.'

'I must admit, it does feel strange.' Nick pointed to his bowl with his fork. 'Great, as usual.'

They both knew he was trying to change the subject. Embarrassingly, they lapsed into an awkward silence as they finished their food.

Afterwards, Nick offered to wash the dishes.

'No, it's fine,' Kate told him, wanting him to leave as soon as possible. 'I can manage.'

But then something changed. Being in such close contact to him was making everything weird. She couldn't concentrate on anything but his eyes. Those come-to-bed eyes that had seduced her over the years. Those same eyes that were causing her to melt again now.

She piled up the plates, trying to ignore the sexual tension in the room. Then, through the reflection of the window, Kate watched Nick move slowly, unsurely, towards her. His arm encircled her waist. So close she could feel his breath on her neck, she shivered as he moved her blouse an inch to the side and ran the tip of his tongue along the length of her bare shoulder.

'Nick...'

He reached around her, put his hands into the soapy water, took the cup she was holding and placed it on the draining board. Slowly, he turned her around to face him.

'Nick... It's...' was all she had time to whisper before his lips were on hers and she melted at their touch. Wet soapy hands found their way into her blouse. Still he kissed her – harder now, more urgent. She pulled out his shirt, then finding no resistance, broke away to undo the buttons. Breathing heavily, she let him remove her blouse. He moaned as she undid his belt; she gasped as he removed her bra and his mouth found her nipple.

Turning her again, he eased her onto the table. Not leaving her mouth for a second, he pushed up her skirt to caress the exposed flesh at the top of her thighs before moving higher. Kate relaxed back as his gentle touch exploded every one of her nerve endings, causing goose bumps to rise on her now so-sensitive skin.

In the split second as he pulled away, she thought he'd changed his mind, but relief flooded through her as he pushed down his trousers. She sat up and reached inside them. Knowing so well every intricate detail of his body, she teased and stroked him exactly the way she knew he wanted her to. When he could resist no more, he pushed into her, letting out a groan as he thrust deeper into her, again and again.

Afterwards, neither of them knew how to react. Their smiles were false, their laughter a little manic. It was as if they had never made love before.

Nick was the first to speak. 'We shouldn't have done that,' he said, his voice almost a whisper.

'Don't be daft,' said Kate. 'Not doing that before got us where we are now.'

'That's not why I came to see you.' Nick's eyes refused to meet Kate's as he handed back her blouse. 'I wanted to talk.'

'We did more than that.' Kate flashed him a sultry smile. Nick didn't return it, so it morphed into a frown. 'Didn't you enjoy it?'

'That's not the point.'

Not the point of what? They'd just had sex, Kate couldn't remember the last time they'd had it so good.

Warning signs shot across her mind as he remained silent, but she buried them rapidly. Instead, she chanced quick glances at him but he was looking at the floor.

'I can't do this,' he said, eventually looking up. 'I can't switch my feelings on and off when it suits.'

'But –'

'You don't understand, do you?' Nick's voice rose slightly.

'No, I don't. Why don't you explain?'

'When I'm not with you, I can be brave about things. Our marriage wasn't working, we both knew that, and I'm not sure we can make it better again. I don't want to hurt you anymore.

Like I said, I just came here to talk things over. I didn't mean to take advantage of the situation. It's just that…' Nick paused. 'You looked so freaking sexy in that outfit. When I saw you tonight, all the feelings I had for you came rushing back. I feel like such a bastard.'

Some of her plan had worked, Kate congratulated herself inwardly. At last he was beginning to come around.

But, wait a minute. All the feelings he *had*?

'So what do we do now?' she asked.

Nick shrugged his shoulders and sat down on the settee. Rosie moved closer and he absent-mindedly stroked her chest. Concentrating intently on *Sky News*, they sat in silence.

'I've got lots of questions,' Kate said when the break came on.

'I haven't got any answers,' said Nick. 'I'm not going to sit here and list all your faults. Some of it was down to me. I think we took each other for granted. Sometimes it happens. We –'

'You could always come back,' Kate interrupted, trying hard to keep things on track.

Nick shook his head. 'I can't.'

'But it's not too late.' Kate switched off the TV, hoping to get his undivided attention. 'I'm willing to try again. I know a lot of it was my fault but I can change. I want to –'

'It's not that simple.' Nick stood up and she quickly followed suit.

'Please give me another chance. I promise this time I won't be –'

'Such a nag?'

'What?' A look of bewilderment crossed Kate's face.

'You used to be so much fun when I first met you. I always enjoyed your sense of humour, your wit. But just lately, you started to direct it at me in a cruel way. Everything I did was wrong, so I bit back.'

'But –'

'I was sick of all the arguing too. In fact, in some bitter and twisted way, I'm sure you were trying to turn me against you. You've wanted me to leave for a long time now, but without it having anything to do with your behaviour. So that you can't be to blame.'

'You're saying it's my fault?' Kate's voice was barely audible. She knew she'd been off with him lately, but it took two to argue with such conviction week after week.

'Yes… No. Maybe it's me who's changed. I don't know, but I can't make it right now.'

'But…'

'For fuck's sake, Kate. It won't work again. Can't you see that?'

Kate sat down with a bump. Tears came fast and freely then.

Nick sat down beside her. 'I didn't mean to be so harsh,' he spoke quietly, 'but I need you to understand that I'm not coming back. I didn't set out to… well, you know, what we did tonight, but you reminded me of the old Kate who used to make me happy. It was wrong of me and I'm sorry.'

Kate said nothing. She didn't trust herself not to lash out at him with her tongue. And even if she shouted and screamed and threw things and smashed things, she knew none of that would make any difference.

'It's over,' said Nick, 'and I'm sorry for any hurt that you're feeling. But you have to get on with your life now, without me.'

Through her tears, Kate gazed into his eyes. Those eyes that she'd often got lost in. All the years she'd seen them shine and now they'd lost their sparkle.

He stopped at the door and turned back for a moment. 'Bye, Kate.'

Only when she heard the front door close behind him did she really start to cry.

CHAPTER SEVEN

'Have you got Freddie?' Ben questioned Chloe as he watched his sister busy pouting at herself, checking her reflection yet again in the visor mirror.

'Yep, I've checked four times already.' Chloe picked up her bag and pulled out Ben's lucky mascot.

Originally the bright green fluffy toy had belonged to her anyway. Martin Farmer had won it for her at the fair when she was twelve. He'd spent all his money trying to score twenty-one with three darts, only for her to finish with him a week later.

'I hope he's as lucky for you,' Ben added.

'He didn't do you any harm,' she teased, rubbing the cuddly toy over his face.

Ben pushed her hand away. 'Yes, but I'm smarter than you. I didn't need luck.' He ruffled her hair as she protested.

Chloe climbed out of the car, slung her bag over her shoulder and walked around to the driver's door.

'Thanks for the lift. I have big plans to get drunk later.'

'Give 'em hell, little sister!' Ben held up his hand for her to high five. 'And don't worry if you flunk it. You'll still have the Ward family charm to fall back on.'

After waving him off, Chloe scanned the crowd for her friend's familiar face amongst the throng of students making their way noisily into the main hall. Manda was waiting for her on the top step. She watched her nervously flicking her pen on and off at great speed as she legged it up the last two steps to reach her.

'You ready for the last two?'

'Not really, but who gives a toss. Let's do it.'

Staring absent-mindedly through the floor-length glass mirrors in front of her, Kate was glad that there weren't many exercisers in the small gym on Saturday afternoon. With heavy feet, she stepped onto the first of four-in-a-row treadmills, punched in a ludicrously high setting and notched in her usual hill program. What she desperately needed was a tough challenge to take her mind off things.

But ten minutes into her run, the cogs were still whirring as she pounded on towards her five-mile target. In vain, she tried to concentrate on the TV screen as the half-naked body of the lead singer of some hot new boy band frolicked around in the sand dunes in their latest video.

Oh, to be young and free of worries, she thought, as she forced herself to go faster. Knowing she wasn't going to go into the zone today, where her mind would be concentrating more on her breathing rather than her worries, she decided to focus on what to do next. Maybe all she and Nick needed was a short break, giving them both time to re-align their feelings and get back into sync. She knew she'd taken him for granted, hadn't really cared about him that much in the end. But the more he wasn't there, the more she wanted him back.

Finally, the treadmill clocked up her target mileage and she allowed herself to take a breather and push down the speed. Although she'd originally come to forget her predicament, her subconscious had worked everything out for her anyway.

After a few days' holiday, rather than face things, she was dreading going back to work on Monday morning. Maybe her work colleagues – with the exception of Louise, of course – would be more concerned about sharing their weekends' stories and escapades rather than concentrating on how pale Kate looked, about how much weight she'd dropped during the longest week of her life, and what her mental state was now that she was on her own.

Not that she was going to tell anyone straight away because, all of a sudden, she'd realised that she might not be there for very much longer.

'Are you sure you want to do this, Lily? It's such a big step to take.'

Lily Mortimer wasn't sure she was doing the right thing at all, but nothing was going to deter her now she'd made up her mind.

'Yes, Mr Stead,' she replied. 'I'm sure.'

'You could bow out gracefully and sell the building as it stands.'

'I could,' said Lily, indebted to him because he'd agreed to call round on his way back to his office rather than have her wait until she next went into Hedworth.

'You could still get a tidy sum for it. It seems that Taylor Constructions are only interested in the land, not the building, to develop.'

'And I won't let them take it as it is now. I have to look after my retirement, Mr Stead. If I have a viable business here, it could be worth more.'

'But you'll have to spend more to get this place up and running again.'

'Speculate to accumulate, I think.'

'I admire your tenacity, Lily.' Mr Stead extracted a large envelope from his briefcase and gave it to her. 'Read through all the details tonight and come to see me next week. We can go over any questions you may have then.'

Lily removed the lid from her pen before pulling out the contents and flicking to the back page.

'Nonsense, Mr Stead. You've been my solicitor for a good many years. I think I can trust you on one last venture.'

'I don't know why they call it rush hour, love.' The taxi driver peered through the rear mirror, adjusting it slightly to catch Kate's attention as he pushed his glasses further up his large nose. 'You can't rush anywhere in this traffic. Where to?'

'Somerley please. Church Square, number 11.'

'Nice town. My daughter lives there. Riley Street. I'm sure you'll find it. Somerley ain't that big a place.'

Kate had heard something similar herself. In Brentside, people would be charging around on their dinner breaks, rushing to stand in another queue in another shop, trying to shove a sandwich in their mouth, to make sure their lunch break was lived to its full potential. There'd be bank queues every Friday when everyone rushed out to spend their wages before declaring themselves broke by Sunday night.

Somerley, she assumed correctly, wasn't that big. She'd read that the town was located in the north-eastern and highest part of the city, and was more of a district really. Although it covered a huge area, it was a drive-through-to-get-to kind of place rather than a park-up-to-shop. To her, it seemed somewhere that would come alive during the day but, once the majority of nine 'til five working hours had been completed, would become silent quite quickly. Although living in a larger town would attract a good deal of clientele for the new business venture, Kate would hate to think that she was living somewhere that poured lager louts out onto her street every night.

On the spur of the moment at the beginning of the week, it had been a great idea to book another day off work and travel to a job interview where she could get board and lodgings thrown in with a little left over for a good time. But now, as the taxi moved slowly along the road, Kate's stomach began to flip around like a full load of washing. What if Nick missed her and wanted to come back after a few weeks?

But surely this was why moving away was such a good idea? It would never be the same again, Kate knew that, but if she bumped into him all the time, she might weaken. Then where would they be in two years' time?

She delved into her handbag as they inched forward in the traffic, pulled out the newspaper cutting and read the advert that had caught her attention almost three weeks ago. Yet again, she wondered if she had the right credentials. Her job as a project officer meant that she had to be a self-starter, have the sheer discipline to keep going – or even worse, scrap something and start over if it wasn't panning out well. She was known to be reliable and kept to deadlines on every project plan that bore her name against an action, something that she hoped might meet the approval of the woman she had spoken to over the phone.

Lily Mortimer hadn't gone into detail about what the cafe looked like. She'd given Kate a little background about its past and asked if she was still interested in a challenge. The word challenge had been the carrot. Working in a café seemed unlikely to stimulate her but last week, as a way to get Nick off her mind, she'd devised a business plan. At the time she wasn't sure if she would use it or not, but now, if she could get the woman interested in it who knew?

She hadn't spoken to Nick since the last time he'd called at the house to say that he wasn't coming back. It had been strange not to receive a phone call or even a text message from him, but then again, she hadn't wanted to contact him. Besides, he obviously didn't want to speak to her, so she needed to stay strong. That way she could start to accept things. She wasn't sure she had yet but the longer they stayed apart, surely it must become easier?

The row of terraced buildings that Kate was dropped in front of seemed passé but fitted well in their surroundings of mature blocks and factories nearby. The paved area in front of the cafe, although in need of a good wash down with a heavy-duty power hose, would be perfect, she thought, if they could get permission to put out a few tables. The properties either side had small enclosed courtyards, each surrounded by a three-foot high wall.

There was a chiropodist next door, a dentist, and a firm of solicitors who had taken over three properties and knocked them through into one huge block. Kate noticed curtains at a couple of the remaining properties and wondered if they were residential.

Once inside, the space captured her heart. It needed time and money spending on it to bring it up to date, but Kate could see it was well worth doing. And, as the meeting got underway, positive thoughts began to replace the doubts she'd had this morning with an image of a brighter future.

'So,' Lily finished Kate's interview with the identical question she had asked all the applicants. 'Do you feel the same way now as you did when you first came through the door?'

'Yes, but at the moment it's like,' Kate stopped until she found the right words, 'time has stood still.'

'It's badly in need of something to lighten it up,' Lily concurred. 'Bring life back into it.'

'Did you have anything in mind?'

'I was rather hoping that you would have some suggestions.'

'Well.' Kate opened the folder she had brought with her and leaned forward. 'I've put together a project plan with the information that you gave me over the phone. I did a bit of research on the internet about Somerley, scoping the competition, that type of thing. There seem to be a lot of factories and industrial estates nearby too. I think they'd be our target market. There are a couple of pubs, a chip-shop, plus a sandwich shop. But what I didn't see was anything special in the line of coffees.'

'Go on,' said Lily, already intrigued.

'My suggestion would be to open a coffee shop. Not just an ordinary run of the mill coffee and cake shop, but one that specialises in coffee. Different aromas and strengths to try, along with different cakes and fancies. We could also sell sandwiches and jacket potatoes to catch the lunchtime trade.

'I think high-quality coffees would sell themselves. We'd only need to stock up on the regular ones and have the others in small doses so they're always available. We could have coffee with whipped cream and flakes of chocolate. Coffee with a liqueur of your choice. Our own hand blended mixtures. Our own coffee shop special even.'

'That seems a workable idea.' Lily signalled for her to stop talking for the moment. 'I see you've thought this through before you came.'

'Yes, and that's why I think it also needs a really good name. Something to ensure it stands out.'

Lily didn't try to hide her delight. 'Well, I don't know what you've sold the most,' she beamed, 'yourself or your ideas. Would you be interested in the supervisory position I mentioned?'

Kate's stomach lurched forward and she tried to slow her breathing. She knew she was being silly but she hadn't felt this excited in ages. This woman was giving her the opportunity to be there from the beginning of a new venture. She'd be able to have some say in the remodelling of the décor, choosing the new menu and variety of coffees. She'd be able to help with the promotion and build-up of the business.

And she'd be able to have a new start, away from Brentside, away from the house, away from the memories and, most of all, away from Nick. She had to give it a chance, even if it turned out to be a temporary thing.

'Yes,' she nodded. 'I would be.'

'Good, then I'd like to welcome you to my coffee shop. Is there anything else you'd like to ask before you leave to catch your train?'

'Actually,' Kate opened the folder again and pulled out the photograph of Rosie she'd pushed in at the back. 'There is one small item I need to discuss.'

CHAPTER EIGHT

'Here's to you then, Chloe.' Ben raised his pint glass high in the air. 'May the female of the family be a successful servant.'

'It's a waitress, actually,' his sister corrected him as she touched her glass to his. 'And I'm going to be the best and the cutest by far.'

They were sitting in Carlo's Pizza House. Chloe had chosen it as her farewell dining treat before she left for Somerley that weekend. It had been a favourite of her mum's and one she knew kept the memories alive for all three of them. The fact that it hadn't changed over the years was an instant appeal. She'd always liked its simple sense of style, right down to the gingham checked tablecloths and wooden chairs with raffia matting that criss-crossed the back of your legs if your skirt was too short. Plastic ivy entwined itself realistically around the window frames, and café nets added a touch of privacy from the passing crowds.

The overpowering smell of garlic brought her back to the present. Even at seven thirty, most of the tables were full of diners.

'What time will Dad be here?' Chloe asked. She reached across the table for a chunk of ciabatta bread.

Ben gently slapped her hand away. 'You know you never finish your meal if you start picking now.'

Ignoring his remark, Chloe grabbed the bread anyway and ferociously ripped it into two pieces.

'He'll be finished around eight. He's told me to order champagne.'

Chloe threw him a look. 'He isn't glad to see me off, you know.'

'Clever girl,' Ben teased, and then his tone changed. 'I still think you should have invited Maddy.'

Although Graham's arrival saved her from the usual lecture, Chloe didn't need reminding of her childish behaviour. She'd regretted not inviting her the minute she'd told Graham of her decision. It had been so obvious he was trying to hide his disappointment at her failure to at least try and understand how important Maddy was to him. But instead of relenting, Chloe had explained how she'd wanted it to be just the three of them. She'd almost gone back on her word when she saw how miserable it had made him… almost.

Ben got up to meet his dad halfway across the room. Chloe smiled. She loved to see men shaking hands and hugging afterwards. It seemed such an intimate gesture.

Graham kissed her cheek. 'You look fabulous as usual,' he remarked. 'I suppose you've ordered a calzone?'

'You know me so well,' Chloe answered. All guilty thoughts around her treatment of Maddy disappeared.

'I do, my little one.' Graham handed her a colourful, squishy parcel. 'Present from Maddy. She says you can swap it if you don't like it, but she usually knows your taste.'

Chloe opened the tissue paper carefully. Inside was a halter neck top she had been looking at in a magazine a few days previously. Maddy must have noticed her coveting it.

'Do you like it?' asked Graham.

'It's okay,' Chloe fibbed, her cheeks starting to burn with embarrassment. She might not like Maddy but she definitely liked the top. Ben raised his eyebrows knowingly but she ignored him as she wrapped it up again, making sure it was put out of harm's way. She didn't want anything to spill over that, thank you very much.

'I can't believe you'll be leaving at the weekend.' Graham sat down and pulled in his chair. 'I'm going to miss you so much.'

Chloe threw her brother another look, this time one of 'I told you so.' Then suddenly the enormity of what she was about to do hit her. She stared at her dad as he studied the menu, his tie hung loosely around his neck, the stress of his day gently easing away as he entered into conversation with his son. She watched her brother as he relayed his working day to his father, giving her a wink as he caught her looking in his direction. Her eyes began to fill up. Trying to concentrate on the words of an Elton John song playing quietly in the background, she gulped down a mouthful of wine.

'Hey.' Graham tilted her chin and wiped away the lone tear that had escaped with his thumb. 'You'll be fine without us.'

'Sure you will,' said Ben, for the first time witnessing how nervous Chloe was about leaving. 'You'll be having too much fun to think of us.'

'My life's not all fun,' Chloe responded indignantly. 'I can be taken seriously once in a while.'

Ben and Graham laughed so loud that even the chef stopped twirling the pizza dough around in his hands. Chloe opened her mouth to answer back, but instead picked up her phone.

'Let's have a group photo.' She signalled for the waiter. 'I need something to remind me of your ugly mugs when you're not around to gang up on me.'

Ben came around to their side of the table and stood between them as they raised their champagne glasses in another toast.

'To Chloe,' they both cried, as Chloe tried hard not to.

* * *

At quarter past eight that same night, Kate sat on the settee in her living room. Nick sat opposite her in the armchair.

'I'm not sure it's a good idea,' he told her.

'It's a solution to our problem. I thought you'd be pleased.'

'I'm pleased about moving back in here again.'

'Well, let's try it then.' Kate sat forward. 'I'll go to Somerley for a month, see if things work out. You move back in and if I don't like it, I'll come back and we'll sell the place, split the proceeds.'

'I can't see why we can't sell it straightaway,' said Nick.

Kate sighed. 'Please. It's only four weeks I'm asking for. I just can't do this without knowing I have a back-up plan.'

'But giving up your job? To work in a café?'

'It's a coffee shop actually.'

'Café, coffee shop, whatever. I just can't see you –'

'Don't you think time apart might do us both good?'

'No. You just don't want our marriage to be over. That isn't a reason for us to stick at it.'

Kate paused then, knowing he was right. She'd realised as soon as he'd set foot in the house that evening that it had felt different. There had been no fireworks, no ticker tape, like she had expected – like she had wanted, even. And, although she had every right to feel sorry for herself because she'd been abandoned again, it wasn't his fault. She had to sort that one out for herself.

'Maybe it's the thought of you with someone else that I can't stand,' she admitted.

Nick shrugged. 'Maybe. Look, I'm sorry about pouncing on you the last time I saw you. Splitting up doesn't mean I've stopped wanting what we had, wishing it could work again… like you do.'

Kate nodded, fighting the urge to run and drape her arms around him. Part of her just wanted everything to be normal again. It would be much easier that way. But after she'd returned from her interview with Lily Mortimer, she'd had a feeling that she was going to be okay. It was simply a matter of time. And what Nick was saying now made complete sense to her. She needed to understand that *she* hadn't failed to keep their marriage together. They'd both played a big part.

Yet she couldn't stop her mind flipping back to their wedding day – ten years ago when they had vowed to love each other forever. It was the summer of 2005, yet even now she could still recall how nervous she'd felt as she'd walked to where he was waiting. She had worn a floor-length sheath of ivory silk and he'd given her the special smile that said he was totally in love with her. She'd taken ages to choose the right setting for the reception, at last deciding on a country hotel they'd stayed at when they had first fallen in love. As Mrs Bradshaw, Kate had been swollen with pride to be led onto the tiny makeshift dance floor, two sets of French doors on either side flung open to let in the balmy July night air.

The day had been perfect and she'd loved every minute of it. Nick had held her close, she had been that precious to him. Once.

Where had it gone so wrong? For a long time they hadn't been satisfied unless they were finding ways to torment each other; childish little things to argue over; stupid little things to disagree about. Usually it ended with Kate bursting into tears.

'I do care for you,' Nick spoke into the silence. 'Part of me always will. But we have to move on.'

Funny you should say that, Kate thought, as she watched him leave the room moments later; waited for the front door to close behind him; listened for the familiar sound of his car reversing out of the drive way.

Because moving on was exactly what she couldn't stop thinking about.

Later that evening, shot through with exhaustion, Lily settled down for the night with a hot drink. It had been extremely tiring work to find two friendly people to help with her plan. She'd been surprised at the amount of letters and phone calls she'd received. Perhaps putting it into five newspapers around the surrounding areas was a bit ambitious of her. At the last count she'd interviewed twenty-four men and women, from all over.

She cast her mind back over the array of strange characters that had made their way to the cafe over the past few weeks. That girl who'd turned up with a mouth full of chewing gum. She looked like a cow mulling over the right amount of grass. And when she talked, after she'd placed the gum on the roof of her mouth, all Lily could get out of her were monosyllables. The girl had no character, wouldn't do at all.

Then there had been Malcolm. He'd come across as a young sprightly man over the phone, but if the truth were known, he wasn't far from retirement age. 'Once I've got over my aches and pains first thing in the morning, I'm as good as any twenty-year-old,' he'd told her proudly. Lily could just imagine. He'd never make the early mornings. He'd probably manage to pull himself out of bed and get to work around eleven. No, he hadn't been suitable at all.

Kate Bradshaw, on the other hand, had seemed perfect. She had a real air of grace about her. Lily had noted the shine on her hair, not a dark strand out of place. Her make-up, subtle yet striking, accentuated her best features, easily her deep set, dark blue eyes. Her business knowledge had been excellent. She had the foresight to look at what the café could be and not what it was. Lily also read between the lines and had surmised that Kate could use the move to Somerley to her own advantage.

Lily's thoughts then turned to Chloe Ward. Lily smiled as she remembered the way Chloe had put her foot into things with the least amount of effort during her interview. She seemed full of life and, oh what beautiful hair. Masses of curls, cascading down her back. Piercing green eyes bewitching her as they sparkled with enthusiasm. There was an actress she reminded Lily of. Used to be married to that small Cruise fellow.

With great pleasure and an immense amount of relief, Lily ran a line straight through the last item on her long list of objectives. At last she could put her plan into place.

CHAPTER NINE

Kate stood on the front doorstep for a moment and looked back into the hallway of her home. For all she knew, it might be the last time that she'd clatter her heels on the flooring, glance through the rectangular mirror to see if she looked decent enough to be let out and try not to get her clothes hooked up on the dried flower arrangement sitting on top of the table.

At first Kate had doubted her idea to move away, but it hadn't taken long for her to realise that she had to do this for her own sanity. Now, it was weird to think that she was leaving. Over the years, how many times had she run through that front door, anxious to see Nick because she couldn't wait to feel his arms engulf her in a bear hug? Rush in with news that she knew he'd be ecstatic to hear?

Sadly, she thought, lately there were far more times when she'd dreaded walking through the front door, knowing that all she'd be met with was a stony silence. The look that said, 'don't bother talking to me.' The body language that said, 'keep well clear, I don't want to know you at the moment.'

With a grave sigh, she pulled the door shut, picked up the last three carrier bags and slung a faded red rucksack over her shoulder, nearly knocking herself off balance in the process.

'I can't believe you're taking all this baggage,' said Louise as she struggled to wheel a bulging suitcase down the short drive-way.

Kate was taking even more baggage than Louise realised – emotional baggage. She frowned, shoving a carrier bag full of Rosie's toys onto the back seat of her car. Rosie was strapped into the passenger seat but still insisted on taking a look. With well-practiced patience, Kate untangled her and sat her straight again.

'Now, be patient,' she stroked Rosie's head reassuringly and gave her a rubber bone to play with.

Maybe that would keep her quiet for some of the journey.

Stretching up to full height, Kate turned back again, this time to stare at the house. The For Sale sign was the first thing that came into view. Nick was moving back in tomorrow. It hadn't been a month yet since he'd moved out, but Kate's life had dramatically changed. In a short space of time, she had separated from her husband, gone for an interview for one job and resigned from another one.

When she'd explained the situation to her team leader, he'd tried to talk her out of it. So too had some of her colleagues.

'You can't just up and walk and leave Nick in the house,' said one. 'You put so much work into it.'

'Are you sure you can't salvage anything?' said another.

'If I could leave here, even if it did mean working in a coffee shop,' said Louise, 'I know I would.'

Last week, on her final day, there had been a long lunch, lots of presents and a few tears. Kate had been scared about moving on, but once out of the building, a weight had gone from her shoulders. Maybe she hadn't enjoyed her job that much after all.

And now the day had come for her to leave and, well, she was ready to go, but her feet were reluctant to move.

'Are you okay?' Louise asked her.

Kate shook her head. 'I'm scared.'

'Don't be. It'll be exciting.'

'But I'm excited too.'

Louise gave Kate a hug. 'You'll be fine.'

Kate pulled back from Louise with a feeling of remorse, wishing that she wasn't leaving her behind too. 'I hope so. You take good care of that husband of yours. Don't wear him out too soon.'

'I won't. And we'll call and see you as soon as you've settled in.'

'You mean once all the mess has gone and the place is looking decent?'

Louise grinned. 'Yep, you got it. When all the hard work has finished.'

'Well, toodle-pip then.'

Kate finally got into her car and started the engine. She forced herself not to look through the rear-view mirror until she had turned out of Marble Close. Her stomach seemed to helter-skelter around. She wasn't sure if it was due to nerves, or happiness, or merely the fact that she hadn't eaten anything for breakfast and had only nibbled at a light lunch. Still, she had plenty of chocolate supplies in the glove compartment and it was only an hour and a half's drive to Somerley at the most.

Pushing all feelings of doubt clearly away and wondering instead what the future would bring for her, with Rosie still securely fastened up by her side, Kate focused on the road ahead and sped off towards their new home.

'Here we are then.' Kate placed Rosie onto the floor two hours later and watched as she proceeded to sniff every inch of her new surroundings. Kate was so thankful that Lily had agreed to let her stay here, if only for her trial period of a month. She knew Rosie would win her over, especially as Lily had shown her a photo of a dog long passed away.

The double bedroom Lily had shown Kate to was situated at the back of the building. Kate pushed up a thick net curtain, mentally changing it to a lighter roman blind, and nosed around at her surroundings. The window overlooked a cobblestoned alleyway, with properties, mostly boarded up, behind. Not a very pleasant view but still, she didn't intend on spending too much time in this room. Throwing Rosie's cushion onto the floor, she wondered what Chloe would be like as she unzipped her suitcase. Lily had told her she was eighteen. She hoped they'd get on well. Fourteen years was quite an age gap.

She didn't have long to wait because Chloe appeared in the doorway twenty minutes later. Instantly, Kate saw how her presence would lighten up any dreary room. Oh, the joys of being eighteen with no responsibilities, she envied, taking in the red, spiral curls, long legs covered in skinny jeans, chequered ballet pumps and the white vest underneath an oversized red T-shirt with a slashed neck. All of a sudden, Chloe's youthfulness brought home to Kate just how different life was going to be. This was most probably a summer job for Chloe. Still, it wasn't her fault.

Embarrassed at being caught with her favourite knickers in her hand, she quickly shoved them into a drawer. Rosie gave a grunt and headed across the floor, immediately demanding attention.

'Hi, you must be Chloe.' She held out her hand, unsure if Chloe would find it too formal. 'I'm Kate.'

'Hi.' Chloe shrugged her right shoulder and her holdall slithered to the floor. Then she shook Kate's outstretched hand and smiled.

'Are you in the room next to mine?'

Chloe nodded, looking over as Kate busied herself grouping her toiletries and cosmetics together on top of the dressing table.

Kate turned back to her quickly, realising how rude she must seem. 'Was your journey here okay?'

'Yes. Lily's making coffee for us. I'm going to dump my stuff and go downstairs. See you in a minute.'

'I'll settle Rosie and then come down to you,' Kate shouted after her.

Hearing her name, Rosie bounced around like a kangaroo while Kate wondered where on earth she was going to put her cushion. It was bad enough that Rosie had to stay in here. With all her snoring and twitching, Kate would be lucky to get any sleep. Hastily, she pushed it under the dressing table and prayed that she'd settle quickly.

Chloe was waiting for her on the landing when she came out of the room minutes later.

'So, what made you come here?' she asked as Kate walked downstairs in front of her.

'Oh, you know,' Kate glanced back shyly. 'A new challenge, a change of scenery. Something like that. How about you?'

'Oh, you know,' Chloe jumped down a step at a time, 'my first job, my first salary, my first taste of freedom away from home. I've just finished my A levels.'

'How did you do?' Kate asked, recalling how nervous she'd been when her results had been due. She needn't have worried though. She'd passed all three.

'I think I did enough to pass but I'm not sure the grades will be good enough for uni.'

'There you are,' smiled Lily as Kate pushed open the door to the café. Catching her breath as she pushed a tray onto a table she had dressed for the occasion, she turned back to the counter. 'Help yourselves while I fetch the milk.'

Kate's eyes lit up. There was enough cake for ten people, let alone the three of them. She spotted her favourite madeira cake alongside scones, a layered chocolate sponge cake and what must be a litre of cream.

Chloe grabbed a mug and added two spoons of sugar before stirring it well. Next she took a slice of carrot cake. She bit into it, her eyes widening in delight.

'This is delish,' she exclaimed when Lily eventually sat down with them.

Kate's eyes rested on Chloe's trim waist. She looked like she'd be able to eat anything and get away with it. She wondered if she exercised or if it was the youth in her that made it easy for her to keep the weight off.

'I made it.' Lily helped herself to the last mug. 'My Bernard said he'd run a marathon if the prize was one of my cakes. We used to sell them in the café.'

'I hope you'll still be doing that once you're up and running again,' said Kate. 'This madeira cake tastes delicious.'

'Thank you.' Lily turned to the first page of her notepad and declared the meeting officially started.

'Now I know that you've only just arrived, but I'd like to know, one more time, what does it suggest to you when you walk into the café?'

'Lots of men coming in to taste your cake,' said Chloe and they all laughed, if a little false and jittery.

'Yes, I'm sure it does,' said Lily. 'And what about you, Kate?'

The first time Kate had walked through the doors into the café, she had been excited at the prospect of making the large space into a bright, yet cosy establishment. The counter situated on the far left wall was in the wrong place for her liking. She felt that it should be in the middle of the back wall and the first thing a customer saw when they came in. She didn't like the floral wallpaper that covered every wall, but that was easy to remove. Once the flooring was covered up, paintwork treated to a touch of white gloss and the windows scrubbed clean, the room would be almost presentable.

Now, sitting here once again, her enthusiasm was still the same.

'Maybe we should go all modern, chocolate and ivory to reflect the colour of coffee,' she tried.

'Ugh, too dark. What about yellow and green?' Chloe flicked back her hair and pouted. 'Anything else could clash with my colouring.'

'Or a traditional look?' Kate offered. Although the look wasn't what she would like, it was Lily's business after all. 'Gingham table clothes, cafe nets at the windows?'

'No!' Chloe shot forward in her chair to protest. 'We'd only attract old biddies that sit resting their legs for two or three hours over one cup of coffee and a scone. We need young blood, people who want to try something different.'

'Old biddies like me, you mean?' said Lily, amused at her outburst.

'No, I…' Chloe blushed.

'It has to be good enough to attract both,' said Kate. 'This is an industrial area so most people may only be able to come here for their lunch and perhaps a quick drink after a hard day at the office. So we need to cater for a morning trade too. It's all good business. Have special deals for pensioners etc.'

Although she hadn't realised until she'd been offered an interview, Kate had always had an interest in coffee shops. She loved nothing better than diving into one, trying out a different drink and watching the goings-on as she sipped it. She'd read online that lots of writers took their laptops with them, and she could see why. There was something about a good coffee shop – the ambience created, the background noises and the varied clientele. And, having done more research after getting the job, she hoped she might have an insight into what would, and wouldn't, work.

'Well, I don't agree with the traditional look,' said Chloe. 'This coffee shop wants new people. New ideas, new recipes. New everything, if you ask me.'

'Some of the stuff is workable.' Kate lifted the lace tablecloth and rubbed her hand over the surface.

'We could jazz these up in no time. How many tables have you got, Lily?'

'Twelve, but –'

'That wouldn't take long. I took a part-time interior design course last year. I learned some brilliant techniques with paint. If we cover everything with a primer, we may be able to colour wash the tables and chairs.'

'Colour what?' Chloe looked bewildered.

'Colour *wash*. It'll get rid of the blue.' Kate eyed Chloe's sceptical look. 'Trust me. It works incredibly well. And it would save a lot of money.'

'I agree,' said Lily, pleased to see her second-in-command was watching the pennies for her. 'But, actually, I've decided to buy some more. I want the new shop to be up to date. I have some brochures for you to browse through. I'm sure you'll come up with something special.'

'What about a couple of settees?' Chloe pointed over to the bay window. 'Maybe over there? People walking past would be able to see customers relaxing.'

'It's a very good idea,' said Lily. 'But I don't want to spend too much.'

'Sorry,' muttered Chloe. 'My dad says I never understand the true value of money.'

'Well, perhaps even you will be surprised when you see the finished result,' said Lily. 'I just want to hear all of your ideas first. So, am I right in saying that the gingham look is out?'

The two younger women looked at one another before nodding their heads.

'Any other ideas?'

'We need really big coffee cups,' stated Chloe. 'As big as boats.'

'And maybe we could wear a uniform to give off the right image?' said Kate. 'I think a black waistcoat over a white shirt looks particularly smart and businesslike. We could have the coffee shop name embroidered across it, which is another thing we need to sort out.'

'Was the old café busy, Lily?' Chloe wanted to know.

'Yes,' said Lily. 'It got busier as the week went on. There's an open air market, run by the council, set up on the public car park around the corner. Hopefully, that will be every Thursday taken care of, as trade used to be steady all day. Mondays and Wednesdays are still bingo days in Hedworth, so there was a bit more trade in the morning but it usually slackened off in the afternoon. Fridays were always busy but Saturday mornings could be just as hectic with the men who did the overtime in the factories nearby all coming in. Perhaps they'll come back again once we re-open.'

'I like the sound of that,' Chloe grinned. Now that she had finished with Christian she was desperate to see what Somerley had to offer in the way of decent talent.

Lily slowly rose to her feet and started to clear the table. 'I'm extremely pleased with your ideas,' she said. 'I'm going to fetch you the catalogues so that you can make a list of what you like and then we'll go through it. And Kate, can you start a list of things to do, please? Obviously I know a lot of suppliers we can still use but I'm always open to suggestions.'

Kate got up to help her, nodding eagerly.

'What else is there around here?' Chloe asked.

Well, apart from the row of shops here in Somerley, there's a retail park about three miles away, with a few well-known stores. But if it's more of a variety that you're after, I'd suggest a drive into Hedworth. It's got everything you can think of and it'll only take you ten minutes.'

'Is it busier there?'

'Yes, the shopping centre is expanding at the same rate as the housing market. There are flats and apartment blocks popping up everywhere. Which is such a shame, as when I first arrived here, all I could see in the distance were rolling fields, farms and outbuildings, cows and horses.'

'Yes, nothing ever stays the same,' Kate said with a sigh.

'Come on,' said Lily. 'I'll show you around downstairs and then you can help yourself to a meal, I'm sure?'

'Do you fancy a walk afterwards?' Kate asked Chloe. She was eager to explore the surrounding streets, as well as take the opportunity to get to know her new work colleague, and Rosie would need to go out soon. 'Get the feel of the place?'

'Do you think we could go for the walk first?' said Chloe. 'Via the chip shop I spotted. I'm starving.'

Yes, Kate mused. Eighteen, without a care in the world, and no need to watch her diet.

Full after their takeaway food, Kate and Chloe had opened a bottle of wine and started the process of getting to know one another. Already it was nine thirty and they were both tired after the excitement of the day. They were in Lily's living room upstairs. Part of the refurbishment would include its decoration, so for the moment all it had in it were two battered armchairs, a mismatched settee, a mahogany sideboard and a television with a lamp on its top. Kate was snuggled into one of the chairs, with

Rosie fast asleep in the tiniest gap between her legs and the arm. Chloe was sprawled full-length on the settee, her pumps lying rejected on the carpet. Neither of them had the energy to watch the police drama that had started fifteen minutes ago. Lily had gone to bed.

Chloe glanced across to see that Kate had fallen asleep. She hoped sleep would come to her as easily tonight, because paranoia was starting to creep in.

Would she like it here?

Was she going to settle in?

Would Lily like her?

Would Kate like her?

More to the point, would she get on with Kate? It was vital that she did as they were going to be spending a lot of time together soon. Kate seemed nice, from first impressions. But what if the age gap was too big, or if Kate was too square? That would never do.

What if they hated each other after a week or two?

What if…?

Chloe didn't have time to finish the sentence. For as quick as her mind started to work overtime, her eyes began to close.

Lily couldn't believe how tired she was as she settled back into bed that night. She'd gone into the living room earlier to check on Kate and Chloe, only to find them both asleep. She'd felt like a wicked stepmother as she'd woken them up. Now, every once in a while she heard a door open and shut. In the distance, she could hear unfamiliar music playing on one of their radios, but it wasn't too loud. Lily was simply used to the quiet, having lived on her own for a while. Besides, it was nice to have people under her roof again. Apart from her own voice alongside the radio, it had been quiet for far too long.

Pleased with how their first staff meeting had gone, at ten thirty-five p.m., on the last Sunday in May, Lily switched off the lamp at the side of her bed and wondered what tomorrow would bring.

And, for the first time since she could remember, she felt a tiny flutter of excitement inside her stomach.

CHAPTER TEN

Kate found herself awake early on her first full day in Somerley so, after lying in the silence of the strange surroundings for ages, she got up. It seemed odd going downstairs to use the toaster in the cafe, and then sitting in a room of empty tables, but the kitchen upstairs that they would use once the coffee shop was reopened was full of boxes of rubbish ready to be taken to the incinerator. Lily had been having a clear out before they came.

She hadn't long returned from taking Rosie around the block when Chloe walked in.

'Morning.' She smiled at her. 'I've just had a toasted bagel. Would you like one?'

'Please.' Chloe nodded. 'Where's Lily?'

'She went to meet a friend – Irene, I think she said her name was. Did you sleep okay? My bed was really comfortable. I went out like a light but I woke up really early.'

'Me too. It was so hot last night. And it looks like it'll be the same today.'

Kate looked out of the bay window. The summer sky was clear at the moment but she knew the unpredictable British weather could change that in a matter of minutes. Already there were a scattering of people around and several groups of school children walking past.

'What shall we do today?' Chloe asked moments later when she took the plate and mug from her.

'I suppose we should make a start on the simple decorating materials,' Kate replied. 'Paint and brushes and the like. I've made a list.'

Chloe kept her sigh to herself and sat down at the nearest table.

Kate pulled out a chair and sat down beside her. 'Sometimes I can't believe I've given up my job to come and work in a café. I suppose I'm excited now I'm here, but I still wonder if I've done the right thing.'

'I'm only planning on staying for the summer until I go to uni.' Chloe held her cup carefully between the tips of her fingers, blowing on the liquid in an attempt to cool it a little. 'It's just an adventure for me.'

Although Kate knew she was leaving a past behind, she could understand that a summer away from home before going to university was just a means to an end.

'So, come on then,' said Chloe. 'I know you told me last night that you've split up from your husband but even me, the queen of prying, couldn't ask about it as soon as we'd met. Is that why you've moved to Somerley?'

Kate didn't want to be reminded of Nick. Being on her own was a struggle and she'd get used to it, no doubt. She'd already done it for four weeks. But, in the meantime, how did she explain to an eighteen-year-old what she had been, and was still going through? Chloe was bound to see the world through stupid rose-tinted glasses. She wasn't old enough to have suffered any real heartache.

Kate was stuck. What should she say? *Mind your own business*, no matter how she put it, clearly sounded rude. Maybe she should tell her a white lie until she knew her better.

'I went away for the weekend, to a hen party,' she blurted out regardless, 'and when I got home my husband had moved his stuff out without saying a word.'

Chloe's vibrantly made-up eyes widened and she put down her coffee. 'Sorry, I'm not known for my tact.'

A silence fell between them. Kate raised her eyes to the ceiling to stop the tears overflowing, blinking rapidly.

'That must have been tough,' Chloe said quietly. 'Look, I know I'm eighteen, but I've been told on *numerous* occasions that I'd make a good agony aunt.'

Kate smiled and quickly wiped away a tear. 'Thanks, Chloe. I'll bear that in mind.'

'Good. My rate is eighty pounds an hour. But for you I'll make an exception!'

'That's the third time we've passed that bloody carpet store.' Chloe pointed it out from the passenger seat of Kate's car as they crawled along in the busy traffic, forty minutes later. 'We're after a retail park. It's only three miles away. It can't be that hard to find.'

Kate indicated right, turned into a side street and parked up. 'This town is supposed to be small,' she mumbled and tried to unfold the map to find their location. In anguish, she threw it on the back seat. 'I'm hopeless with directions.'

'Where's the sat-nav when you need it?'

'Never mind sat-nav.' Kate wound down her window as a man approached them on the pavement. 'There are simpler ways of getting what we want. Excuse me!'

Once they'd located the DIY superstore, they spent an hour searching for everything on Kate's list.

'It's a good job we decided not to paint all the tables and chairs,' she groaned as she pushed the loaded trolley towards her car. 'This is heavy enough as it is. I knew I should have put my flatties on.'

As she struggled to manoeuvre it, Chloe grabbed one end of the handle and they steered together.

'I hope we've remembered everything,' said Chloe. 'I don't fancy coming back here in a hurry.'

'But you've spent a fortune in *Topshop!*'

Chloe smiled. 'Well, there has to be some consolation.'

Kate attempted to crush the last tin of emulsion into the boot of the car. Admitting defeat, she threw it onto the back seat, where it landed with a thud before rolling onto the floor.

'I'm glad they do refunds,' Chloe added.

Kate slammed the tailgate down. 'Well, I'm not taking any of my tins back. I have to dampen down some of the pink with that creamy colour I found. Pink must be Lily's favourite colour.'

'I was referring to *Topshop*,' said Chloe.

Kate smiled.

Chloe watched Kate as she returned the trolley. Her manner had been positive when they'd first met yesterday, and she seemed like someone who would listen as well as share her own problems. Maybe she'd turn out to be the older sister she'd always craved. Or she could be another Maddy… Chloe shuddered, no thanks.

One thing was for sure, she realised as she waited for her to catch up. They definitely shared a common interest.

'I really like your shoes,' she said, looking down to admire them.

'Thanks,' said Kate. 'They were half-price in the sale. What size do you take?'

'Seven.'

'Oh. Pity.'

'I wish I was the same height as you,' Chloe whined as she got into the car. 'I get sick of walking with the Gods.'

'But you're so tall!' Kate started up the engine. 'I'd love to have longer legs.'

'You want to try catching decent looking six-foot fellas all the time. And I hate going out with anyone smaller than me. I'm five-foot-eleven in a heel.'

'Chloe, have you never been to a rugby match?' Kate shook her head in amusement.

It only took them a matter of minutes to find their way back to Somerley and unload the car. Chloe's face was flushed when she finally came through the front doors a few minutes after Kate. She flexed her arms in relief as she put down the last of the tins on the counter.

'Can you imagine what this place is going to smell like in a couple of days?' she said. 'We'll have to buy loads of those plug-in air freshener thingies.'

'Either that or customers can have a gas mask provided with their first drink. Where did you get to?'

'I've been talking to the men who're working on the church. They saw us earlier and wanted to know what was happening with the shop. One of them invited us to the pub later. I said we'd meet them there, about six.'

Kate's eyes widened. 'I'm not doing that!'

'Why not?'

'Because I'm not.'

'But why?'

'Do I have to give a reason?'

'But it'll give us a chance to get to know people. There'll probably be more of them in the pub too. We can –'

'You'll have to go on your own,' said Kate. 'I can't feel comfortable around others yet. I need time to settle in, get used to my surroundings first.'

'Well, sorry I spoke. Anyone would think I'd asked you to roller-skate around the square naked!'

Kate lowered her eyes from Chloe's stare.

'Remind me what you did for a living before you came here,' Chloe said when Kate had been quiet for a minute.

Kate sighed. 'I worked for a housing association.'

'So I bet you're used to arguing your corner, speaking out?'

Kate shrugged.

'Don't be all fuddy-duddy and lighten up.' Chloe folded her arms. 'It's a drink in the middle of the afternoon.'

'I'm just not as confident as you,' Kate owned up.

'There's nothing scary about it.'

'I know, but let me get used to things in my own time.'

'Okay.' Chloe's tone was easier now. 'I'll give you until… tomorrow.' She grinned and then clasped her hand over her mouth. 'Ohmigod! We've just had our first row and it wasn't me who started it!'

When Lily came back later in the morning, Chloe had made a start on stripping the main walls of paper.

With the warm weather continuing and the steamer on full, the job was turning out to be worse than expected. Chloe had thought it would be easy when Kate had suggested that they do it together, so when she went to visit a few suppliers, Chloe had decided to get on with it by herself. But so far, in just over an hour, she had managed to clear all of a square metre of wallpaper from the dubious walls.

'I thought you might like this,' Lily said minutes later, placing two mugs of coffee on a table. She pulled out a chair as Chloe made her way over. 'I can see you've been working hard even though it's so warm in here now.'

'Cheers,' said Chloe, thankful for a break from the heat of the dingy room. She didn't dare look at the state her hair would be in.

'Did you sleep well last night?'

Chloe wiped her hands before picking up her drink. 'Yep.'

'And your room? Was that all right? Not too warm – or too cold?'

'Everything was fine.'

'Good. I know it's going to take you time to settle so I wanted to get all the little details right, if I could.'

'It's great at the moment, though I don't think I've ever worked this hard in my entire life.'

Lily shifted in her chair. 'It'll be much better in here when it's decorated and light again. Oh, please sit down, child. You're making my neck ache.'

Chloe giggled before doing as she was told. 'Was it always so dark before?'

'No. The walls had been whitewashed at first. Then we decorated it properly but it always got dirty quickly. It was hard to keep up with, but Bernard tried his best.'

'How long were you married?'

'Fifty years.' Lily beamed with pride. 'We just managed to celebrate our golden wedding anniversary.'

'Oh, congratulations.' Recognising her mistake, Chloe turned scarlet in a millisecond. 'I mean...' She decided to change the subject. 'Do you have any children?'

'No, we weren't able to.'

Chloe looked down at her hands, cursing inwardly. Talk about putting her foot in her mouth, twice.

If Lily noticed her discomfort she ignored it.

'We had a long time together, so many beautiful memories,' she continued. 'When we started out, Somerley was fairly quiet – a friendly town where everyone knew everyone else's business. Not that it was always a blessing.'

Chloe smiled shyly. 'Have you always lived around here?'

Lily shook her head. 'Bernard had but he was living in Chesterfield when I met him. We'd been married less than a year when he spotted this place. It was completely run down then, far more than it is now.' Lily's face lit up as she slipped back in time. 'I can still remember the excitement shining in his eyes as he looked over the building. "Think of the potential, Lil," he'd said, sweeping an arm around the dark room. "We know this is going to be an industrial part of Somerley. Once other business developers get wind of it, lots of custom will come our way. There are always people to be fed. We could do a sandwich round. There'll be plenty of scope to expand."'

'What did you think?' Chloe leaned forward and rested her chin in the crook of her hands.

'I hadn't been too sure. I didn't have a clue how to run a café. I couldn't cook that much in those days. But Bernard didn't have the odd bacon sandwich and fry up in mind. He wanted a tea shop.'

'A tea shop?'

'Yes, something with a character of its own, selling home-made cakes, scones and cream, and only the odd sandwich. Somewhere with a bit of class, he would say, for the ladies. Somewhere the men could get mugs of milky tea and thick, buttered toast. Well, as usual, I'd been swept up by his enthusiasm. Bernard always had that effect on me.'

'What did he look like?' Chloe was intrigued by now. 'Do you have a photo down here?'

'Oh, yes.' As Chloe helped herself to a chocolate digestive, Lily shuffled over to the counter and rummaged behind it. Moments later, she handed Chloe a photograph.

Chloe looked down at a couple in their early twenties. Bernard was marginally taller than Lily and stood proud in a black suit with a carnation buttonhole. Hazel eyes smiled at Chloe as he posed with his bride-to-be, Lily's arm linked through his as they stood at the side of the church. Lily wore a pink shift dress and matching short jacket. She held a tiny posy of carnations.

'So you agreed to a tea shop?'

'Yes.' Lily sat back down. 'I remember Bernard carrying me over the threshold on the day we collected the keys. And after two months of hard work, painting and cleaning everything in sight,' she smiled at Chloe, 'just like you're doing now, Lil's Pantry was ready to open.'

'Lil's Pantry. I like that. So was it a success?'

'It was steady. I can remember lots of things going wrong. We experimented with new ideas and products. Sometimes they didn't work out quite as planned but we persevered, helped each other and got through many a muddle or mishap. We had a visit from Prince Charles, you know.'

'You mean he came *here*?'

'No! He was coming to open a car factory around the corner on the main road. Oh, what was its name?' Lily frowned. 'Bernard had hung bunting and concocted a makeshift flagpole and hung a union jack. I can still hear him muttering his disappointment when the chauffeur-driven limousine had gone straight past. Did he honestly think Prince Charles would stop for a cup of tea?' She smiled. 'The future King of England might just have caught a glimpse of a red triangle if he'd turned his head at the right moment.'

'That's classic!' said Chloe. 'He seems such a lovely man. What was the rest of your family like?'

Lily's smile faded. 'He was my family. My mother died when I was five and my father never re-married. He raised me well on his own, but I had to clean the house and do all the shopping from a very early age. Not that I minded," she added quickly. 'Though it would have been nice to have someone to talk to.'

Chloe could sympathise with that but in a different kind of way. So many times she'd come home from a night out and longed to have a female to share her feelings with. And not just a mother, a sister, even.

'I know what you mean. It gets lonely on your own.'

'I suppose that was what kept us together,' Lily said. 'Bernard had three brothers: he'd already lost two of them through cancer, and he lost the other one the year after I met him.'

Chloe wondered if she should change the subject as she saw Lily's eyes misting over. But she was so enthralled with the love story that she couldn't stop her questions. She loved hearing about the 'good old days'. Her friend, Manda, thought she was strange. Said she had weird taste for liking anything old.

'I bet you'd like to see this place busy again,' she added.

Lily glanced around the dismal room that had seen better times. 'Yes, but some of the family run firms have been taken over by the larger conglomerates as well as local entrepreneurs. They have their own canteens now,' she explained. 'With age as well as illness against us, the business began to slide. Bernard had…'

'I'm sure we can make it work again,' said Chloe, sensing her sorrow.

Lily leaned over and covered Chloe's young hands with her own. 'My dear,' she smiled, 'you bring light into a dim place. I'm so glad that you're helping me.'

The door opened behind them and in walked a flushed Kate.

'Oh, very cosy,' she said, spying the two of them around the table.

'It's my fault,' Lily admitted. 'I kept Chloe talking. It was rather a nice chat actually.'

'About anything in particular?'

'Oh, you know,' said Chloe. 'This and that.'

'Yes,' said Lily. 'Something and nothing.'

'Well, listen up!' Kate looked like she was ready to burst with excitement. Her eyes skimmed over the walls as if they refused to be drawn in by the enormity of the task ahead. 'I've sourced out a shop that could make your cakes, Lily, and I've found a bakery that will deliver to us on an as-and-when basis, so there'll be hardly any waste while we build up trade. They mentioned a warehouse that stocks every type of coffee you can think of so I called in there too. They advised us to sell a few at a time at first, to test the market. And I've got ideas galore for cups and saucers, menu designs, table decorations, you know, simple things that add to the overall ambience.' She finally paused for breath. 'This coffee shop is going to be amazing when it's finished.'

Lily rubbed the small of her back as she made her way gingerly up the stairs. Her legs were aching, her head was throbbing. She needed to rest.

She looked up, suddenly imagining Bernard standing on the landing above, arms folded and a stern frown.

'Never mind giving me that look,' she spoke inwardly. 'I'm doing it – the café you loved will be restored.'

She smiled as she held onto the banister to negotiate the next step. Even though her body was more or less worn out, getting the café ready to re-open as a coffee shop had certainly given her a new lease of life. So too had being around Kate and Chloe. They were so young, so alive, so full of hope. They seemed to instill in her the will that she could do anything.

With their help, Lily might just be onto a winner. Which would make her plan work out a lot better too.

CHAPTER ELEVEN

On Wednesday morning, Kate was on her way to the news-agents in the next street when she heard a voice calling from above. Feeling low and in need of a large bar of the thickest, creamiest chocolate, she was off to see Harry, the proprietor, on the pretence that they needed some rubbish bags.

'Hey, gorgeous,' she heard. 'Not seen you around here before. What's your name?'

Kate shielded her eyes from the mid-morning sun and could just about make out a group of men leaning over the scaffolding attached to the side of the church. The one on the far right waved and she indulged him with a smile.

'She's here again,' she heard minutes later as she walked back.

Kate knew what would come next. Most builders were so predictable, they wouldn't be able to resist.

'You're not shy, are you?' one of them shouted down. 'They say the quiet ones are the dirtiest.'

They were behind her now but Kate stopped and looked up again. She counted four of them leaning over, pretty much like quads in their jeans, obligatory yellow hard hats, fluorescent vests and steel toe-capped boots. Apart from one young apprentice, they all looked about her age.

Right, Miss Chloe Ward, Kate thought as she watched them childishly point fingers at each other amidst choruses of 'it wasn't me, it was him.' *Let's see who's a fuddy-duddy now then.*

'I could be shy, I suppose,' she shouted, 'but not when I'm fastening handcuffs and doing things involving chocolate sauce. So which one of you wants to be first?'

'Me!' shouted one.

'No, me!' shouted another.

'Take no notice of them two. I'm older and have far more experience!'

'Patience, patience. You'll have to wait for me to make up my mind!' With another smile, Kate walked away, dismissing their pleas for her to stay with a shake of her head. The smile broadened as she jogged the few yards back to the safety of the coffee shop and she began to giggle. Although they were doing all the chasing – or to put it mildly, flirting – Kate flounced, a little lighter on her feet than when she had left earlier, suddenly no longer in need of the chocolate.

'Do you think we should make a start soon?' Kate was suddenly feeling guilty as she and Chloe sat down to rest again. It was still only ten thirty that morning, but already her motivation was dissolving. Stripping the walls was taking what seemed like forever. In two days, they had only managed to remove half of the paper from the four walls.

Chloe shook her head. 'We deserve a break after all the work. My arms are killing me after using that steamer.'

'At least you have a steamer,' Kate protested on deaf ears. She had drawn the short straw after going on about what a good job hot water and washing-up liquid did if it was left to soak. But the shiny surface of the paper was so thin it was coming off like chewing gum. She'd already ruined one pair of jeans.

'Shi-i-t-t!' shrieked Chloe and quick as a flash, her feet were off the table and she was across to the other side of the room. 'Lily's back.'

Kate got up pretty sharpish. She didn't want to be caught resting, especially after they *had* worked so hard.

'My, you've been busy,' Lily greeted them both with a smile. Chloe winked at an embarrassed looking Kate.

'There's still a lot to do… oh, hello.'

The lady standing next to Lily was dressed in all the colours of the rainbow. Two thin legs in blue tights popped out from beneath a red pleated skirt. Black shoes were the only drab colour she had on, probably to make up for the canary yellow of her cardigan.

'Kate, Chloe, this is Irene,' Lily introduced, stepping to one side. 'She's what you two would call my best friend.'

'It's about time there were some young people working in this place,' Irene smiled and then just as quickly changed it to a scowl. 'Although I don't think Lily should be working at all, at her time of life.'

'I'm not going to be working here as much as overseeing.' Lily pretended to sulk. 'You make me sound like I'm ancient.'

Irene put down her tartan shopper. 'You *are* ancient. And so am I.'

'Says the old lady who's swanning off to stay with her daughter and her family in Australia for the next six months and leaving me here all alone.'

Irene sighed. 'You had the opportunity of coming with me, Lily,' she chided. 'But you just didn't want to.'

'I know.' Lily gave her friend a quick hug. 'I am going to miss you, though.'

'I suppose you two wouldn't say no to a cup of tea?' Chloe offered, with a sideways glance over at Kate. 'We were about to stop for a break, weren't we, Kate?'

Kate grinned. 'Yes, we've been working so hard – although I'm not sure you can tell that much.' She cast an eye around the room, failing to recognise any relics of the old café. It did look dreadful now that some of the paper had been removed. She was amazed at what it had been covering up, or even holding up. The counter and the one remaining table and chairs that had survived the skip yesterday were shrouded in remains of dreary curtains and there were stacks of black bags piled up in front of the window.

'I never knew decorating was so long winded.' Chloe wiped her sticky hands on a clean towel. 'No wonder my dad always gets someone in to do it for us.'

Lily was only half listening. She'd decided to take a closer look at the wall nearest to her. Furtively, she rubbed a hand across the surface. 'This wall has more bumps and wrinkles than me!' she exclaimed.

'What colour is this supposed to be?' Irene exclaimed at the top of her voice, sliding her glasses down the bridge of her nose before blinking exaggeratingly at the patch of lilac on the tin. 'Lily, I wish I'd had my cataracts done at the same time as you.'

'It's lilac, Irene,' said Lily. 'It's exactly what the old place needs. And you hadn't got cataracts to remove. You just have poor eye sight.'

'At last I understand why your eyes are so blue,' said Kate.

Lily nodded. 'I had them done a while ago now. It was worth all the pain. Now, what else was I going to say? Oh yes. I've been given the name of a builder this morning, he's been highly recommended. Terry Allen – his son and nephew help him out. They're a couple of jokers by all accounts, but Terry keeps them in order. Alex and, what was the other one called?' Lily paused. 'Tom, that's it. I'm going to call him later.'

'Sounds interesting,' Chloe commented. 'But I'm sure we can do better than any men.'

Lily smiled at Chloe's self-assurance. 'What I'd like you two to do now is source out some wallpaper books and we'll sit down together to pick out a scheme. There's no way we can paint these walls without it looking like it's been done on the cheap.'

Lily carried her bag through to the kitchen and set it down on the table. She sat carefully, slipped off her court shoes and rubbed her stocking clad toes, smiling to herself when she heard the squeals of laughter erupting from the other room. They seemed to be getting on well, but it was early days yet. The crunch would be when they'd lived together for a few weeks after the coffee shop had opened. Once the fuss had died down and the excitement had been exchanged for hard work.

She sat back in the chair and visualised Kate and Chloe in the uniforms they'd picked out yesterday.

Letting them have the final say had been a good idea, she'd realised, when she'd seen their reactions. The coffee shop would be a success, Lily was certain. So young, so full of ideas, she knew they'd attract a decent type of clientele.

'Sorry, Lily, I was about to make a brew, wasn't I?' Chloe rushed in as if on the tail of a whirlwind, interrupting her thoughts. 'I was talking to Irene. She's a lovely old dear, shame about her dress sense though. That cardie looks as old as the ark. Now, about that drink.'

After a tiring week, Kate headed off to a gym on Saturday afternoon. Somerley Leisure Centre was only a mile away from Church Square so it took her all of twenty minutes to drive there and enrol as a member. Easy to do at the weekend, she surmised, but she knew it would more than likely take her ages to get there in the rush hour traffic which would be trying its best to inch its way onto the ring road.

The gym was similar in size to the one she'd been a member of in Brentside. Rows of cardio machines stood in line like toy soldiers. Aside from the many sets of dumbbells arranged neatly in racks, there were machines to work every different muscle in the body. Mirror after mirror adorned the walls, making the room double in size immediately, the remaining spaces covered with posters explaining how to change from a Teletubby into a Barbie doll in a matter of six… years.

She'd just started to walk over towards the stepper equipment when a man in a blue T-shirt beckoned her over.

'Hi, I'm Eddie, your instructor for today. Do you need any help?'

Kate might not have been into appearances as much as the teenager she was working with, but she was impressed with anyone who took the time to improve their body. Not more than twenty-five at a guess, her eyes roamed over his firm torso barely covered by the thin-ribbed material stretched over it. Biceps bulged from underneath the sleeves and, as he ran a hand over his hair, she waited for his eyes to catch up with hers as he gave her the once-over. She blushed at his look of appreciation.

'I've never used that model of treadmill before,' she pointed over to the far wall, forgetting all about the Stairmaster. 'Can you show me how it works?'

Kate's nerves began to settle as Eddie set the control panel to a steady pace for her. After a few minutes walking, she upped the speed and began her run. Through the mirror in front of her, she took a sneaky glimpse behind her reflection.

Considering it was a weekend, the gym was pretty full. A guy in his forties was barely moving his legs on a stationary bike while he read a Lee Child novel. A young woman lay back, taking a break, reclining on the leg press. Two plump middle-aged ladies walked side by side on the treadmills along from her, deep in conversation. None of them seemed in any way intimidated by the group of men puffing, panting and screeching as they used the free weights over in the far corner.

Kate cast an eye swiftly over the display panel and found she'd already been running for twelve minutes. The young woman was now working hard on the chest press. That particular set finished, she drew a hand across her brow and wiped it dry with a sweatband, a matching scrunchie held back her hair in a ponytail. Kate caught her eye, smiled shyly and was pleased when the smile was returned.

Finally, she was done. Totally de-stressed as the endorphins got to work inside her body, she wiped her brow with a towel. The gym wasn't so huge now. It seemed more inviting and she couldn't wait to try out the other machines.

An hour later, she was in the changing rooms when the young woman she'd seen earlier came out of the shower.

'Hi,' she smiled at Kate. 'I'm Lucy. I haven't seen you here before.'

'I joined this morning.' Kate smiled back. 'It seems like a friendly place.'

'Yes, I've been a member for three years. Mind you, I don't think I would have been as regular if Eddie wasn't one of the instructors, seeing as I've got my own gym at home. He certainly gets me into a sweat every time I see him.' She laughed. 'I suppose there's no harm in looking, even though I'm married. Do you live around here? I live on the other side of Hedworth. It's only a few minutes away. We've been there since we got married. Are you married?'

'Well, I –'

'You have a fantastic figure, by the way. You've obviously worked out for a while. Your muscle definition is amaaaazing.'

Kate spotted her looking down. For a split second, she thought she could see envy in her eyes. 'Oh, get off with you,' she squirmed. 'I hate my legs.'

'I wish mine were like that rather than thin and gangly. Yours are lovely!'

'No, they aren't. I'm five foot three – which is the reason I wear heels most of the time. I'd love to have longer legs. Mine are just stocky, which would be great if I wanted to be a footballer.'

'Honey,' Lucy said in a melodramatic tone. 'You need to learn to love yourself more.'

'I tell you it was bizarre,' Kate declared as she relayed her morning to Chloe over a lunch of jacket potato and tuna salad. 'One minute I'm swooning over this young fitness instructor, who is way too young for me by the way, and the next I'm listening to a woman I barely know telling me her life story in thirty seconds flat and then telling me I have fantastic legs when I know I absolutely do not have!'

'There's nothing wrong with your legs,' said Chloe. 'Did you ask if we can put a poster on the notice board?'

'Yes, and we can put one in the reception too, by the front doors.'

'Great. Let's hope we drum up some business.'

As Chloe went off to pour them both a cold drink, Kate thought again how quickly her life was changing. Going to the gym and meeting Lucy made her realise that she was finding her feet, starting to establish old routines. Suddenly she was making friends away from her home. She was settling down and leaving her old life far behind. And sometimes it didn't seem such a chore.

Maybe everything would work out okay after all.

CHAPTER TWELVE

Lily shuffled around, knowing so well that it would be impossible to get comfortable on the chair. As well as its hardness, she knew getting up in the early hours when she couldn't sleep last night had been a bad idea.

She totted up the huge column of numbers, double-checked and transferred the figures to another notepad. Already she'd exceeded her budget, but still she wasn't sure they'd created the right ambience for the coffee shop. Oh, what the heck, she sighed and put down her pen. It was only time and money and it shouldn't take long to do the few alterations that Kate had suggested. Both she and Chloe had come up with some wonderful ideas. Lily might as well get it right the first time and it always saved money in the long term.

'Good morning, Lily.' A familiar face greeted her as the mechanism of a silent bell sprang into action on the front door.

'Good morning, Alf.' Lily smiled, genuinely pleased to see him. Alf was a friend of both hers and Bernard's. They had met when Bernard's van had had a punctured tyre. Alf kindly helped him out and Lily had given him free tea and a scone filled with homemade jam and cream. They'd all been friends since. Alf's wife, Joan, had died suddenly when he was thirty-six and he'd never remarried.

'How are you this morning?' Lily enquired as he sat down across from her.

'I'm good, thanks.' Alf's face broke into a smile. 'Just thought I'd rest my legs for a while.'

Lily didn't know which she envied about him the most, his wonderful hardly-a-wrinkle-in-sight skin or the fact that he always seemed to be happy. Even though the day outside was fairly mild, he wore a black blazer, his huge stomach protruding from above his trousers, his braces pulled taut gripping them. As he strained to see what was behind him, his burly hands, although ravaged with age and slightly twisting at the knuckles, gripped the side of the chair to stop him toppling over. Once he'd finished his inspection, he turned back to her.

'So,' Lily swept an arm around the chaos, 'what do you think of my plan so far? Do you think it will work?'

Lily knew Alf was as sceptical as Irene, so a little teasing was in order. After Kate and Chloe had finished the arduous task of stripping the walls, they'd been left with a completely blank canvas, which even she had to admit was more oppressive than the floral wallpaper. Terry Allen was coming to see her this afternoon to give her a quote on the work that was needed to make it look special again.

Alf removed his cap and placed it down on the table. 'You know what I think. You're mad to try again.'

'That's not the answer I had in mind.'

'It's the only answer I have. You don't have to do this.'

Lily sighed. 'I need something to occupy my time.'

'But we can do things together. We could go dancing. And play bingo.'

'We already go dancing and play bingo.'

'What about the cinema?'

'We went last Friday.'

'To the museum, maybe on a picnic…'

Lily mentally switched off as he went through his endless list of possible outings that they could enjoy together. The twinkle in his eyes worked overtime to convince her, but she couldn't return his affection.

Not now, not ever.

At last she held up her hand to silence him. 'Before you talk yourself hoarse, maybe it's time for a nice mug of milky tea?'

'I'll tell you what you could improve,' he said before she disappeared through the kitchen door.

Cautiously, she turned back to face him, and then hid a grin as he rubbed at his bottom.

'These chairs are too hard for the likes of my well-worn flesh. I think you need some new ones.'

'Delivery for Mrs Mortimer,' a voice shouted through the open doors an hour later. A short and round man with the most outrageous shorts carried one end of a rectangular box. His equally short colleague appeared at the other end.

'From Denleys? I'm sure it wasn't supposed to arrive until the end of the month.' Lily looked puzzled and went off in search of the order form.

'What is it?' Kate asked Mr Short and Round.

'Coffee machine, love.' He wiped his brow with the back of a grubby looking hand. 'Which is what we both could do with – a good cuppa. Isn't that right, Markus?'

Markus nodded but Kate shook her head without more ado.

'Sorry, but we're not open for business yet. If you could put the box on the counter over on the far wall please, I'll sign for the order.'

'Here it is.' Lily was out of breath when she returned to find them gone and Chloe spraying air freshener abundantly around where they had stood. 'It shouldn't have been delivered for another two weeks.'

'Never mind, at least it's here now,' said Kate. 'It's one thing we can cross off the list.'

'Yes, I suppose it is.' Lily looked through the window where another van had pulled up to the kerb.

This one was definitely on time. Thankfully Terry Allen was quite the opposite of the delivery men. For starters, he was tall, clean-shaven and smelt of shower gel.

'I'll show you through to the kitchen first,' Lily said after a quick introduction to her staff. 'That's where most of the work is needed.'

Two minutes later and curiosity had got the better of Chloe. She had the coffee machine stripped of its plastic bubble wrap and was busy filling a stainless steel jar with milk.

'Maybe you shouldn't meddle,' Kate advised. 'I don't know about you, but I've never used a machine like that before.'

'How hard can it be to make a cappuccino?' Chloe flicked up a switch, pulled down a lever and pushed a jug up the spout as the machine kicked into life. Spluttering and gurgling with all its might, the frothy concoction had soon filled the jug and was spilling over the sides.

'Oh, no. Help me!' she cried.

Kate pulled another jug from its wrapping and moved Chloe aside. 'Switch it off,' she shouted over the din as it filled pretty quickly.

Chloe flicked a switch, then another and another, but the machine continued to moan and groan. Quickly, she crawled under the counter to locate the plug. Once she'd switched off the power supply, the noise, along with the coffee machine, stopped. There was a dreadful smell of burning.

'Just what I like to see,' a voice called out from behind them. 'A woman on all fours directly in front of me. And, may I add, with a delightfully toned butt.'

Kate turned around as another voice cried, 'Move out of the way and let me see. You always have the first shot at everyone.'

Chloe carefully backed out and pulled herself up. Standing in front of her were two men, she guessed in their early twenties.

'Ohmigod, it's Nicole Kidman!'

'Like I've never heard that before,' Chloe muttered.

'I'm Alex,' he grinned, 'and this is my cousin, Tom. You won't hear him say much, he doesn't get a chance when I'm around.' His eyes came to rest on Kate. 'Well, *hello*, you must be Catherine Zeta-Jones.'

'Spare me the bullshit,' said Kate light-heartedly. 'We've been warned about you two already, so don't push your luck.'

Tom shoved Alex out of the way. 'Will you let me see?' He flashed a cheesy smile at the girls. Apart from the distinct tramlines shaved into his hairstyle, he was so much like his cousin the two of them could pass for twins at a glance. Both had dark hair and not an ounce of excess fat between them. It was Tom's crooked front tooth that made his smile just that bit cheekier.

'Any of you two know how to fix temperamental coffee machines?' Chloe asked.

Alex fiddled with a strand of his hair and threw her a smouldering look. 'I'll have it working in no time. I've always been good with my hands.'

Kate headed for the door that led her to the safety of the hall. 'Chloe, I'll leave you to it. I'm sure you can handle these two while I go upstairs to check on my baby.'

'Baby?' Tom groaned. 'Did I just hear her say baby? No one mentioned that when we got this job!'

'What's that?' Chloe asked Kate as she joined her in the living room later that evening.

Kate moved her feet out of the way so that Chloe could sit next to her. Rosie, not to be outdone, jumped in between them.

'It's just an email.'

'What does it say? Or is it too personal to share?'

'It's from Nick. He's still keen to put the house on the market and there's a couple of forms that he needs my signature on. I'll have to meet up with him soon.'

'Sounds like you're not sure if you should.'

Kate shook her head, too upset to talk. Although she'd only been here for two weeks, one tiny reminder of her previous life was all it had taken to make her go to pieces. She folded the paper in half and shoved it into her dressing gown pocket, wishing again that she'd brought along her portable TV from home. She'd only come in to the living room to catch the weather report before taking a shower.

Sensing Kate's mood, Chloe picked up the remote control and was soon channel-hopping. 'Now there's a guy to make you forget your troubles.' She pointed the remote control at the screen. 'I'd forget an ex-husband if his hands were squeezing my tits.'

'He's not my ex-husband,' said Kate.

'He soon will be, though. Mmm, check out that six-pack.'

'Is that all you ever think about? Men and sex?' Kate shook her head in exasperation. Maybe eighteen wasn't such a good age to be, after all. Too many hormones.

CHAPTER THIRTEEN

Kate pressed the button to illuminate the time and then swore under her breath. She'd been in her room for over an hour with still no sign of sleep. Tossing and turning in a strange bed wasn't her idea of fun.

Neither was crying herself to sleep, which she'd done for the past few nights. Reluctantly, she switched on the lamp but the dim lighting did nothing to cheer her.

Although she'd made the room as welcoming as she could with a lick of paint and the odd knick-knack, she couldn't help but compare it to the bedroom she'd shared with Nick. Kate had copied the idea from an article she'd seen. She'd had to adapt it slightly with sand coloured carpeting and walls, owing to Nick's refusal to have laminate flooring in *every* room of the house. The bed was crafted out of solid wood in a natural oak stain, boasting thick chrome legs and ivory faux suede headboard panels. They'd chosen it together to create a focal point – and now she couldn't enjoy it, stuck in a single bed for a single girl.

Just exactly when had everything started to go wrong, she wondered? Her mind flipped back eleven years to the night when Nick had come hurtling into her life. It had been two weeks before Christmas and Kate had been on her work's night out. She'd been employed as an insurance clerk then and had to work every Saturday morning – one of the reasons why she'd chosen to drive that night; the other being how hard it was to get a taxi with everyone else on their Christmas outings as well.

They'd enjoyed the usual mass-produced dinner of cheap turkey and cold roast potatoes and then noisily made their way to

Shades, the local late haunt at the time. As they'd squeezed into a space by the side of the dance floor, Nick had been dancing with his friends. Kate had emerged from the even more packed ladies loos to find he was the hot favourite with the girls.

'He's lovely,' Deb, the part-time receptionist remarked, even though she was wearing beer goggles.

'And he's a nice guy too. Used to go out with my sister's best friend's cousin. Or was it my cousin's best friend's –'

'LOVELY?' Libby, one of the underwriters, interrupted. 'He's more than lovely! He's the best looking guy I've seen in ages.'

'Yeah, and you've seen a few lately,' Lesley the temp, who covered everything from typing to toilet paper supplies, screeched.

Immediately Kate turned to look, and liked what she saw. After she'd caught Nick's eye a few times, he sauntered across the crowded dance floor towards them.

'Dance, lady?' He held out his hand, which was a bit steadier than his feet.

Kate chanced it.

She'd been the talk of the office the next morning but Kate had always kept her private life close to her tiny chest. At work, the women desperately tried to worm every last detail from her.

'Did you snog him?' Lesley the temp wanted to know. She'd long ago abandoned the typing in favour of the bacon run and was enthusiastically tucking into her sandwich.

'I'd have done *more* than snog him,' Libby the underwriter informed them all.

Kate had no trouble believing her.

'Did he give you his number?' Deb the part-time receptionist asked.

'No, but he took mine.'

'Oh dear. Now the waiting game starts,' Libby enlightened her, biting into a cheese and sausage baguette before pointing a greasy finger at her. 'They say they'll call, you wait like a deranged cat and they never do.'

'He'll call,' Kate told them.

But he didn't need to call. An hour later, with the office still smelling like a takeaway shop, Nick walked in with a bouquet of flowers and a smile on his lips that said far more than it should have. Jaws dropped, giggles erupted from each desk with every word he'd uttered, and Kate's cheeks continued to glow the colour of Santa Claus's tunic when he offered to buy her lunch because he couldn't wait to see her again. She finished work at one and stayed at his flat for most of that weekend. Within a month, he'd invited her to stay permanently. Within a year, they'd bought their first house together.

They *had* been happy: for ages. They'd planned to have at least one child, but not too early. Mid-thirties they reckoned would be the right time for them. They made their house into a comfortable and stylish home, worked hard to get promoted and enjoyed a more than reasonable standard of living. They took lavish holidays twice a year and weekends away at the drop of a hat. They saved hard for a rainy day but would think nothing of going shopping and blowing a few hundred pounds on whatever took their fancy.

Kate drew up her knees, wrapped her arms around them and let the tears fall. She wished she had Louise to talk to but she'd gone a bit quiet on her lately. She was still waiting for an answer to the text message she'd sent at the beginning of the week, which was strange but not unusual for Louise.

But if Louise was here, she'd put her straight and cheer her up. If Louise was here, she'd tell Kate to get on with her life and leave the past behind. If Louise was here, she'd tell her to – Kate gulped back tears.

How could she still miss Nick, even though she was sure she didn't want to be with him anymore?

It had been Alex who'd first reminded her of him. A long time ago, she and Nick had joked and played around together like she'd observed him messing about with Chloe. Then it had been Sam. Finally giving in to Chloe's constant pleas, Kate had gone to the pub and met up with the builders. It had been quite a laugh actually. Along with Brendan, the foreman, Sam, one of the brickies, had taken the responsibility of looking after her, seeing as Chloe had explained her circumstances loudly to the group. They'd been across a few times since and the email she'd received from Nick had made her feel guilty about it, even though she shouldn't feel that way at all. Surely she should be able to enjoy the company of other men now that she was separated? But, with this thought, she began to cry again. Nick was moving on, why couldn't she?

The bedroom door opened moments later.

'I couldn't help but hear you,' whispered Chloe. 'Are you all right?'

'I'm fine,' Kate managed to say through her sobs. 'I'm just having a girlie wobble.'

Chloe pushed open the door and moved quickly across the room. 'Don't worry. I've already had mine tonight.'

Kate was momentarily stunned. She hadn't thought that Chloe might be struggling with her emotions too.

Chloe grinned. 'What? You think I haven't cried oodles since I've been here?'

All of a sudden, Kate felt better and decided to trust Chloe with a few more details. Slowly, she unfolded her past. She kept back some of the details because they seemed too personal, and in some cases too petty, to share. But it felt good to offload to someone she didn't know very well.

'Didn't you realise it was that bad?' Chloe questioned afterwards.

'There were signs that the marriage wasn't working but I didn't think he'd leave me.'

'Perhaps he didn't mean to hurt you. And no matter what he did, it was bound to remind you of your dad leaving.'

'Father,' Kate muttered. Joseph Portman had never been a dad to her.

'What does Nick look like?'

Kate stretched over to the current book she was reading and pulled out a photograph from the back. She was standing in front of Nick and he was hugging her tightly. She was laughing, her hand reaching back to touch his cheek.

'You both look so happy,' said Chloe.

Kate gnawed on her bottom lip. 'That was taken a while ago. It was the last couple of years that were so false. I suppose we irritated each other more as time went on, but I still loved him. I'll never forget him, no matter what happens.'

'No, you probably won't. It's a woman's pre… perog… prerogative – I can never say that word – to feel miserable one minute and ecstatic the next.'

Kate glanced at Chloe. Her curls tied back with a band emphasised how pale her skin was without makeup. If it weren't for the Playboy bunny logo on her short nightdress, along with the breasts spilling out of it, you'd think she was barely in her teens. How had she got such a mature head on such youthful shoulders?

Suddenly, Kate realised that she didn't know much about Chloe's past. She'd been too wrapped up in her own to find out. That was going to change right now.

'Look,' Chloe spoiled her moment. 'I was on my way to get a drink. I don't know about you but I fancy a midnight feast. How about it?'

It wasn't a welcoming sight when they turned on the kitchen light downstairs. After a more than reasonable quote, Terry had started on the alterations. Alex and Tom were due to join him at the end of the week. Half assembled units were piled in every available space, remnants of the old kitchen packed away in boxes stacked high.

Chloe fought her way over to the fridge while Kate prepared coffee. She picked up a piece of wood before the nail spiking out of it found its way into her foot and placed it on the remains of the worktop.

'They'll never finish this in time. It's like a war zone back here.' Chloe moved a small length of piping and threw it over her shoulder.

'Be quiet,' Kate whispered loudly as it clattered to the floor.

'Sorry. There's cheese, coleslaw, hummus, cooked ham. I'm sure there's some crusty bread left and there's a packet of crackers.'

Kate spied a small piece of MDF and gave it to Chloe who carefully piled the food on to it.

'Excellent,' she said. 'The makings of a perfect late night snack.'

'You've cheered up,' Chloe remarked later as they ate their food.

Kate cleared her throat ready for the next bite. 'I might watch my weight but I'm always happy when I'm eating,' she stated. 'So, tell me about you and yours. I hate to admit it, but I've been a bit wrapped up in myself lately to show concern for anyone else.'

'You don't say! It's a good job I have an iPod. At least I can switch off every now and then.'

Kate pulled a face at her before helping herself to another cracker. 'Go on, anyway.'

'There's not much to say really. I live with my dad and my brother. My mum died in a car accident when I was seven. I've already told you that.'

'Do you remember much about it?'

Chloe shrugged her shoulders. 'Not really. We were on the way home from a wedding when a car raced towards us on the wrong side of the road. Apparently, Mum was alive when the fire and rescue unit freed her from the wreckage but she'd died soon after that.' She put down her sandwich and sighed. 'The stupid teenage driver received a six-month suspended jail sentence and a fine, can you believe that?'

Kate shook her head. Chloe seemed more mature about things than she had ever been about her parents, even though she hadn't lost either of them through death. Since Kate had met Nick, her relationship with her mother had become even more estranged. Somehow she felt it was easier not to go and see her, the time between visits becoming longer and when she'd moved to Lincolnshire with Trevor, it had seemed a perfect way out of what had become an awkward situation. She'd only been to visit their new house once in the past three years.

'So you had to be the woman about the house?' she probed gently.

'Most of the time,' Chloe scoffed, thinking of Maddy trying to muscle her way in.

'Girlfriends got in the way?'

'One in particular. The one he's with now, in fact. Maddy's been on the scene for three years. She's forty-two.'

'Does she have any children?'

'A son, Craig, but he doesn't live with us. He's off at uni.'

'I bet she's good for your dad, though?'

Kate felt the temperature in the room go decidedly chilly. An awkward silence followed so she stirred her coffee noisily while she waited for the atmosphere to change.

Kate raised her eyebrows, urging her to continue. 'Chloe?'

'I just –'

'– don't like her?'

'I… I was just a kid when Mum died,' Chloe tried to explain, 'and it changed my life so much. It was my dad who took me to dance classes until I got fed up of them. It was my dad who made me look like a shaggy dog instead of a princess when he'd attempted to do my hair. It was my dad who I had to drag to the shops to buy me new clothes. I should have done all that with my mum. Maybe being robbed of that made me too dependent on him. I've had him to myself since then, I suppose.'

'So, is she nice?'

Chloe's curls flailed about as she nodded her head. 'Maddy hasn't let herself go in her forties like so many women seem to. I suppose, in a way, she's a perfect role model – she's a really successful business woman. But I know that my dad loves her… really loves her. And it hurts.'

Kate could see tears glistening in Chloe's eyes. She'd always thought there would be a young girl in there somewhere, underneath that grown-up exterior.

'Is that why you moved away?' she asked gently. 'To give them time to be together?'

Chloe was confused. 'What do you mean?'

'Maybe you'd feel threatened by any woman who tried to muscle in on your dad? It's understandable. I would have felt the same.'

'I tried really hard to get on with her but I was so jealous. I'd hear them laughing in the conservatory and I'd be so annoyed that I'd storm in and start moaning about something or other, just to change the mood. Ben was forever having a go at me. It's caused no end of rows.' Chloe took a sip from her drink and guiltily averted her eyes for a moment. 'I've been a right bitch, really.'

'Don't worry,' Kate tried to appease her. 'It'll work itself out. One day you'll see the funny side of things.'

'I bet Maddy doesn't find things funny. I love my dad, Kate. I suppose I owe it to him to try and get on with her.'

'What does your dad do for a living?'

'He sells shoes. We have two factories and five outlets with his name above the doors.'

'And you've never wanted to work for him?'

Chloe shook her head. 'My brother hasn't either. Luckily for us, Dad's been really understanding about it.' Her voice became lower for a moment as she imitated her father. '"I'd be proud to have someone to take over when I'm old and grey, but I won't push either of you into working for the family." But we have benefited from it really. He gave us each a second-hand car on our seventeenth birthdays and an allowance to help us through college. Ben's training to be a solicitor. I haven't decided what to do yet.'

Their conversation changed back to lighter subjects and they talked about the new items that they'd chosen for the coffee shop and how the refurbishment was moving on. Before they knew it, they were back onto the subject of Nick and it was Kate's turn to talk.

'You must have been happy at one time,' said Chloe. 'You did marry him, after all.'

'Yes, I suppose it was good for most of the time.' Kate switched the kettle on again. Picking up Chloe's mug, she tried to explain how she felt about the relationship without raking up too many gory details. 'I loved him so much when we first got together. I suppose that's why it's hard to let go. I've been with him for so long.'

'I just don't see why you split up.' Chloe's face sported a puzzled expression. 'Then again, I've never been in love, not like you and Nick. I thought I'd loved Joe Broadman when I was in high school, but I soon tired of him after the novelty wore off.'

'It's complicated.' Kate didn't expect Chloe to understand. 'I don't know why but we started to argue all the time, over nothing really. On the odd occasion I went out with friends, he'd accuse me of flirting with other men. If I was going anywhere with Louise, my friend from work, he'd goad me, try to start an argument to make me feel guilty. I think I made him feel insecure – maybe because I was growing away from him.' She spooned coffee into the mugs, added sugar for Chloe and turned back. 'Sometimes it wasn't worth the hassle and I'd stay in to keep him quiet. But then I'd become resentful and we'd end up arguing anyway. I felt like I was trapped.'

'Maybe you and Sam should get it together then?'

Kate frowned. 'Where did that come from?'

Chloe flicked her a knowing look. 'It's obvious he fancies the pants off you. I can't understand what's taking you so long.'

Kate felt herself blushing. 'God, I'm not ready for that yet. Besides, he's far too young for me.'

'But it's obvious that you fancy him, too.'

'No, it's not!' Kate baulked. 'It isn't, is it?'

'There's no shame in it.'

'Maybe not, but –' Chloe stared at her. 'Stop it. You're making me blush.'

'Why don't you ask *him* out?'

'Because.'

'Because?'

'Because…' Kate grinned, finally finding the funny side. 'I'm not ready to go out with anyone yet.'

'But you could have some fun.'

'Look, it's hard to explain why, so leave me be.'

Chloe wasn't put off by her resistance. 'What you need is a good seeing-to by another man. If you stay on the shelf much longer, your fanny faloo will be sealed over if you're not careful.'

'My fanny fa… what?'

Slow footsteps alerted them to someone coming down the stairs.

'Oh no, it's the ghost of coffee coming to drown us in his brew,' Chloe whispered.

Kate giggled.

'So, this is what you get up to once my back is turned.' Lily tutted good-humouredly.

'Did we wake you?' Kate pulled out the empty chair beside her and Lily sat down.

'No,' said Lily. 'I was already having trouble sleeping. What have you been chatting about?'

Kate and Chloe shared a smile.

'Oh, you know,' said Chloe. 'This and that.'

'Yeah,' Kate winked conspiratorially at her. 'Something and nothing.'

'I've decided to let you know the name of the coffee shop,' Lily announced at their next meeting. They'd had so many over the last few days that, for purposes of comfort, they'd changed tactics and were now congregated in the living room. Lily sat in her favourite armchair by the window. Kate and Chloe shared the settee.

'Thank god for that,' said Chloe. 'I'm getting fed up of people asking me when "the caff" is going to open.'

Lily unfolded a piece of paper and held it up for them both to see.

'Mi Tierra?' Chloe frowned. 'I've never heard of that. What does it mean?'

Kate, too, racked her brain but failed to come up with any understanding of the words.

'It's pronounced me ti-air-a and it means my homeland,' Lily explained. 'Seeing as *home is where the heart is*, or so the saying goes, I thought it would be rather appropriate. And rather quirky and modern. What do you two think?'

Kate sat in thought then raised her eyebrows. 'It's different,' she said.

'I like it,' nodded Chloe. 'Sounds quite cool, really.'

Lily folded the paper in half again. 'Good. That's settled then. The coffee shop name is Mi Tierra.'

As Lily moved onto the next thing on her list, Kate repeated the words to herself.

Mi Tierra?

There was something not quite right about it, but she couldn't put her finger on it.

She thought about it all that night. Since she'd arrived in Somerley, Kate had got to know the lay of the land and the people who came and went about their business during the day. There were several professional office blocks around, but more down-to-earth blue-collar workers than white. What would the name Mi Tierra conjure up to them?

Perhaps she could have a word with Sam and some of the other builders to see what they thought of it. Would it put them off coming in? Would they think it was a fancy restaurant and not want to try it out to see regardless?

Did it really give off the right vibe? Kate wasn't sure it did at all.

CHAPTER FOURTEEN

Lily wiped floury hands on her apron as she waited for the next batch of baking to cool down, whilst keeping a watchful eye on the timer so that she didn't burn the chocolate-chip cookies. It was only seven a.m. but she had a lot to do today. As she sat in the bay window, watching all the commotion in front of her as the stall-holders parked up on the road to unload their vans, she made a mental note to remind herself that she needed to make another appointment with Mr Stead. There were lots of things she had to see to before time ran out. Everything seemed to be happening so fast.

In roughly one hour's time, she'd be able to cross her pen straight through the words 'baking for the market'. It hadn't been an easy task to complete, what with Terry and his boys around to get in her way but they were working extremely hard to finish on time. Terry had informed her last night before he left that they were on schedule.

Kate's idea about hiring a stall to promote the coffee shop had been an excellent idea. Free pieces of their wares to sample would be far more tempting than leaflets that would be discarded for the market cleaner to sweep up. And, hopefully, it would entice customers in to try other things.

So far, near on three weeks had produced an enormous effort to transform the café into a coffee shop. Lily had been astounded at how much had changed in that short time. She'd thought she'd been optimistic about opening up in four weeks but Kate and Chloe had treated it as a challenge during the first three so that she now knew it was possible. Just as well, because

Lily had been used to a far slower pace when she had worked with Bernard.

When Lily next glanced at her watch, she pulled herself to her feet. It was time to check the oven. The cookies would be done by now. And, along with everything else she'd baked, surely there'd be enough to last out the morning.

Somerley market wasn't a huge affair – there were thirty stalls at the most, only one of everything, apart from clothes and shoes – but it was hugely popular with the locals. Kate didn't have a minute to look around as she had planned, to try and gauge the type of clientele that might frequent the coffee shop. By the time the church clock chimed out eleven noisy times, they had practically given away most of the morning's allowance, on schedule. Thankfully, she could mark her idea down as a success.

She sighed. Even giving cake away was a hassle, she'd found out that morning after people had flocked around her, pushing and shoving as if they hadn't got a minute of their time to spare.

'Would you like to try a piece, sir?' Kate greeted the elderly man who stood in front of her. He took a tiny square of ginger cake, dipped his cap, and continued with his walk. Well, at least he had manners.

She turned to see where Chloe was, only to find her deep in conversation with three young teenagers.

All boys about her age, they congregated around her like she was the real Nicole Kidman. Kate watched as Chloe pulled back her head and did that irritating flick with her hair that had them all but panting. She rolled her eyes, secretly envious of Chloe's natural ability to laugh and joke with the boys.

'Not many left to go,' Chloe nudged her arm minutes later. 'It didn't take as long as I thought.'

'It didn't take *you* much time at all.' Kate glared at her. 'I've done most of the hard work.'

'Chill out. I'm only doing PR.' Chloe laughed at the scowl on Kate's face. 'One day, you'll realise how much hard work it is to flirt. Oh, maybe you'll get your chance now.'

Busy organising what was left on top of the table, Kate was unaware that Sam had crept up beside her.

'Hey, Katie,' he smiled. 'Can I bite into your cookie?'

Kate scooped up the crumbs she'd wiped into a pile before coming up level with a pair of sparkly eyes. While Sam treated Chloe to a smile, she flicked her eyes from top to toe and back again, deciding he was a real treat to behold. A hand ruffled the blond hair where his hard hat had flattened the spikes.

'Of course you can,' she replied, automatically mirroring his action by running a hand through her own hair. She hoped her lipstick was still intact as he dipped his head to one side and gave her a wink of a brown eye. He was taller than her, she realised, aware that standing next to him was much better than staring up at him from the pavement.

Chloe loaded her tray with the remainder of Lily's cakes. 'I'm going to shift these, seeing as *you're* too busy to help.'

Kate's jaw dropped as Chloe strolled past, tongue in cheek. 'And you accuse me of flirting?' she had the audacity to whisper before Kate could retaliate.

After finishing off the morning at the market, they were back in the coffee shop getting ready to go over Kate's latest list of things to do. Chloe and Kate had barely started talking when Alex came barging in.

Patiently, Kate waited for him to find what he was searching for, knowing full well that he wouldn't just go when he found it. Both him and Tom had been great fun to have around while they had been completing the refurbishments but they were always interrupting, wanting to know what was going on.

'You two are always on a break,' he said, picking up a piece of paper from the table. 'What's this for?'

Kate snatched it back from him. 'It's the agenda for the meeting. The meeting we are in the middle of, *if* you don't mind.'

Alex held up his hands. 'Pretend I'm not here. Or maybe I can take notes?'

'Stop taking the piss and go away.' Chloe made to slap him but he dodged her hand.

'Where's the boss lady today?'

'She's gone to a bakery that I visited last week,' said Kate. 'Now, find what you're looking for and out!'

'Do you think we'll be busy on the opening day?' Chloe wanted to know as he searched around behind them noisily. She scanned the agenda again to see what was left to discuss.

'It's hard to say,' said Kate. 'We'll do another cake day next Thursday. Lily has also suggested putting an ad in the local paper. Surely that will catch anyone we've missed.'

'You ought to have me and Tom working here,' Alex joked. 'Two good-looking guys like us are sure to bring the female clientele flocking.'

Observing him in his paint splattered overalls – although not a single dark hair out of place – humming along to this week's number one on the radio, made Kate realise how well he'd scrub up. She rubbed her chin thoughtfully.

'That's not a bad idea,' she said.

Chloe shrugged one shoulder. 'Maybe a couple of guys *would* bring in the girls?' she questioned, already knowing the answer. 'You'll have to ask Tom.'

Alex perched on the edge of the table. 'No way, I was only messing.'

'Well, I think it's a great idea.' Kate nodded encouragingly. 'Although I don't suppose you two will be up to it.'

'Yes,' said Chloe. 'It'll be a long day. You'll need plenty of stamina. Maybe we'd better keep it all female.'

Alex jumped guiltily to his feet as his uncle came into the room.

'Thought I'd find you resting in here,' said Terry. 'I need that hammer to finish off. Can't you leave them alone for one minute?'

'They've asked us to help out on the opening day,' Alex said, in order to avoid his question. 'A bit of eye candy, you know?'

'Is that right?' Terry rubbed his hands together excitingly. 'What would you want us to do?'

'They want *you* to do nothing. It's me and Tom they need. You can spare us for the day, can't you?'

Kate winked at Terry. 'We're opening next Saturday.'

'Oh, that's a different matter,' Alex replied curtly. 'I'm usually hungover on Saturdays.'

'See?' Kate shook her head. 'What did I tell you? No stamina.'

'Well, I suppose if you put it that way.' He flicked his eyes accusingly from one to the other. 'Count us in.'

'Looks like we've covered everything then,' said Chloe as Alex finally left them to it.

'Not quite,' said Kate. 'I've been thinking about the name, Mi Tierra.'

'I know.' Chloe nodded as she chewed on her fingernail. 'It sounded a bit posh for me, but I like it now.'

'I agree it's a nice name, but I don't think that it symbolises a coffee shop.' Kate paused. 'What would you think it was if you drove past in your car?'

Chloe gave it some thought for a moment. 'Now you come to mention it, I'd probably think it was a restaurant. But people will be able to see through the windows, I suppose.'

'Which suggests?'

Chloe nodded, catching her meaning. 'It's a restaurant. Maybe we should talk to Lily about it? Before any signs or logos are finished?'

Kate sighed. 'I'm not sure we should. It is her business, her idea. And, timewise, it's pushing it.'

They were still discussing the problem when Lily arrived ten minutes later with Irene. She had a huge bag in her arms and she struggled to get it through the front door. Kate rushed to her aid.

'Ooh, thanks, love,' said Lily appreciatively. 'It's not heavy but it's awkward to carry.'

'What is it?' asked Chloe. Already, she was opening the ties.

'It's a beanbag for Rosie. I thought she could have her own bed in the living room now, rather than you keep carrying the same one back and forth.'

'Oh, Lily, thank you. That's so thoughtful.' Kate smiled as Chloe pulled it out. As if released from a jack-in-the-box, it sprang across the floor. All at once, she realised this was not the time to discuss the name of the shop. How could she explain to Lily now that she didn't like her choice?

But Chloe took the matter into her own hands. 'Irene, what do you think of the name Mi Tierra?'

'Not much.' Irene pulled out a chair and sat down. 'You'll have everyone asking you what it means all the time.'

'That's exactly what we thought.' Kate looked across at Lily shyly. 'I think Mi Tierra sounds like a restaurant name, a foreign restaurant actually. It doesn't suggest a coffee shop. I know I wouldn't give it a second look during the day if I was passing. I would think it wasn't open until evenings.'

Lily sat down next to her. 'I thought it was rather a nice name, actually.'

Kate was horrified to see the look that crossed her face. 'It is!' she said quickly. 'I just thought it –'

'She's right, Lil,' said Irene, emphasising it with a nod of her head. 'It isn't catchy enough. You want something simple, something easy to recognise. I don't know, something like… Coffee Time… The Coffee Stop… Coffee and Friends…'

'Ooh!' said Chloe. 'The Coffee Stop. I like that.'

'Yes', agreed Kate. 'It's simple and effective.'

'I was only joking,' said Irene, quite taken aback at their outburst.

Lily wasn't sure. 'I chose Mi Tierra because I thought it would stand out. Doesn't The Coffee Stop sound a little amateur?'

'But it captures everything this shop has to offer,' Kate enthused. 'It's going to be a friendly place to stop off –'

'– Where you can gossip with your mates –' interrupted Chloe.

'– And enjoy a different type of coffee.'

Lily frowned. 'Let me think about it,' she told them.

The last weekend before the newly named coffee shop opened found Kate and Chloe going their separate ways.

On Sunday, Kate went back to Brentside to see Nick. She'd arranged to meet him at two thirty, in a city centre Starbucks. She didn't feel ready to meet at the house.

Aware that her heart seemed to have flown into her throat when she spotted him sitting at a table, she swallowed.

'I've got you your usual,' Nick said as she sat down opposite him. He slid over a cappuccino, quickly followed by two documents.

Kate ran a hand through her hair. 'In what way?'

Nick shrugged his shoulders. 'I don't know. Lighter, I guess.'

'Well, I have been doing a lot of physical work lately. We've –'

'I meant your face,' he jumped in.

Suddenly Kate understood. She smiled at him and her heart settled back into its normal position. 'I feel okay at the moment,' she said truthfully, because as she sat there, so close to him, she realised that she did.

'Where do I need to sign?'

Nick pointed to four crosses. 'The policy is worth seven thousand, cash-in price. I'll send you your half when I get the cheque. I'm still waiting on the others.'

'Thanks.'

'And you still don't want to put the house on the market yet?'

Kate shrugged. 'I suppose you've been letting clients know anyway?'

Nick took a gulp of his drink, glancing over towards a group of teenagers sitting at a table to their side.

'I've figured out what price is best for it,' he told her. 'But I'm in no rush to move out, if you're okay waiting.'

Kate nodded and followed Nick's gaze to the teenagers. They were laughing and joking loudly, like they hadn't got a care in the world. Suddenly, she realised *she* had all the time in the world, too. It didn't matter how long she had to wait, she wasn't going to be here to deal with any of it.

Kate turned back to Nick and nodded again. 'Yes, that's fine.'

And as she said it, for the first time in ages, she realised that actually, she was going to be okay.

* * *

On Saturday evening, Chloe had gone out with her friend, Manda. They'd met a few more friends and then went on to a club, and she'd come home a bit later and a lot tipsier than she had planned. On Sunday morning, she woke up in her own bed with a sense of déjà vu. She went downstairs at half past eleven, only to find her dad in the kitchen with Maddy.

'Where's Ben?' she asked, helping herself to a banana.

'He's gone to play golf,' Maddy informed her. 'He said he won't be back in time to see you before you leave, so said to wish you luck for the opening.'

'Chloe, come and see this.' Graham beckoned her over and showed her a framed photograph. There were around eighty small boys in a group, some standing, some sitting on rows of chairs.

'Can you see which one is me?' he asked, putting an arm around her shoulders.

Chloe studied the photograph for a moment and then shook her head.

Graham pointed to a gangly boy on the back row. 'That's me, there,' he said with a laugh. 'I showed the photo to Maddy last week and she's had it framed for me.'

'You are so nice to *my* father,' Chloe replied, glaring at Maddy.

'I bet you can't wait to get back to the coffee shop,' Maddy ignored the jibe. 'It sounds like a really cool place to hang out. I bet it will be –'

'You're not getting rid of me that easily,' Chloe said nastily.

'No, I didn't mean –'

'Of course you didn't.' Graham patted Maddy reassuringly on her arm. 'Chloe knows exactly what you mean.'

Chloe sloped off to the conservatory. Graham joined her minutes later and handed her a cup of coffee.

'You really should try being nicer to her,' he said. 'She tries hard to get involved, but you just shut her out.'

'I'm sorry,' Chloe relented a little. Now that Maddy had left the room, she felt easier knowing she had her father's undivided attention.

'So, come on then,' he said. 'Tell me all about what you've been up to. I know you're dying to.'

Lily had a quiet day without the two of them. After a hectic week, a trip to the church graveyard was her first port of call on Sunday morning, followed by the church service. On the way home, she called in to see Irene, surprising herself by craving company. But Irene had been none too pleased when she'd caught her checking her watch again.

'For goodness' sakes, Lil,' she said. 'Why don't you go and see if one of them is back?'

Lily didn't need asking twice, but there was no one there to greet her when she walked up the stairs into the living room. Apart from Rosie, that was.

'Hello, little madam,' she said, bending down carefully to fuss her. 'I'm so glad I offered to look after you or else I'd be all alone.'

'Are you talking to yourself again, Lily Mortimer?' Chloe shouted up the stairs.

Lily turned round, just as Chloe reached her.

Chloe bent forward and flung her arms around her. 'I couldn't wait to get back.'

For an instant, Lily was stunned at her show of affection. Then she smiled and hugged her too. She looked up. 'I've missed you too. I was just telling Rosie how quiet it had been.'

Chloe moved into her room and came out seconds later without her holdall. 'Is Kate home?'

'Not yet,' said Lily, secretly bursting with pleasure. Chloe had called it *home* already. 'I'll put the kettle on, shall I?'

They were on their second cup of tea when Kate finally arrived back. Rosie shot down the stairs as she shouted up to them.

'Hey,' said Chloe, hanging her head over the banister.

'Hey, how did it go with Maddy?' Kate asked as she reached the top of the stairs.

Chloe screwed up her nose. 'It was okay, I suppose. She had an old photograph framed for my dad. He was over the moon. I think she did it on purpose, because she knew I was coming home.'

'Oh, come on, Chloe. I'm sure –'

'Oh, never mind that. How did it go with Nick?'

'Fine,' Kate said with a smile. 'It wasn't anywhere near as bad as I thought it would be. We were quite civil actually.'

'What, no heart beating rapidly? No pulse pulsating wildly?'

'Not really,' she replied.

'Well, that's good to hear,' said Lily as she joined them. 'Would you like a cup of tea?'

'Ooh, Lily.' Kate touched her arm. 'I could murder one. Only how you make it, mind.'

Lily walked back into the kitchen and flicked on the kettle again. 'I don't know about you, Kate,' she heard Chloe saying, 'but I couldn't wait to get back. I'm so excited about the opening day. My dad told me off for talking about it all the time. "It's The Coffee Stop this, Kate that, Lily this, The Coffee Stop that", he said and…'

Lily smiled again. It seemed they had missed her just as much as she had missed them. She bit her lip to stop herself from giggling excitedly.

CHAPTER FIFTEEN

After moving all the new tables and chairs backwards and forwards downstairs, to maximise the available space, Kate's back
and shoulders were aching as if she had worked out at the gym.
It was ten thirty and all she wanted to do was relax. She was lying in bed reading a book when her phone rang. Nick's name
came up on caller display.

'Kate?' she heard above some kind of rocky background music. 'Kate, is that you?'

'Yes, Nick. It's me. What do you want? Do you know what
time it is?'

'Oh, Katie, Katie, Katie,' he slurred. 'I miss you so much.
When are you coming home?'

'What… what do you mean?'

'After seeing you yesterday afternoon, I realised how much I
need you. I'm not good without you, babe. I want you to come
home.'

Oh, no, she didn't need this now.

'But… I can't.'

'Yes, you can. You can move back in with me. I'll support
you until you get another job. I love you, Katie.'

Kate held her breath for a moment, sensing the power of
three small words as tears sprang to her eyes.

'Come home, I need you. Please,' he yelled, due to silence at
her end of the line.

'I have to go, Nick.'

'But I love you, Kate! You have to come back –'

Kate disconnected the call, switched off her phone and burst into tears. Then she proceeded to analyse his every word for the next two hours.

'Morning, sleepyhead,' Kate greeted Chloe as she walked into the coffee shop the next day.

'Morning.' Chloe shielded her eyes from the sun's bright rays. 'Looks like another hot day on the horizon.'

'It does indeed. What do you fancy to start this fine morning off? A tall or a skinny? Cappuccino or latte? Decaf or regular? I still feel like I need more practice so you can be my guinea pig.'

Since Chloe's attempt to produce a cappuccino had resulted in burnt offerings – she'd no idea before then that you could *scald* milk – Kate had taken it upon herself to oversee some staff training. After Tom had kindly explained that the water needed to be plumbed in first, so that it was hot all the time, she'd grabbed the instruction book and read it from cover to cover. Once it had been fitted correctly, she and Chloe had pressed every button, pushed every lever and made every coffee concoction going, just in case.

'I'll have a mocha, please.' Chloe scraped a high stool across the floor and jumped up onto it. 'Did you manage to catch up with Louise?'

'No.' Kate shook her head. 'She wasn't in when I called. I really wanted to see her this weekend too. I feel like I haven't spoken to her in ages. Maybe I should have rung her first.'

'Then it wouldn't have been a surprise.'

'I know but I should have made more of an effort to keep in touch.'

'You can't be in two places at once,' said Chloe.

'Hmm.' It didn't do anything to assuage Kate's guilt.

Moments later, Kate slid a cup and saucer towards Chloe. Chloe glanced down at it; lilac with delicate cream swirls and gold edging around the rim. To say it was a cup was a bit of an understatement. It seemed enough for two ordinary cups of coffee. But then, this was no ordinary coffee shop.

With pride, she took in the ambience she'd helped to create. Three walls were covered in delicate striped cream and lilac wallpaper. Beech wood panelling on the front of the counter blended pleasingly with the bold colour of the lilac-painted wall behind it, and was the same colour as the flooring. The serving hatch was barely visible due to Terry's expert joinery skills. Mirrored tiles behind the counter added extra depth without trying and there was a place for bits and bobs to authenticate the shelves above. Kate had added a few bits of local pottery, some quirky coffee mugs she'd found in a charity shop and a teapot in the shape of a country cottage.

Kate was pleased that Lily had acted upon her suggestion to move the counter to the back wall. With the till situated at its far end, it gave them more room to manoeuvre. And they'd installed a narrow worktop beneath the smaller window, allowing four people to sit on high stools and look over the square instead of into the coffee shop.

There were only a few minor details to sort out now. The windows had to be dressed. Chalk boards needed to be fitted to either end of the tile panels. Once Terry had finished the window seat in the bay window, the two settees Lily had ordered would be placed either side.

Lily had decided that the first coffee and slice of cake were to be free. If the shop was busy on its first day, they'd be off the starting line. All they had to do then was keep the whistle blowing, get over the hurdles and head straight to the finish.

'Penny for them?' Kate clicked her fingers in front of Chloe's face. 'Are they hot or are they not?'

'Huh?'

'Your thoughts! You've been sitting in a trance for a few minutes now.' Chloe swished the remains of the coffee around the bottom of the cup. 'It looks great, doesn't it?'

'It does. We should be proud of ourselves.'

'It's a little scary though, don't you think?'

'I'm terrified!' Kate grimaced. 'I'm scared that the first cup I carry will tip up in the lap of the first customer we have. Forcing a headline such as "Coffee shop clown throws a party – all over the first customer. Woman to sue."'

Chloe giggled self-consciously. 'It's not going to be that bad, but I want it to work so much. I can't imagine having to go home, tail between my legs, admitting defeat.'

Suddenly, Kate's light-hearted mood changed as she remembered the unwelcome reminder of home she'd had the night before.

She sighed, not wanting to share too much with Chloe. 'Well, at least you've got a home to go back –'

'Hey.' Chloe stopped her in mid-flow with a pointed finger. 'Come on now.'

'I know, I know.' Kate practised that stuck-on smile again. 'I'm as strong as I want to be, so you keep telling me. The only problem is that I'm unsure how strong I *need* to be.'

Just before the staff meeting that afternoon at three, Kate made a visit to the retail park and bought another mobile phone. She didn't want to risk Nick ringing again when he was feeling low.

'Been treating yourself?' Lily picked up the box that Kate had discarded on the counter top.

'Nick caught me off guard last night,' Kate explained, 'so I thought I'd better get a new one. I've wanted to update mine for ages anyway.'

'Ah, I wondered what was bothering you. You've been really quiet today.' Lily sat down. 'Did it upset you more than you thought to see him at the weekend?'

'Actually, I was more relieved to think that I might have done the right thing.'

'And now?'

'Now, I'm not so sure.' Kate screwed the plastic wrapping up into a ball and launched it toward the bin, secretly pleased when it landed where it should.

'Do you miss him?'

'I think I miss being part of a couple more, if I'm honest. But I *do* have to know that I did the right thing. Maybe I should go and see him again, talk it through. Just to be sure.'

Kate looked up to see Lily pondering over what to say. When she remained quiet, she pressed a button on the phone. It burst out a tune and she switched it off again quickly.

'Are the boys ready yet?' Lily asked.

'In the kitchen.'

'And Chloe?'

'I'm here.' Chloe's curls bounced freely behind her as she walked across the room. She smiled at Lily.

'The diva has arrived. So now we can begin.'

The kitchen door crashed open. Tom walked steadily across the room with a tray of glasses.

'Champagne!' Alex came up behind him with Chloe. He held a bottle in each hand. 'It's Lily's treat.'

'This place looks amazing now,' said Chloe.

'I'm glad it's all finished,' said Kate, as Chloe pulled out a chair beside her. The new ones had silver powder-coated metal frames and high backs, with upholstered seat-pads in complimentary colours. Lily had disagreed on glass-topped tables, instead choosing a chunky beech effect for hassle free cleaning, but it had still had the desired result.

Chloe raised an empty glass as Lily joined them all. 'To The Coffee Stop and all that sail in her.'

Lily smiled. 'We're not in a ship, Chloe.'

'Definitely not!' said Kate as the cork flew across the room, narrowly missing the mirrored tiles behind the bar. 'This is one business that isn't going to sink.'

'Here's to us,' said Chloe. 'For being such a kick-ass team.'

'Here's to Lily,' said Kate. 'For giving us the chance to work together.'

'Here's to the lads!' Alex chirped up.

'Yeah, yeah.' Up went Chloe's hand. 'Whatever.'

'Down to business, I suppose,' Kate began as she checked the list in front of her. 'Can everyone be here around nine on Friday morning?'

It had been Chloe's idea to change the opening day from Saturday to Friday. She'd been people watching and wasn't sure if there was enough passing trade at the weekend. Lily and Kate had thought it was an excellent idea.

Before anyone could answer, Kate moved swiftly on. 'Although we don't officially open until twelve on our first day, there will be lots to do. Here's hoping we don't get a break. Our aim is to be rushed off our feet.'

'Do you think we should practice what to say to the media?' Alex looked directly at Kate for an answer.

Already she was forecasting a sarcastic one. 'What do you mean?'

'In case we say the wrong things!' He slapped a palm on his forehead. 'What if I slip up and start revealing all my darkest secrets to a reporter? You know what they're like. Once they get you talking, they twist and turn the best tale you've got and make it into *The Exorcist*.'

'And me,' said Tom. 'I have so many ex-girlfriends that could tell tales. It might ruin your reputation if you mix with us.'

'You can't have had that many – you're barely in your twenties!' Chloe chided. 'Besides, who would want to know about you anyway? They'll be more interested in us lay-dees.'

'Oh, but you don't know –'

'Come on now. Let's get back on track.' Kate moved them along. 'I'm finding it hard to keep up with you all talking at once. Are we all clear what we need to be doing?'

'Yes,' said Alex. 'Tom is to hand round cakes and sandwiches and I have the respectable job of clearing tables.'

'I'm glad you've listened to something,' remarked Chloe. 'Or else there'll be no time for champagne.'

'If you'd let me continue,' Kate said haughtily, 'we can finish the agenda.'

Chloe giggled and then held her head down as Kate frowned. 'I've left school. Remember?' she muttered.

Kate smiled shyly. 'Am I coming on a bit heavy?'

Three bobbing heads acknowledged Kate. Lily chose to abstain.

'Well, I'm nervous too,' said Kate.

It was true. Only last week, she'd woken in a panic thinking she'd forgotten to lock up – and they weren't even open yet.

'I just want everything to be perfect,' she added.

'With you at the helm, I'm certain it will be.' Lily touched her arm lightly to let her know everything was okay. 'You've done a brilliant job. You all have, actually, and I'm so proud of what you've achieved in such a short space of time.'

'But we're not in a ship,' Chloe mocked, to break up the tension.

'Let's check the agenda one more time,' smiled Kate, before looking down. 'The local newspaper reporter is due at eleven thirty, Lily, is that okay? He wants a few words from you.'

'Yes, that's fine,' Lily replied. 'Although I'm so nervous, I can feel butterflies in my tummy already.'

'Butterflies?' snorted Alex raucously. 'I've got pterodactyls flapping around in mine and I'm only here for the day.'

When the meeting finished, Kate shared out the champagne. 'Here's to The Coffee Stop!' she said as she raised her glass.

'Here's to our first day.' Chloe followed suit. 'May my feet stand the pace.'

Lily stayed seated as she spoke. 'Here's to my Bernard. God bless his soul.'

'Well,' Alex stood up. 'Here's to the boys!'

Tom whooped in agreement.

Three pairs of eyes bore into Alex's, so much so that he could feel himself colouring.

'Okay, okay,' he relented, throwing up his glass again. 'You women are so mean! Here's to the girls too.'

Once Alex and Tom had left, and Kate and Chloe had gone upstairs, Lily turned off the lights, taking a moment to glance over her shoulder at what they had created. It had started off as a silly dream. How had she been blessed with two young ladies to help her create The Coffee Stop? Someone was certainly looking down on her.

'Is it you, Bernard?' she whispered as she stood in silence for a moment.

Once again, Lily made her way upstairs after a long but wonderful day. All she wanted now was a good night's sleep. And for the Coffee Stop to be the success that she craved. Only time would tell if she would get either.

CHAPTER SIXTEEN

At half past ten that same evening, Kate was still mulling over Nick's words. Even though she knew she shouldn't, she wanted to ring him. The words of an article she'd read popped into her mind. It said something about speaking the truth when you're drunk. Perhaps this was Nick's way of saying he'd made a mistake. *He sounded sincere,* she thought, and he'd been really nice to her yesterday.

But was she reading too much into things? Maybe she *wanted* to read too much into his words. Maybe the fact that they hadn't given their relationship another try would haunt her until they did. The perfectionist in her still refused to give up. It was that thought that scared her the most.

It was no use. She'd have to speak to him to sound him out – but not on the new phone. She picked up her rejected mobile and rang him.

'Hi, Nick, it's Kate,' she said in a sing-song tone when he answered.

'Oh, hello.'

'Feeling a little more sober today?'

'I suppose so.'

'You said –'

'Look, Kate, I was a little worse for wear last night. I may have said some things that I shouldn't have.'

'You said you wanted me to come home.'

'We both know that wouldn't work.'

'But I thought –'

'I'm sorry,' he interrupted her again, 'but it was just the alcohol talking. I wasn't thinking straight. Obviously, I shouldn't have called you.'

'Obviously,' she answered, realising that she'd lost a night's sleep over nothing.

After a few more sentences of small talk, she disconnected the call and went through to the living room, only to find it empty. She switched on the TV. In lengthy detail, the news presenter spoke about a blazing fire at a paint factory but Nick's face kept appearing before Kate's eyes.

What was going on? Why had he been so flippant after the things he'd said last night? Kate wished she could switch her affection on and off like that. Things would be much easier.

Familiar feelings started to creep back and, in frustration, she shook her head to rid it of his image.

How could she have let herself be taken in by his charm again?

When Chloe joined her a few minutes later, Kate felt the need to share her thoughts.

'If you ask me, you've had a shock,' Chloe said afterwards. 'You haven't seen Nick in ages, yet he used to be there every day. He's bound to have that effect on you.'

'I know,' Kate agreed. 'But I wasn't prepared for the rush of feelings I had when he said he wanted me to go back.'

'I thought you were getting over him?' Chloe sounded confused.

'So did I. I was okay when I saw him. I realised that I'd made the right decision, no matter how painful it was to move on. But he really got to me last night, made me think all sorts of things.'

'So tell me, what would be different if you went back?'

'I'm not too sure, if I'm honest. Maybe it's the fact that we haven't tried again that bugs me.' Kate thought back to the last time they'd had sex on the kitchen table.

'You're blushing!'

'Let's just say we did try at some things.'

Chloe rolled her eyes. 'Don't tell me you had a goodbye shag? It's never the same, you know.'

Kate recoiled at her words. 'How would you know that?'

'How would I know that you'd had a goodbye shag? Or how would I know because of my age?'

Kate looked away in embarrassment.

'Well, did you?'

She nodded.

'And did it do the trick?'

'If you must know, it scratched an itch.' Kate sighed. 'You're right. We lost our way. There was no spark left, nothing to aim towards. We hardly did anything as a couple. I wanted nights out together instead of me waiting for him to come home… quality nights in instead of him going to play football. I wanted *conversation*!'

'And you think you can still have all that?'

Kate paused. 'No, the magic has gone.' She grabbed a cushion and pulled it to her chest. 'It's just so confusing. My head seems to be over him but my heart hasn't caught up yet.'

Chloe reached for her magazine and flipped her legs up onto the settee. 'You should have told him to naff off while you had the chance. Switch off that phone and use the new one now.'

'That's not practical. What if he needs to speak to me regarding the house?'

'Give him the landline number. Or he can email you.'

'But –'

'Look, he's bound to ring you again, and when he does, you shouldn't give him the satisfaction of answering. He has no right to play with your feelings like that.'

Later as she tried to soak her cares away in a hot bath, Kate found she still couldn't get Nick out of her mind. Was she just annoyed that he was being so blasé about the phone call, after all the angst he'd caused her? Because he *didn't* want her to go back, whereas she had thought the opposite? Or was her heart telling her things her head didn't want to listen to?

Part of her was humiliated. She'd been thinking of him all day but she now knew he hadn't given her a second thought. Another part of her was annoyed that once again Nick was in control. Not only had he walked out on her, it was him who was selling their home and, after last night, it was him who had put her in turmoil by messing with her emotions.

Trying to concentrate on her paperback, after ten minutes she found that she'd read the same paragraph over and over again and still couldn't remember a word of it. She threw it to the floor in a temper.

How dare he keep on messing with her feelings. The sooner things were sorted out with him now, the better.

The following morning, Kate and Chloe were handing out cakes and biscuits to anyone entering the market. It was their last attempt to drum up trade before their opening day.

'Kate! Chloe!' Tom shouted above the sound of the meat man advertising two-lamb-chops-for-a-fiver over his infuriatingly loud speaker. He weaved his way through the crowds before continuing. 'Lily's sent me to get you. You *have* to see the coffee shop. All the signwriting has been finished. There are lights above the main sign and it looks…' he paused for effect, as well as to catch his breath after running all the way, 'it looks like a proper coffee shop *daann sarrth*. I'll look after this little lot while you go and see.'

Once Kate and Chloe had slalomed their way through the crowd, they walked a little faster. Then they walked a lot faster. A quick glance at each other was all it took for them to break out into a run. They laughed and pushed each other all the way back to the shop.

This is stupid, thought Kate. *Surely this much excitement isn't warranted for a sign going up?*

But it wasn't just the sign. They slowed down enough to take in the full effect as they walked along the row of properties towards the cobbled-frontage of number eleven. Or The Coffee Stop, as it was now saying above the double doors.

'Kate, I feel like crying,' said Chloe.

'I know what you mean.' Kate couldn't take her eyes away. Tom was right. It looked amazing. The sign was made of cream Perspex, The Coffee Stop written in gold. The letters seemed more pronounced due to a shadowing technique, three round lights hanging down to illuminate it. A deep purple awning was spread out above the smaller window where Lily, Alf and Irene sat at one of the new tables they'd brought outside. Signwriting in the bay window advertised some of the regular coffees, as well as cakes they would be providing, and there was an A-frame menu board ready to be written on propped up by the low wall.

Alex stood with his hand high on the frame of the open doorway, one ankle flicked over the other.

'Well, what do you think?' he asked.

Lily hadn't heard Kate and Chloe arrive and turned her head to catch their reaction. She only had to look at their faces to know how pleased they were with the end result.

'It's finished,' gasped Kate. 'We actually have a coffee shop.'

'I'm...' Chloe's hands rose up in mock surrender. 'I'm lost for words.'

'Must be good, then,' teased Alex. 'Let me show you how it looks with the blinds shut.'

He disappeared into the shop and for a few crazy moments shouted through the door, 'Blinds open... blinds shut... blinds open... blinds shut.' Kate watched as the vertical slats flew to one side of the window and back again. 'Blinds pulled across... blinds shut again.'

'What do you two think?' Kate spoke directly to Alf and Irene.

Kate had met both of Lily's friends now on several occasions as they had kept an eye on things – or rather, kept an eye on Lily. Whereas Alf was polite and chose his words carefully to say that he was worried when Lily looked a bit worn out, Irene just spit out what she was thinking.

'It looks okay,' Alf replied.

Lily tutted. 'It looks far better than okay,' she told him. 'They've worked so hard to get it finished. I'm really proud of them.'

Kate wasn't perturbed as she sat down next to Lily. They'd get around Alf eventually and she knew he was only protecting his friend.

'And you, Irene?' she asked. 'What do you think?'

Irene pushed her glasses further up her nose. 'It's a darn sight better than it was,' she admitted.

Kate smiled with gratitude at the same time as Lily.

'Although,' Irene continued, 'I still think she's mad to open it up again.'

'Yoo-hoo! Kate!'

Kate turned her head to see Lucy, from the gym, tottering across the road. When Lily had suggested getting someone in part-time, to work a few hours ad hoc, Kate had mentioned it to Lucy and she'd jumped at the chance.

'Lucy! You look fantastic.' Kate walked towards her, admiring her golden legs on show beneath her short denim skirt. 'Good holiday?'

Lucy air-kissed her dramatically. 'It was fabulous. Plenty of sea, sand and lots of the other!' She pulled off her sunglasses and looked Kate up and down. 'I hardly recognise you with your clothes on,' she shrieked at her own joke.

Kate turned to everyone, praying they understood that Lucy was referring to always seeing her in gym wear.

'This is Lucy,' she introduced the petite blonde to everyone. 'She's going to be working here in the mornings, on an "as and when" basis, until trade builds up. Oh, and all day on a Thursday, if that's okay, Luce?'

Lucy nodded and gave a royal wave to the group. 'Sorry I missed all the fun while you've been busy working but I've been to Benidorm for a week – hence the tan.' She held out a bronzed arm for them to see. 'I'm so lucky to have skin that browns easily. You must be Chloe,' she said to the wary looking young woman.

'And I'm Alex.' He shot forward and held out a hand. 'It's a pleasure to meet you.'

'Oh,' Lucy tittered, 'the pleasure is all mine.'

'Are you helping out tomorrow?'

Lucy shook her head, layered hair flicking around her chest. 'I have to go to a wedding this weekend. We've hired a room for two nights so I won't be back until Sunday. But I'll be here on Monday. Bright and early.'

'What a pity.' Alex's shoulders dropped sensationally. 'Our next job is in Birmingham. Looks like I'll have to do a detour on my way home.'

'Glad you could make it – *after* all the hard work has been done,' Chloe said to her, pointing at Lucy's long acrylic nails. 'Mind, you wouldn't want to be breaking any of those.'

Kate's look was puzzled as she caught the sarcasm in Chloe's tone.

But Lucy wasn't fazed.

'Oh, don't worry about me,' she said. 'I have a nail technician on standby for such a thing. He's a friend of mine. I'll get him to do yours if you like?'

Chloe folded her arms to hide her hands. 'No thank you,' she answered. 'I like all my body parts to be real.'

Lucy looked puzzled for a moment before roaring with laughter. 'Oh, you're referring to my puppies,' she said, flicking her eyes down to her chest. 'No, I can assure you they're every bit real. You and I are going to have to watch where we're walking – we'll be bouncing off ourselves if we're not careful!'

Kate laughed, then glanced covertly at Chloe to see her scowling at Lucy. She hadn't thought that Lucy coming to work with them would cause any problems but she could definitely pick up an underlying current of tension. She'd have to keep an eye on them both, otherwise she had a feeling that there would be trouble.

Lily couldn't believe that it was twelve thirty at night and she was still wide awake. Unable to toss and turn in her bed any longer, she'd moved into the old living room. Although clean and tidy before, it had now been transformed into another bright place. The walls had been treated to a dash of cream, and the paintwork was back to its original white. A calligraphic printed throw had taken care of the badly worn settee and it had been pushed back as far as it would go. It provided much needed space, especially as Kate and Chloe had persuaded her to part with the old sideboard she'd had since her wedding day – which wasn't much of a problem, as she'd only kept it because it belonged to Bernard's mother. Much to her amazement, Lily hadn't had to fight to keep her cream armchairs. They'd been seen as stylish accompaniments.

The heavily patterned curtains at the three single sash windows had been replaced with horizontal wooden blinds. A plain cream rug hid most of the tatty brown carpet that was due to be replaced next week and the picture Kate had brought with her had pride of place over the fire. A concoction of modern art, Lily had been informed.

In an effort to get comfortable, she reached for an embroidered cushion from the chair and then rested back into the settee. Slowly, she pulled her slippered feet onto her low footstool. Rosie, who had padded in behind her a few minutes earlier, stirred by her side before stretching her legs and settling again. Lily smiled. Even though she had jumped into the new beanbag as soon as Kate had put it onto the floor, Rosie still preferred to sit on the settee when there was anyone in the room.

Anxiously, Lily tried not to think about the list of things to do before they were ready to open in the morning. Instead, she thought about her dress hanging on the wardrobe door, along with its matching jacket. She was really looking forward to wearing something bright for a change. The last time she'd worn a suit, she'd been saying goodbye to Bernard. The new clothes seemed like a symbol of the future.

She wanted everything to be perfect. For herself. For Kate and Chloe. Most of all, for Bernard.

Lily must have dozed off because the next thing she knew, it was quarter to seven. She sat still for a few moments. It always took her a while every morning before she felt steady enough to stand. Often, she'd find the room spinning or she'd be left with a queasy feeling. A sign of old age, Dr Warren had told her when she'd been worried enough to question her about it during her last appointment. But Lily was more concerned that her worst fear was about to rear its ugly head.

Once back in the real world, she slowly got to her feet and let in the day as she pulled up one of the blinds. The square was quiet, except for the odd bird flitting about here and there. Lily yawned and felt her stomach flip again as she thought of what was to come. She might be fit for nothing at the end of today, but she was looking forward to it immensely.

She went through to the kitchen and switched on the kettle. A minute later, she checked to see if it was switched on at the socket. It was. She flicked on the light switch but nothing happened.

In a rush of panic, Lily realised that the electricity was off.

CHAPTER SEVENTEEN

'Chloe, get up!' Kate banged on her bedroom door. 'The electricity has gone off. We need to check the food in the fridge.'

Chloe shot out of bed. Without thinking, she turned the light switch on and then off just to make sure.

Then she shook her head. Why *did* she do that? Quickly, she dressed and ran down the stairs.

'Have you checked the fuse box?' she asked Kate, who was flicking through the pages of the telephone directory.

Kate clicked her fingers. 'Of course! Now why didn't I think of that?' She threw Chloe a look of exasperation. 'Be my guest, if you know what to do.'

'I was only trying to help.'

Lily passed Chloe a teacloth. 'Here, you can mop up the water. The electricity must have been off for hours. I've managed to salvage most of the cakes, but some of them are sodden.'

'We won't be able to open now, will we?'

Kate looked over to see tears welling up in Chloe's eyes. 'Oh yes, we bloody well will,' she replied. 'Don't worry. This will only be a hiccup. I'm just going to fetch my mobile. The cordless phones aren't working.'

When she came back ten minutes later, the floor was practically dry. Chloe was complaining sorely of wet patches on her knees.

'The electricity supplier doesn't know how long we're likely to be off,' Kate told them. 'The problem is underground and until they get to it they can't say what it is. If you stand on the forecourt, you can hear them digging.'

'Oh no,' said Lily. 'What are we going to do?'

'That's not all,' said Kate. 'It's only Church Square and Williamson Street that have been affected.'

'Typical.' Chloe huffed. 'It couldn't happen on any other day. Have you rung Alex? He'll know what to do.'

'Gone straight to voicemail. We'll have to wait until he gets here.'

'What about trying Terry's number?' Lily looked at the clock. Ten past seven. 'I know it's early, but he will be up.'

'Good idea.' Kate grabbed his business card from off the notice board. 'In the meantime, Chloe, would you help Lily load as many things as you can into both our cars? We'll have to rely on other people's good natures, try and blag some room in their fridges for now.'

'It's not the contents of the fridges that are the real problem,' said Lily forlornly. 'We can't provide any coffee.'

Chloe and Kate both stopped what they were doing. Suddenly the extent of the situation bore down on them.

'Let's not panic yet.' Kate tried to stay positive. 'There are nearly five hours until we open. Let me speak to Terry first and see what he can suggest.'

While Lily started to pack things up, Chloe rushed upstairs to get changed. Kate was just finishing on the phone when she dashed back down again. Chloe sat on the bottom step to fasten her laces.

'What did he say?' she asked when Kate had been staring into space for a while.

Kate frowned. 'Oh, that was Lucy. She was ringing to wish us luck before she left for the wedding. Terry's wife says he's on his way to Birmingham so I'm not going to try his mobile phone. But Alex has rung me back. Him and Tom are on their way.'

'Whoop-de-do,' Chloe tried to make light of the situation. 'It's Batman and Robin to the rescue.'

Kate smiled. 'Come on, you. Let's go and see if Lily's coping.'

Lily was muttering to herself in the kitchen as she loaded another box with cakes.

'What was that?' asked Chloe as she helped her close up the lid.

'Oh, nothing,' Lily laughed. 'I was cursing Bernard. This fiasco must be all his doing.'

'Oh, look!' Kate pointed to the ceiling where the light was shining away. In all the commotion they'd missed it. 'The electricity is back on.'

Lily sighed. 'Thank goodness for that. Maybe things can become a little less manic now.'

But their good fortune didn't last as over the next few minutes the electricity went off… then on again… then off again… and stayed off. At ten to eight, they decided that they couldn't wait around for it to make up its mind.

Alex arrived a few minutes later. 'Well, what do you know? We only leave you alone for a few hours and look at the state you're in!'

'Thank God you're here,' said Kate. 'We don't know what to do.'

Alex raised his hands. 'I don't know why you're looking at me. I can't conjure up electricity just like that. But I can try to get you a generator sorted out.'

'No need, I've got one outside,' a voice said from behind him.

'Lucy!' Kate rushed forward. 'I thought you were on your way to London.'

'I couldn't let you down on your big day.' She threw a thumb over her shoulder. 'My husband Karl is outside. Apparently the generator he has won't run everything but it will do most of it, for a while at least.'

'That's so kind of you,' Lily told her with a huge sigh. 'Thank you so much.'

'I'll go and help him,' said Alex. 'There'll be lots of cable extensions to fit. And Tom's on his way to the hire shop. I'd better ring him and let him know we might be fixed up.'

'Where are you going to put it?' asked Chloe.

'It'll have to stay outside on the forecourt.'

'Why? Won't it fit in the kitchen?'

Alex laughed before shaking his head. 'I suppose it might, at a push, but have you thought about where the fumes will go? I didn't know we were supplying smoked sandwiches.'

'Sandwiches!' Kate slapped her palm on her forehead. 'We haven't even started them yet.'

In a split second, Lucy pulled off her jacket and hung it on the back of the door. 'I might as well help out while I wait for Karl, but don't expect me to do anything that involves smell or colour. I've just had my nails done yesterday.'

'Great!' Chloe handed her a loaf of bread and grabbed Kate's arm. 'You can start buttering with Lily while Kate and I get the cakes shared out!'

By nine o' clock, the cakes had been distributed around to anyone who would take them in. Everyone was looking forward to the opening and commented that, as they were getting free coffee and cakes, it was the least they could do. Rachel from the tiny bank next to the Co-op lent them a tea urn and Ivy from the chemist said they could use their staff room if they needed to prepare anything.

'Right, I'm off to Harry's,' said Chloe, once they had returned to the shop. 'He says I can use his iron and I'm taking my hairdryer.'

Kate looked on in astonishment. 'You haven't ironed your uniform?'

'Of course I haven't.' Chloe shook her head, curls flailing. 'I only iron things when I need them. How was I supposed to know there'd be no electricity on when I woke up?'

'But we need you here to help out. There's so much…' Kate stopped, and ran a hand through her hair, rebellious at the moment without the means of straightening it. 'That's a great idea. Do me a favour, please. Run upstairs and fetch my straighteners and take them across too. You know I can't function if my hair's a mess.'

Chloe took the stairs two at a time. She had just pushed everything into a carrier bag when her phone rang.

'Hi, Chloe. How's it going?'

'Oh, Dad, we're in a right mess. We've had a power cut. The electricity is likely to be off for most of the day. Lucy's husband, Karl, has loaned us a generator. Kate and I have been taking all the cakes and sandwiches around to the other shops and stashing them in there. It's only the two streets, you see. Typical we had to be one of them. There's an underground fault.'

'Oh dear, I won't keep you long, then. I just wanted to wish you luck and to see if you'd had any more thoughts about which course you're going to choose. You know there isn't long to go.'

'Oh, Dad,' Chloe sighed loudly. 'I told you on Sunday, my exam papers are barely dry.'

'I know that, but every time I speak to you, you seem like you're settling in there. You sound so excited.'

'It's not so much excitement that you can hear in my voice. I'm in a mad panic. If we don't get on, there'll be no opening today. And we've worked so hard to make sure –'

'I'm worried that you're getting too attached.'

'I'm getting *involved*, Dad. The coffee shop looks fantastic now, far better than I ever imagined it would. You should be proud of what I've achieved.'

'I am, but I'll be prouder still when you wear your cap and gown. You'll have better prospects. Just you wait and see.'

Chloe sighed again. 'I've got to go now,' she finished off when she knew he wasn't to be fobbed off. 'I can't talk now. I need to help out.' She paused. 'Wish me luck then?'

'Luck? Chloe, you were born under a star.'

Hearing him laugh made Chloe smile, but as she disconnected the call his words echoed through her head. Why did he have to spoil her mood, today of all days?

'Are you finished in there yet?' Kate banged on the bathroom door an hour later. 'Hurry up, will you!'

Chloe appeared within seconds. 'Keep your knickers on, I'm done. I can't remember the last time I had a strip down wash at the sink.'

Kate sighed. 'No shower – I forgot. Was that your Dad I heard you talking to earlier on?'

'Yep, I've only been here for four weeks and already he's hounding me to leave.'

'You can't do that! Not today anyway.'

'He's still going on about college. This job is meant to be a stopgap but I want to have some fun too. And there's all the customer research to do as well.'

'*Customer research?*' Kate frowned. 'Lily hasn't mentioned anything to me.'

Chloe rolled her eyes. 'Keeping an eye on the talent coming into the shop. I've got some serious flirting to catch up on.' She grinned cheekily before flying up the stairs.

Back in her bedroom, Chloe tried to detach herself from the noise, and the smell, caused by the generator.

Hopefully, she flicked the light switch but the electricity was still off. She doubted it would return in time for the opening. It was quarter past eleven now.

She stood in the middle of the room, wanting to savour the moment as she examined her reflection in the wardrobe mirror. This was the first time she'd seen her outfit altogether. Black skirt, newly-ironed white shirt topped with black waistcoat, neat black apron, practically unnoticeable as it blended in with the skirt, note pad and pencils pushed into its deep pockets out of the way.

Proudly, Chloe fingered the purple and lilac embroidered logo and then pinned on her name badge.

Finally, she brushed an imaginary speck of dust off her shoulder, scrutinized her eyeliner, pouted her lips and pronounced herself ready to go.

'Chloe!' Alex gestured to her when she joined everyone downstairs. 'There's someone here to see you.'

'Dad!' Chloe ran into his open arms. 'But I only spoke to you earlier… You never said you were coming. Is Ben with you?'

Graham released his grip and smiled at his daughter. 'No, I've brought Maddy along with me. She's just parking the car. Ah, here she is now.'

'Hello, Chloe,' said Maddy as she joined them, linking her arm through Graham's. 'We thought we'd surprise you.'

'Hi, Maddy.' Chloe nodded curtly, at the same time noticing how fresh and youthful she looked in her outfit of dark jeans and a plain red T-shirt. She had her hair tied back from her face in a French plait, her brown eyes not really needing any make-up as they sparkled of their own accord. Even her red lipstick was the right shade of young.

Chloe turned back to her father and took his free hand. 'Have you met everyone?'

'Not yet. I –'

'Kate, come and meet my father.'

Kate slid a tray of sandwiches onto the counter alongside the sausage rolls and wiped her hands on a tea towel before going over to them.

'Hello, Graham. I'm very pleased to meet you at last. I've heard so much about you.' She turned to the smart looking woman by his side. 'And you must be Maddy?'

Maddy smiled apologetically as she held out a manicured hand. 'I suppose you've heard a lot about me, too?'

An awkward silence descended. Graham looked at Chloe, his eyes twinkling with mischief. 'You never told me how beautiful Kate was.'

'I… I… why, thank you,' Kate stuttered, her face colouring rapidly.

'The uniform looks great.' Graham switched his gaze between them and then stopped at Kate. 'I hear you've had a disastrous morning?'

'Oh, I'm sure everything will work out as planned. We're starting as we aim to go on, spitting in the face of catastrophe. Can I get you both a coffee?'

Chloe stepped forward. 'No, *I'll* do that.' She dragged her father over to the window seat. Maddy followed behind like a sheep.

Kate went over to join Alex and Tom at the counter. They were both in white shirts and black trousers.

'Nice togs,' she said approvingly. 'You actually do scrub up well.'

'But of course,' said Alex. 'Would you really expect anything else?'

Kate grinned. Suddenly, as she stood there with twenty minutes to go before they opened, after the mad rush of the morning, there seemed to be a sense of calm in the shop. Whatever *could* go wrong had gone wrong. With a rush of emotion, she realised that they were still going to make it on time.

'This wasn't how I'd envisioned the start of our first day in business,' she said when Chloe came over to them a few minutes later. 'I do hope the electricity comes on soon. I know we'll be able to shift all the sandwiches we've made but I don't want anything to –'

Chloe nudged Kate as Lily entered the room. She looked up just in time to see a picture of health in a blue shift dress and matching jacket walk slowly, yet proudly, towards them. Lily pulled the open jacket towards her middle, then let it fall as she reached them. Low-heeled navy court shoes finished off the outfit, as did the diamante brooch pinned to her collar. Nervously, she reached up to her neck. Fingering the blue and lilac scarf, she smiled hesitantly.

'Do I look all right?' she asked.

Before Kate or Chloe could speak, Alex sighed in dramatic fashion. 'As beautiful as a real flower, Lily,' he said.

'An absolute picture,' agreed Tom.

Lily beamed. 'Actually, I hate to admit this to you both, for fear of what comment will come from it, but you do look very smart, for a change.'

'Didn't we tell you that we loved dressing up?' Tom gave her a twirl.

'Yeah, but we look more like James Bond today than what you normally have in mind!' quipped Alex.

As everyone laughed, Kate signalled to Chloe. 'Before we open,' she announced to the room, 'there's one thing we'd like to do.'

Chloe took Lily's hand, walked with her behind the counter and presented her with the photograph she'd shown to her during her first week in Somerley. Kate had managed to find a frame with a lilac insert that complimented the style of the coffee shop, surrounding the picture of them both.

'We think Bernard should be here too,' said Chloe.

'We thought you could hang it over the mirrored tiles so that you can see him every day,' said Kate.

Tenderly, Lily ran a finger over the image.

'Thank you,' she managed to say eventually. Before turning back to face them all, she wiped away a lone tear. 'This means so much to me.'

Kate had tears in her own eyes as Lily tried desperately to compose herself. Her expression gave away just how hard today was going to be and she admired her for the courage she was showing. She was a remarkable lady. Not much like a boss, more like a hen clucking around her chicks. Chloe had mentioned that Lily and Bernard hadn't been able to have children. It must have been agony for her, she reflected now. Lily would have been a superb mother.

Lily took a deep breath, checked her watch and took a quick glance around the room. Apart from the noise of the generator outside, everything was as it should be.

She looked up at them. 'Shall we do it then?'

'You bet!' Chloe held up her hand for Kate to high-five as she walked past. 'Let's declare this place open!'

CHAPTER EIGHTEEN

The grand opening seemed to go as expected after the chaotic start to the day. Chloe ushered Graham and Maddy outside so that the shop would be completely empty. She and Kate held a ribbon across the front of the double doors while Lily cut through it with a pair of scissors. Already a dozen people had congregated on the forecourt. The good old British weather turned and the light rain that had started twenty minutes ago lasted another two minutes before a burst of thunder ushered them all indoors.

Once inside, the staff fell over each other's feet as they barged professionally around, apologising for the lack of lighting, trying to keep the doors shut so the fumes from the generator weren't too awful, sitting people down at tables, showing them menus while they prepared their drinks, managing not to trip over the array of extension cables.

Sam, Brendan and the builders came in around one o' clock. Kate was delighted that they'd made the effort and spent at least twenty minutes tending to their needs. They were definitely good for business, she noted with a slight pang of envy, when three teenage girls wearing the tiniest of vest tops and skirts no wider than some of her belts, hoisted themselves purposefully onto the high stools next to them.

Harry, from the newsagents, called in around one thirty, along with Vic from the post office, Ivy and Sheena from the chemist, Nina and Simon from the chiropodist, the gang from the trendy solicitor's three doors down and Rachel from the bank. Lily fussed around them all, thanking them for coming and hoping they would call again.

At quarter to two, the electricity came on. There was a huge cheer from everyone when it was still on ten minutes later. Lily gave Chloe a selection of cakes to take to the workmen.

By three thirty, Kate had burnt herself twice on the beast of a coffee machine, Chloe was fed up of being called *excuse me*, Alex and Tom wanted to go back to joinery immediately and no one could hear the seventies compilation CD that had been put on in the background due to the amount of people milling around.

Chloe didn't have as much time to spend with her father as she would have liked but she kept an eye on him from wherever she was. She was just about to see if he wanted a refill when she noticed Kate had beaten her to it. When she heard them all laughing, she rushed over.

'Kate was just telling us about your antics with the coffee machine.' Graham smiled and patted her on the arm. 'That's so typical of you, Chloe.'

Chloe pulled a face. 'I did tell you it was a genuine mistake.'

'I'm sure it was,' Kate appeased. 'Still, we've cracked it now.'

'You've created a fantastic place to relax in,' said Maddy, spotting a chance to join in. 'It's so inviting. I wish we had something like this in Penlingham.'

'I'd second that.' Graham looked up at Kate again. 'I think I'm ready for one of your coffee shop specials. Shall I have a regular or grande, miss?'

'Dad!'

Graham looked at Chloe then at Maddy. 'What?'

'You're embarrassing me,' said Chloe.

'I don't see how. Would you like a grande, Maddy?'

Maddy nodded, while Chloe scowled. When another customer beckoned for her, she flounced off.

Lily was oblivious to Chloe's strange frame of mind when she joined Alf at the back of the room. He'd been sitting there with Irene since they had opened, the chairs around their table coming and going depending on how busy it had been. Irene had disappeared to the loo, no doubt due to all the cups of tea she had drunk.

'I'm absolutely worn out,' Lily told him as she sat down. 'I'm so glad the electricity came back on again – and stayed on this time.'

Alf folded his arms across his stomach, wrinkling up his red polka-dot tie in the process. 'You should be letting the young ones do the running around,' he said.

'It's their first full day. I'm sure it won't be as busy on Monday, nor as hectic.'

'How are you doing, Alfie?' Kate patted his shoulder as she whizzed past.

Alf flashed a knowing smile at Lily and raised his eyebrows. 'You'd better be quick or else I'm going to be spoken for.'

'Don't be silly, she's far too young for you.'

'The younger the better, I say. And don't be so sexist. Haven't you heard of equality? That goes for age too.'

'More like sexual harassment, if you ask me. Honestly, Alf, you're nothing but a dirty old man.'

By four thirty, Lily's legs had given up supporting her tiny frame. She couldn't remember the last time she'd been so busy. An elderly couple sat at table seven, sharing a pot of tea. A man at table four with dark, wavy hair that he kept blowing away from his face, sipped at his drink. When he caught Lily look-

ing, he smiled over the top of his laptop. A group of young ladies decorated the leather settees, being entertained by Alex and
Tom sitting in the bay window. There was something going on
between Chloe and Kate that Lily couldn't quite put her finger
on, and the music had gone off, having been forgotten due to
no one listening to it.

When she'd first had the idea to start again, Lily had never
imagined it would be like this. Everyone had pulled together
today. They'd all been rushed off their feet. Twice they'd run
out of mugs and had to dish out the old china ones from Lily's
days gone by. But they'd served their purpose, if only for one
more day.

An hour later, Kate followed the last customers to the doors,
turned the open sign around and leaned her back against the
glass. 'Thank god that's over.'

Across the room, everyone had congregated around Lily.
Graham was finishing the last of his coffee before he and Maddy
would be on their way.

'I'm bushed.' Chloe sat down heavily. 'I've never washed so
many dishes in my life.'

'I can't remember you washing that many.' Alex tapped her
feet. Reluctantly, she removed them from the chair next to her
so he could sit down. 'That dishwasher doesn't hold enough
cups. And have you seen the state of my hair because of all that
steam?'

'Relax, it's still got style.' Kate tousled his gel-logged hair and
sat down next to him.

'Really?' He looked pleased, even when she wiped her hand
on her apron with a grimace. 'You mean you do fancy me, after
all?'

'That's not the only person she fancies,' muttered Chloe, giving Kate a dirty look.

For a moment, Kate frowned, but then she turned to Lily. 'Well, I think that went well, considering our earlier misfortune, don't you?'

'Yes.' Lily smiled. 'You've all done a marvellous job. I can't thank you enough.'

Tom popped his head around the kitchen door. 'Would anyone like any more cake?'

'Not me,' said Kate. 'I couldn't eat anything else. I have room for a cold glass of wine, though.'

'You shouldn't eat so much anyway,' said Alex. 'You're getting on now. You need to watch every calorie or else you'll soon be on that slippery slope. Besides, didn't you say you were on a diet?'

Kate threw him a scowl. 'Diets begin on a Monday. Everyone knows that.'

Chloe took off her shoes and rubbed at her aching toes. 'Did you see that man who came in around twelve thirty? What was his name again? It sounded strange.'

'I think it was Serle.' Alex sat down beside her. 'He scared the shi– life out of me and I'm tall. He seems cool, though. I bet he'll be back.'

'I hope that some of the others come back too.' Chloe grinned. 'It's nice to see there's some talent in Somerley.'

'Chloe Ward!' said Graham, joining them after a trip to the lavatory. 'Not in front of your father, please!'

Chloe opened her mouth to speak but caught Maddy's warning glance.

'Well, I hope we don't get too many regulars, not all at the same time, anyway. I, for one, don't want to be that busy every day,' said Kate, although secretly she knew it had done her the world of good to keep busy.

'Right, Maddy,' said Graham. 'I think it's about time we made a move.'

Maddy got to her feet and Chloe stood up too.

'It's been a pleasure to meet everyone.' Graham glanced around the room. 'Congratulations on your achievements so far and I wish you every success for the future.'

'Yes, me too.' Maddy smiled. 'I hope it goes well. You deserve it, after all your hard work.'

A few minutes later, Kate stood behind Chloe on the forecourt as she waved them off. Once the car was out of sight, Chloe turned and walked back, ignoring Kate completely.

Kate called to her. 'Chloe, could I have a word? I think we need to clear the air.'

Chloe swivelled round to face her. 'Yes, I think we do. I don't know how you could do that to me.'

'Do what, exactly?'

'You were flirting with my father!'

Kate's eyes widened. 'I was doing no such thing.'

'Yes, you were. "*Oh, I'm sure everything will work out as planned. Yes, we're going to be very successful. We're spitting in the eye of catastrophe.*" And bringing up that bloody coffee machine *again*.'

'You *always* bring it up. It's a funny story.'

'At one time, I even heard you *giggle* when he whispered something to you.'

Kate was lost for words as she thought back over the day. She couldn't recall anything untoward and besides, Graham was with Maddy. She wouldn't do that to anyone.

'You've got it all wrong,' she tried to explain.

'No, I haven't.' Chloe sat down on the wall.

Kate sat down beside her. 'I didn't flirt with your father. He's the last person on earth I'd want to get involved with.'

'Why, what's wrong with him?' Chloe snapped. 'He's a good-looking man.'

Kate sighed. 'I know he is, but he's with Maddy.'

'Maddy noticed too.'

'What do you mean?'

'When he said you were beautiful, Maddy looked hurt.'

'No, it was a bit of banter. The kind of thing you say to someone to break the ice. It was very nice of him to say so but it didn't mean anything.'

Chloe huffed. 'It did from where I was standing.'

All of a sudden, Kate understood. 'Is that why you've been funny with me all afternoon? You thought I was trying to steal your thunder? Oh, Chloe, I'm sorry. I was only being friendly.'

Chloe shook her head and quickly looked at her feet. 'I suppose we don't really know each other yet, do we?'

Kate waited for her to look up again. 'I think it'll take time for us to trust each other,' she said, choosing her words carefully. 'I know there's a huge age gap between us and that's something we need to overcome, but I thought we were friends.'

'We *are*.'

'Then why would you think I fancied your father?'

'I… I don't really know,' she admitted. 'Maybe it was seeing him turn up with Maddy today.'

'Maddy is comfortable with your dad, Chloe. That's why she didn't feel threatened. It shows the kind of relationship they have, built on mutual trust.' Kate paused. 'If you ever have a problem like that again, then you must *talk* to me. Little differences like these have a way of blowing up out of proportion, and if that happens, working here is going to be hell. And neither of us wants that, do we?'

Chloe shook her head again. She was about to speak again when Alex and Tom erupted onto the forecourt.

'What are you two doing out here?' Alex wanted to know. 'We've left loads of good wine in there. If you're not careful, Lily will drink it all.'

Lily was following up behind them. 'Less of the cheek, young man.' She smiled at Kate and Chloe.

'Come on, you two. I'm sure you've got things to do tonight. You've worked so hard today. I can lock up.'

'Because, guess what?' screeched Tom as he whisked off his tie and threw it up into the air. 'You've got to do it all again on Monday! And we haven't.'

When she'd finally locked the door behind Alex and Tom, and Kate and Chloe had gone upstairs, Lily poured herself a small glass of wine and sat down again to relish the silence. After the hustle and bustle of the day, everything seemed so peaceful.

She'd been dreading this moment for weeks now. It was good to finally have the coffee shop up and running – but it was also the first time she'd done it without Bernard. Today, she'd felt so many emotions, desperately wanting to enjoy the opening but also wishing that Bernard could have been there too. If she could have only one wish, it would be to share this moment with him, to be able to sit and talk over the day with a glass of wine apiece.

Lily lifted her eyes to the heavens, then, in a silent tribute to the man she would always love, raised her glass.

CHAPTER NINETEEN

The clock had barely reached half past ten on Monday morning before Chloe started to moan. It was their first full day open for business and so far there had only been a disappointing handful of customers.

'I'm so bored.' She pushed back her chair and stretched out her legs.

Kate stirred a spoon around in her coffee. 'We should be prepared for these lulls while the business is building up.'

Lucy thudded down on the empty chair next to Chloe. 'You said it was really busy on Friday. I thought we might have at least half of the customers back today.'

'People always take advantage of something when it's free. Now look at the place.' Chloe stuck her thumb over her shoulder. A couple sat in the window drinking their second cup of coffee. In the far corner, a middle-aged lady sat idly flicking through a slimming magazine whilst demolishing her second chocolate-chip cookie.

'Where does your husband work?' Chloe asked Lucy as Kate sloped off to find something to do.

'He has his own building firm. He's extremely talented. He can put his hands to anything,' she said with a grin.

'Does he work away a lot? I'd hate it if my boyfriend did. You never know what he might be getting up to.'

'Oh, I trust Karl. He would never have an affair.'

Chloe huffed. 'And you're so certain, are you?'

Lucy giggled like a five-year-old. 'Of course I am. I'm his wife. You should see the things he treats me to. Jewellery, clothes, shoes, handbags. I can have whatever I want. He treats me like a queen.'

Chloe kept her thoughts to herself. It wasn't the word she would have used.

Five minutes later, the middle-aged lady picked up her cup, finished her drink and left.

'Another one bites the dust.' Lucy sighed wearily as Kate sat back down again.

'We need to chill out,' Kate told them. 'We should only worry if it's like this in a few weeks.'

'But time's going so slooooooooooooowly.' Chloe leaned back in her chair. 'And it's too quiet without Alex and Tom.'

'I know. I keep waiting for one of them to pop their head around the door and interrupt us. Not that we're doing anything they can interrupt.'

'How long will they be working in Birmingham?'

'I think Terry said the job would last them for the rest of this year,' said Kate. 'So it means they won't even be popping in anytime soon.'

'They won't come in here now that the work is finished,' said Lucy. 'They'll be off to the nearest Wetherspoons for a cheap pint.'

'How would you know?' said Chloe. 'You don't even know them.'

Kate sat upright as the door opened. 'Oh, we have a regular. He came in on Friday.'

'He's the one I was telling you about,' said Chloe with a nod. 'The one with the funny name. I'll see to him.'

Lucy jumped to her feet. 'No, I'll go. I need something to do.'

Chloe got to him first.

'Hi. It's Serle, isn't it?' In her eagerness, she forgot to stop and landed with a thump in his chest.

'Oops. Sorry.' She flashed him her sweetest smile.

Serle smiled back, revealing a set of straight white teeth, which contrasted with his ebony skin. The scar of quite a recent accident was visible under his left eye and a red woollen hat hid what little hair he had.

Huge black hands held Chloe at arms' length. 'Hey, it's not often I have girls fighting over me.' His voice seemed to fill the whole room.

'What would you like?' Chloe stood poised with her note-pad.

As Serle studied the menu on the wall behind her, Lucy sloped away.

'Never mind, someone else will be in soon,' said Kate as she practiced her little knowledge of origami on a paper napkin.

Tuesday and Wednesday were pretty much the same as Monday. So when Thursday started off busy and stayed that way, no one had actually been prepared. Chloe lost her temper when a squat, weedy man accused her of short-changing him. Lily rushed in with apologies, which had made Chloe even worse.

Lucy seemed to be getting on with things nicely, despite the frosty looks coming from Chloe every ten seconds and Kate lost count of the times that she'd been moaned at by people kept waiting because Chloe wasn't working hard enough.

Friday was much steadier. Saturday started off well but by eleven thirty, the coffee shop was completely empty. It gave them a chance to take stock of the first week and keep their chins up regarding the second. At their next meeting on Monday morning, over a working breakfast of tea and toast, Lily offered congratulations as the first item on the agenda. Kate, Chloe and Lucy smiled, relishing the praise after all their hard work.

'All in all, I think our first week went pretty well,' Lily continued. 'We had a marvellous turnout on Thursday and Friday and, even if the earlier part of the week was quiet, the end certainly made up for it.

'Moving swiftly on.' She checked the next item. 'We need to keep The Coffee Stop in the spotlight, so to speak. Have you any ideas?'

'What about a takeaway service?' Chloe suggested. 'Let people come in and take a drink away with them. That way we could catch some of the workers as they pass by. They might then buy a muffin or a cookie to go with it.'

'That's a great idea,' said Kate. She looked at Lily. 'Shall I look into that?'

Lily nodded.

'What about handing out more cakes?' asked Lucy.

'It isn't cost effective now that we're open for business,' explained Kate.

'We could have some sort of a promotion,' agreed Lily. She tapped her pen lightly on her upper lip. 'Something that will help people to remember us.'

'How about the local radio?' Kate suggested.

'Yeah, I've listened to that in the mornings,' Chloe joined in. She swallowed her toast before continuing, 'That Reg Barker's really quirky. Do you think he'd let one of us do an interview? Or a jingle, maybe?'

'Is that something you could look into, Kate?' Lily wanted to know.

Kate shook her head slowly from side to side. 'Not me,' she said. 'You know how tongue-tied I get.'

'Oh, go on,' said Lily. 'You said you'd done presentations before. It must be similar to that.'

'It's nothing like a radio –'

'I'll do it,' piped in Lucy. 'I think it'd be a laugh.'

'I don't think so!' Chloe shook her head fervently. 'You've only been here two minutes. It should be me or Kate.'

'I'm only saying if Kate doesn't want to. You can't force her to do it.'

'It isn't fair if she does it.' Chloe looked at Kate for support. 'I want to do it then.'

Lucy frowned at Chloe. 'Don't be a baby. You only want to do it so I can't.'

'No, I –'

'Okay, you two! Enough of the bickering!' Kate raised a hand for silence, rolling her eyes at Lily. 'I'll do it, if it means you two being quiet.'

'So tell me, Katie Cool,' Reg Barker spoke in a practiced velvet tone. 'What does a man have to do to get a good time at your place?'

Kate tried to calm her nerves before she began to speak on the Thursday morning breakfast slot. She skimmed her eyes around the studio, trying not to take in the vast space filled with buttons, dials and microphones. 'Don't think about the thousands in the audience,' Reg had told her on her brief induction.

'Just clear your throat before you go on air and you'll be fine.'

Fine? I bet he doesn't get palpitations, or sweaty palms, probably not even a frog in his throat on a bad day. Kate cleared her throat anyway and was mortified to hear it amplified around the room.

'He could always request a house special,' she finally spoke. Reg's assistant screwed his face up in agony as he pulled his headset away from his ear and frantically started to fiddle with buttons.

'Oh, you do specials, do you? A bit like extras?'

'Not exactly.'

'And what about the other girls working there? Do they do specials?'

'Oh yes. And we have many different varieties to choose from. We do –'

'Different varieties, huh? Do you do different sizes too?'

'Of course. Grande and regular.'

'Tell me what size I'd like,' Reg said huskily.

'Hmm, let me see…' Kate paused for effect. 'I bet you'd like a café grande, the top of the range with oodles of froth, and plenty of whipped cream.'

'That sounds good to me. Tell me something else, Katie Cool. Are you footloose and fancy-free?'

'Well, I wouldn't go so far as to say free.'

'Ah, sounds like you're heading for a break up? Am I right?'

'No, I'm –'

'So, there you have it folks,' he interrupted her again. 'Another exclusive here on the *Reg Barker Show* on your local radio station Hedworth FM 107.2. Here's a message for all you single guys out there. Get yourself down to The Coffee Stop, because Kate could possibly be in the mood for love.'

The sound of Lionel Ritchie telling everyone that it's easy on a Sunday morning came into range as Kate pulled off her earphones. Reg stuck up his thumb in appreciation.

'That was fantastic,' he said when they came off air. 'You played me well and that's what people will remember when they hear your jingle. They'll be coming to see you in droves.'

'You made me sound like a complete tart,' said Kate, visibly relaxing now that her nightmare was over.

Then panic set in. 'I didn't sound too desperate, did I?'

'No,' Reg assured her. 'You sounded flirty. It's just a laugh, anything to keep the public interested. You did a great job.'

On her way back to the coffee shop, Kate couldn't stop grinning. It had been nerve wracking to go on air like that, worried that she'd slip up and make a fool of herself, therefore letting everyone down. But she seemed to have made a good job of it. Once again, she'd stepped out of her comfort zone and, once again it had felt really good.

'Shush, here she comes.' Chloe ran from the window as she caught sight of Kate marching across the forecourt. She joined Lucy and Lily at the counter.

Kate opened the door and jumped as she heard one almighty cheer.

'Yay!' screamed Chloe. 'You were fantastic, Kate. It sounded real cool!'

'I agree,' said Lucy, with a lot less noise.

'Okay, okay, you two,' Kate interrupted. 'Give me the low down. Did I sound pathetic?'

'It was *brilliant*,' reiterated Chloe, heading towards Serle with his takeaway coffee and muffin tucked neatly inside a brown paper bag.

'It was okay,' sulked Lucy as she strode off into the kitchen.

'I heard you.' Serle took off his baseball cap and ran a hand over his head before putting it back on again. 'It was really funny.'

'You were very good.' Lily smiled her approval.

'It was humiliating!' Kate feigned a hurt expression as she stood in the middle of the room, not sure what to do with herself. It had been a nerve-wracking experience but she had yet to come down from the high. 'I've never heard a conversation with so many double entendres,' she added.

'People will certainly remember our name now.' Chloe jumped onto a stool against the counter. 'What was the jingle he made up for you?'

'I can't remember,' Kate lied, hiding her crimson face in her hands.

'Come to The Coffee Stop and see the tart with a heart!'

'Please tell me it didn't sound that bad!' Kate pulled herself up beside Chloe and unzipped her fleece jacket. 'I'm never doing anything like that again. Next time you want free publicity, Lily, I'll leave the young ones to do it.'

Kate smiled at Lily as she came into the living room the following morning at six thirty.

'Are you having trouble sleeping too?' she asked with a yawn.

Lily nodded. 'My stomach was off but it seems all right now.'

Even though Lily gave the impression of being all right, underneath Kate could see she was exhausted. Her skin had hardly any colour to it and for once her perfect grey curls had dropped nearly as much as her shoulders.

'What about you?' Lily asked her. 'Is there something on your mind?'

'Oh, I'm just feeling a little lost, that's all.' Again last night, Kate had gone to bed and not been able to sleep. Nick had emailed to say they should meet. She'd replied to say this weekend would be good but immediately after she'd sent it, she'd started to worry about it.

Lily nodded. 'I still feel that way about Bernard.'

'You miss him a lot, don't you?'

'Never a day goes by when I don't think of him. Some nights I even cry myself to sleep. Stupid, I know.'

'There's nothing wrong with that. You were together for years. You must feel like you've lost a limb.'

'You have a funny way with words.' Lily smiled at Kate. 'But I do know what you mean. And I do know that you will get used to life without Nick. When are you going to see him again?'

'I don't want to go back,' she admitted.

'Do you still love him?'

Kate paused. That was the million-dollar question and one she was having trouble answering. 'I miss being with him. I miss him holding me. I miss sharing things.' Her eyes brimmed with tears. 'Maybe it was a stupid idea to move away.'

'Nonsense, it took a lot of courage to do what you did. Why do you think it was stupid?'

'I thought I could forget him if he wasn't around to remind me. But that phone call really threw me. I can't stop thinking about him, yet I know that I don't want to be with him anymore. It's like his ghost is following me around. Watching my every move in case I do something he disapproves of.'

'And I suppose Chloe has no sympathy for you?'

'She tries to help, but doesn't understand. She keeps telling me the best thing I can do is find another man but it's not that simple.'

'Of course it's not. Chloe is young. Just wait until her heart is broken, and then she'll know what you're going through.'

'You're a good listener, Lily,' Kate told her, which brought her neatly onto the subject that was intriguing her. 'I think you would have made a great mum. Chloe mentioned that you and Bernard couldn't have children. That's a shame.'

Lily gnawed softly on her bottom lip. 'We tried for many years before admitting defeat. It was hard to watch Irene's daughter grow up while we were still trying to conceive our child. In the end, we decided not to go for tests, just let nature take its course. And nature never did.'

Kate gave a weak smile.

Lily had gone off into a world of her own too. Kate saw her eyes glistening and realised she must have touched a nerve. She smiled at Lily to make amends. 'Thanks for listening to me going on,' she said. 'I'm still getting used to everything changing. It's good to have someone to confide in.'

'You mean someone old, with more wisdom and experience, don't you? I'll get you for that.' She smiled and patted Kate on the leg. 'Don't worry. Everything is still new. All these feelings are part of the healing process.'

Kate shrugged. 'I can't understand why I feel so guilty, Lily. It's never going to work out between us again.'

'Then it's right to see him now. It's best to get it finished. That way you can let go of the past and put your heart into Somerley.'

'I thought I did that the last time I saw him.'

'Oh, that was just a wobble he had when he called you. That's understandable.' She smiled. 'I know you've had your fair share.'

Kate smiled back, beginning to realise just how much Lily had noticed without her saying a word. She *had* had doubts since she'd arrived six weeks ago. She'd been fearful that she'd made the wrong choice to move to Somerley. She'd felt sorry for herself to find her marriage in tatters. She'd felt utterly rejected because Nick didn't want to put up a fight to keep her with him in Brentside. She'd felt... Jeez, she felt exhausted thinking about it!

So was going to see him the right thing to do? Get it over and done with, as Lily had stated? Well, there was only one way to find out. She decided to seize the day and ring Nick to see if she could visit once the coffee shop was closed for the weekend.

When the morning shift had finished, a nervous Kate left for Brentside. An hour and a half later, she indicated right and turned into Marble Close.

Suddenly feeling nervous as she caught the first glimpse of their house up above, she pulled into the kerb for a breather. Number 25 had been their first home and was situated at the head of a cul-de-sac.

Hidden by a thick row of conifers, she could only see a part of it but already it seemed like years since she'd lived there.

Anxiously, she checked her reflection in the rear-view mirror. Her hair had been recently dyed, leaving it with a vibrant shine, *dress to impress* had been the words of wisdom to come from Lucy and Chloe had shown her some tricks with this season's make-up, persuading her to try some new shades to give her a confidence boost. The effects had been stunning. Nick would certainly see what he was missing.

Not that she really wanted him to, Kate thought.

Or did she?

Even though she was twenty minutes early, she started up the engine to move along the last few yards. Might as well get it over and done with.

She turned her car into the driveway and slammed on the brakes. Nick was standing in the doorway. Her friend, Louise, had been getting into her car, parked next to his. Before she noticed Kate, she ran back to Nick, straight into his arms for a kiss.

CHAPTER TWENTY

Kate tried to get out of her car so fast that she got trapped in the seatbelt. In frustration, she pulled at it. It flew backwards, almost hitting her.

'Kate!' Nick spluttered as she finally reached him. 'I – I wasn't expecting you yet.'

'Oh, I bet you weren't.' Kate slapped him hard across his cheek. 'And I bet you weren't expecting that either. How could you?'

'Kate, stop!' cried Louise.

'Don't *speak* to me, you bitch!' Kate watched Louise visibly pale in a matter of seconds. 'You, of all people. "You've got to leave him," you said. "He's a bully, if you ask me," you said. Not a phone call, not a text – was that because you were fucking my HUSBAND?'

'Whoa!' Nick rubbed at his cheek to ease the sting. 'Can we take this inside? I still have to live here, you know.'

Kate pushed past him and through to the kitchen. As she fought to compose herself, she could hear Nick and Louise talking. Moments later, they came into the room, Louise staying behind Nick, peering over his shoulder.

'So, you're not even married for a year.' Kate shook her head in disbelief as she glared at Louise. 'Does James know about this, I wonder?'

Nick took a step forward. 'This has nothing to do with Lou, Kate.'

'Like hell it hasn't. In case you've forgotten, she's married to a good friend of ours. She was my best friend at work, my confidante.' Kate involuntarily shuddered, thinking back to all the things she had told her. 'Everything I said to you,' she pointed at Louise, 'you used against me to get him for yourself.'

'It wasn't like that,' said Louise. 'Nick and I... We're in love.'

Kate saw Nick's eyes widen for a second before he looked away. She laughed.

'Now would that be love as in he *loves* you or love as in he's *in* love with you? And where does that leave James? Do you love him or are you still *in* love with him, even when you're screwing around?'

Nick opened his mouth to speak but Kate moved closer to him.

'She's the one you used to slag off all the time. He used to have a go at me for going out with you,' she glanced pointedly at Louise, 'saying that we dressed up for a night out as if we were on the pull. Like a couple of tarts. The office bike, he used to call you, isn't that right, Nick? What was it, some kind of love–hate relationship?'

'Look,' said Louise, 'you have every right to be angry. But don't you think you should give Nick a chance to explain?'

'Oh, please! I don't want to hear another word from you. You're the one who used to sympathise with me when I went on and on about his bad habits. My God, how could I have been so stupid!'

A silence spread around the room as each one of them worked out their options. Kate sat down with a thump at the kitchen table. This wasn't how she'd imagined her chat today with Nick. She'd thought she'd be coming back for one last time, to settle things in her mind. To make her realise that she had done the right thing. Well, Nick had certainly gone some way to making her mind up for her once and for all.

She looked across the room where glances were going back and forth between Nick and Louise. Nick, her husband, and Louise, her best friend. It was a joke, a cliché. It was her worst nightmare.

Yet now, as she sat here, Kate wondered if she actually did care. Maybe Lily was right and all her feelings for Nick had gone. The distance between them had obviously been far more than forty miles and had grown considerably since she had left.

Maybe it was the thought of the two of them going behind her back – not the fact that someone else was messing around with what was still rightfully hers.

She needed to talk to Nick.

'I think you should leave, Lou,' she said. 'Go back to your husband and leave me to talk to mine, alone.'

'I don't think that's a good –'

'She's right, Lou,' said Nick, much to her dismay. 'This is our argument, me and Kate. I'll call you later, yeah? When it's all settled.'

'But –'

Nick touched her gently on her arm. 'I'll call you later.'

Louise's eyes were full to the brim as she turned back to Kate. 'I'm sorry. It shouldn't have happened but it did. I've hated myself ever since. That's why I stopped calling you, texting you, whatever.'

'I think you'd be better explaining that to James.'

At the mention of her husband's name, Louise winced and her tears fell. 'Please don't tell him.'

Quickly, she wiped them away and, with one last look at Nick, she left.

Kate had no intention of telling James anything. She knew he idolised his wife; why should she be the one to burst his bubble?

As soon as the front door had closed, Nick joined her at the table.

'I'm sorry, too, Kate. But, you and me, we were going nowhere fast. I just clicked with Lou at her wedding.'

'Her wedding!' Kate gasped. 'But that means –'

'No, it doesn't,' Nick interrupted sharply. 'I never thought anything of it at the time. Then I saw her, maybe a week after you'd left. She was walking towards me in the town. We stopped to chat. She asked me how I was doing and, well, you know the rest. But it wasn't meant to happen. And I know you probably won't believe me, but nothing happened before you left.'

'You're right, I don't believe you,' Kate scoffed. 'I can't believe you chose her, either.'

'What happened with me and Louise was down to the two of us.'

'By us, you mean me and you?' Kate shook her head. 'Don't you dare blame that on me!'

'I'm not blaming you!' Nick sighed. 'I'm just saying that if we were happy, then I wouldn't have met with Louise.'

'So you *are* saying you saw her before I left?'

'No! I –'

'No wonder she was so keen to show me the advertisement about the coffee shop. The two-faced cow.'

'It's not her fault.' Nick stood up. 'I'll make coffee. I know I could do with one.'

Kate sat in silence again as he prepared their drinks. She had no idea what to say next. For one thing, she couldn't work out how she felt. Why wasn't she ripping his head off for screwing her best friend?

Why wasn't she feeling slightly hard done by? Nick had clearly moved on while she had spent her time thinking about him in Somerley, often feeling guilty, yet at the same time, he'd probably been with Louise. She thought back to that late night phone call. Maybe the guilt had got to him.

Suddenly she realised that she'd been let off the hook, emotion wise. If Nick *had* been having an affair before she left, it would have been more of an ordeal to get over him. She would have wondered what was wrong with her, why did he need to find love with someone else. But Nick was right. This way she could see that they had made their marriage collapse, without any interference from a third party.

Somehow, it made it more acceptable.

There could only be one explanation. She couldn't love him anymore.

'You do know, if it wasn't me, then it would have been you eventually,' Nick broke into her thoughts as he sat back down. 'Our marriage was over. We just didn't want to let go.'

Kate knew he was right. It wasn't easy to try again, no matter what other people thought. Like she had told Chloe during their midnight feast, once the magic had gone, it was hard to get it back.

'I know,' she replied. 'I suppose sleeping with someone I could understand – but did it have to be Louise? I thought you got on with James.'

'I do!'

'Well, I'd hate to be you when he does find out.'

'He won't find out from me.'

'Oh, me neither, but you're bound to slip up soon. Someone will see you when you least expect it and then BOOM. Have you thought about what might happen then?'

Nick picked up his mug and looked over the garden. 'I haven't really looked that far ahead.'

'But you must! It isn't fair not to.'

'I thought this conversation was going to be about you and me.'

'Well, it is, kind of.' Kate shrugged her shoulders and sniggered. 'It's about you and me being definitely over, isn't it? That much is plainly obvious now, don't you think?'

Nick's bottom lip twitched.

Kate smiled, picked up her drink and took a sip. Indeed, the conversation hadn't gone as she'd expected but it had sorted out a few problems for her. She didn't love Nick anymore and for that thought alone the afternoon had been worthwhile.

'You must really hate me,' Nick said, taking her silence for distress.

Kate shook her head and did something impulsively. She reached across the table and took hold of his hand. 'I don't hate you at all. I think you're right. It would have been one of us sooner or later because the love had gone. And… well, love makes the world go round, so they say.'

Nick covered her hand with his free one. 'I do still care for you, Kate. I think I always will.'

'Me too,' she told him.

Two hours later, they were still chatting. Being into financial advice, Nick had insisted on taking out new insurance policies whenever they'd had a pay rise so there had been a few more papers to sign. Kate had pooh-poohed the idea every year – saying that she'd rather spend her well-earned money on shoes – but now, she realised, she could finally appreciate his expertise.

'Don't you find this weird, Nick?' she asked him as she finished off another coffee. They had moved to the settee now. 'Three hours ago, I slapped you for playing around with my best friend. Now, we're talking about things in a civilised manner.'

Nick rubbed his hand over his cheek. 'There was nothing civilised about that. It stung like hell.'

'Well,' Kate nudged him, 'you deserved it.'

'I suppose I did.'

Nick's eyes glistened as he gave a weak smile. Blinking rapidly, Kate looked up towards the ceiling, trying to stop her own tears falling. But they fell anyway when he pulled her into his arms. She hugged him back fiercely.

'I'm sorry,' Nick told her. 'For everything.'

'Me too,' she replied.

It didn't feel awkward to hug for one last time at the front door. Kate would miss him, there was no doubt about that, and she would always have fond memories to recall. But it was time for them both to go and create some new ones.

'Take care, Kate,' Nick said, giving her hand one last squeeze.

Once again, Kate reversed the car out of the drive. She was leaving, but this time it was final. It had been an ordeal seeing him but now that it was over with, both of them could get on with their lives.

Lily was right, Kate would never forget him and, even with the revelation about Louise, she knew one day she'd remember some little anecdote, some memory, and she would smile. Because she had been happy with Nick for a long time.

But now, as she turned out of Marble Close, the only thing Kate had on her mind that afternoon was going home.

And that home, she realised, was with her new friends in Somerley.

CHAPTER TWENTY-ONE

'What did you get up to last night?' Kate asked Chloe, curious to know before they opened up the next day.

She'd been in bed when Chloe had got home the night before.

'Josh and I went to the pub – again,' Chloe told her. Josh was one of the builders working on the church across the square. 'I hooked up with him but that's his lot now.'

'Chloe! You didn't!'

Chloe laughed at the shocked expression on Kate's face. 'Hooking up doesn't mean shagging him in full view of everyone. It means I had what you and Lily would call a good old-fashioned snog.'

'I knew that,' Kate acknowledged, trying to act cool but knowing that she had failed miserably. 'I'm merely jealous. Are you seeing him again?'

There was no time for any more questioning, as the first rush of the day began when all of three customers came in together.

'I still can't believe you've had enough of Josh already,' Lucy remarked afterwards.

'A woman can only take so much boredom,' said Chloe.

'But since you've been here, as well as dating Josh, you've already been asked out by two fellas that I know of,' said Kate.

'That's not many. Not by my normal standards anyway.'

'We haven't been open that long,' Lucy commented.

'You're jealous too!' Chloe ribbed, knowing she had the upper hand.

'I'm not jealous. I already have a man.'

'When he's at home.'

Kate noticed Lucy scowling at Chloe but she didn't say anything else.

'Oh, look,' said Chloe, completely going off the subject. 'He's back again. Laptop Man.'

Kate's eyes immediately looked towards the door. It was the man who had been working on his laptop on their opening day. She noticed he was wearing another sharp suit, a few dark hairs escaping above the white of his open shirt collar. He wore the suit well; she wondered what he'd look like in casual attire – or maybe no clothes at all. When he caught her eye and smiled, she felt the start of a blush.

'He's quite dishy,' said Lucy as she continued to fill up the rack with packets of salted crisps. 'But he's more your age, Kate. He must be mid thirties?'

'I reckon so,' Chloe continued before Kate could speak. 'Although I'd rather like to try the older man for myself sometime. So, if you don't want…'

'Stop discussing him and go and take his order,' said Kate.

'Why don't you go?' Lucy grinned at her.

'I'm busy here and –'

'You're blushing,' cried Chloe. 'You fancy the pants off him, don't you?'

Just then they heard a shout.

'It's good to see you again, mate.' Laptop man shook hands with Serle who had just walked in and they embraced in a bear hug. A lot of manly pats on the back later and Serle sat down opposite him.

Chloe was over to them in a flash, leaving Kate wondering if she would ever get to grips with her candour.

* * *

Lily came to see Kate just before The Coffee Shop closed for the night. The last customer had left about twenty minutes previously. Chloe had already gone upstairs.

'How is everything here?' Lily asked her.

'Fine, I think.' Kate sat down at a table and pulled out a chair for Lily. 'There's a little tension between Chloe and Lucy, though. I'm not sure how to handle it.'

'Then don't. I think it will sort itself out.'

'I keep thinking that, but then another petty argument starts and they're off again. They seem to be purposely trying to outdo one another. Maybe I made a mistake by employing Lucy.'

'Oh?' Lily questioned.

'I thought that Chloe would like someone more her own age to work with but she seems to be the bitchier of the two. And her remarks are far more hurtful.'

'She'll calm down in time. At the moment, Lucy has come in and knocked everything off balance. It's *you* they're fighting over.'

Kate frowned. 'Me?'

'Yes, your friendship. You and Chloe were in this from the beginning. Lucy coming in has altered the dynamics for a while. Chloe and Lucy are vying for your attention. Chloe has the upper hand because she works and lives with you. Lucy probably feels left out of things as she's only here for a few hours at a time. It's up to you to either chastise them or let them work it out for themselves.'

'I'm not sure which way will be best.'

Lily shrugged. 'That's why you're my second-in-command, Kate. It's your choice. You'll have to reprimand Chloe if you feel she needs it. And you have the authority to hire and fire, if you want to finish Lucy.'

'No, I don't want to do that. I like Lucy and I think if they weren't so stubborn, they'd get along really well. I just want them to be friends.'

'I'm sure they will be in time,' said Lily.

Once Lily had gone back upstairs and she'd swept the floor, Kate sank back into a chair and rested her chin in her hands. This supervising thing was turning out to be a nightmare. Because she'd never had to discipline anyone before, she couldn't make her mind up if she was overreacting to a bit of close-to-the-bone banter or whether Chloe was really overstepping the mark. Perhaps she should have a quiet word with her, nip things in the bud, so to speak. But how would she react? What would happen if she made things worse?

Kate sighed loudly. This was awful. She didn't want Lily thinking she wasn't capable of doing her job.

Because now things had changed with Nick, there was no way she was going back to Brentside.

Early on Thursday morning, Chloe had just come out of the bathroom after a shower when she heard a thud.

Knowing Kate had already gone down to open up, she dismissed the noise. Until she heard someone whisper her name loudly.

'Lily!' Chloe spotted her lying on the floor at the bottom of the stairs. She was wearing her nightdress, but one of her slippers lay across the room. Her knees crumpled beneath her every time she strived to get to her feet. Shocked by her pasty complexion, Chloe rushed down to her.

Lily grasped Chloe's hand and whimpered in pain.

'What happened?' Chloe asked.

'I'm… I'm… not sure. One minute… I was walking across the hallway… the next thing… I'm on the floor.'

Chloe let her catch her breath before asking her another question. The clock on the wall said ten past eight. 'How long have you been here?'

'Not too long. I just went down to have a quick word with Kate. I must have tripped over my slipper.'

Chloe could see how much pain Lily was in as she helped her up. 'You really need to see a doctor. I'll –'

'No!' Lily's tone was sharp. 'I only need to rest.'

Chloe squeezed Lily's frozen fingers to warm them up. 'But you might have broken a bone. You look like you've fallen hard.'

'It's a bit of cramp. I'll be fine.'

Knowing she wasn't going to be heard, Chloe turned to leave but Lily stopped her.

'I'm sorry I was short with you, love. Please don't tell anyone you found me like this.'

Chloe spotted her chance. 'Okay,' she nodded. 'I won't say anything, but only if you'll ring your doctor. You might be better with a course of antibiotics or strong painkillers. That leg is going to be sore.'

Lily nodded too. 'If it still hurts tomorrow, I'll definitely ring.'

Chloe observed the pleading look on her face. 'Okay,' she relented. 'If you're sure.'

'How are the plans going for your wedding, Vicky?' Kate stopped at table two and glanced at the magazine the young woman was reading. 'I like that one there,' she added, pointing to a dress. 'It's really elegant.'

Vicky worked in the chemist and had become a regular customer in a matter of days of the coffee shop opening. She looked up, eyebrows raised. 'I won't get into that if I don't eat anything for the next two years, never mind the next two months. Besides, I've already chosen my dress last year. I'm going for the final fitting next week.'

'You're going to look gorgeous,' Kate patted her reassuringly on her shoulder and moved back to the counter. 'I think I'll check on Lily,' she told Chloe as she walked past. 'I haven't seen her since first thing this morning. It's gone midday already.'

'She's resting,' Chloe replied without thinking. 'I said I wouldn't disturb her.'

'Oh. Why?'

Chloe felt a rush of red flooding her cheeks. 'Well, I…'

But it was too late.

'You should have said something,' Kate said, after she'd told her how she had found Lily. 'Have you any idea how dangerous a fall could be for someone of Lily's age? She could have broken her hip, or caused a blood clot. Anything could be wrong. What time did you see her, was it first thing?'

Chloe nodded. 'Yes, but she told me not to tell you.'

'She would, she doesn't like to be fussed over.' Kate flicked her eyes towards Lucy as she came in from the kitchen to see what all the commotion was about. 'Did you know that Lily was poorly?'

Lucy shook her head. 'You know I would have told you if I did.' She turned to Chloe when Kate relayed the story. 'I can't believe you haven't said anything.'

'But she told me not to tell you!' Chloe's bottom lip began to tremble. 'I didn't do anything deliberately.'

Kate headed for the door. 'Well, you'd better pray she's okay when I see her.'

Upstairs, she tapped lightly on Lily's bedroom door, hoping that she wouldn't be waking her if she were asleep.

'Come in.'

Kate went into the room. 'Chloe told me you'd fallen, Lily. Are you okay?'

Lily gave a faint smile. 'Yes, I'm fine thanks, just a little shaken.'

'What happened?'

'I felt a bit faint and the next minute I was on the floor.' Lily laughed. 'It's old age catching up with me. I seem to get every bug that's doing the rounds.'

Kate gave a sympathetic smile. 'Would you like me to get you anything before I leave?'

Lily shook her head. 'Is everything okay downstairs?'

Kate nodded. She left Lily then but, later that afternoon, popped in to see her again.

'You still look pale,' she said, handing Lily a glass of water and an aspirin. 'Are you going to make an appointment to see –?'

With a wave of her hand, Lily dismissed the idea. 'I'll be as right as rain in a day or two.'

Kate wasn't too sure but gave Lily the benefit of the doubt. If she said she was feeling better, then Kate would have to believe her. No matter how exhausted she seemed.

CHAPTER TWENTY-TWO

Kate noticed the man who had come in last week sat at table four again. No matter how many times it happened, it still gave her an immense feeling of pride when someone kept returning. More so with him, she noted, feeling her skin reddening slightly when he came to settle his bill.

She slipped him a chocolate muffin into a paper bag. The smile he gave her lit up his whole face, taking emphasis away from the mean and moody darkness of his eyes.

'Third visit gets you a treat,' Kate offered in the way of explanation.

'Thanks. I've been to the solicitors along the way again so I thought I'd try another one of your lattes.'

'Oh, you're a legal type?' Kate drew a conclusion from the sharp suit he was wearing.

'Nothing as glamorous I'm afraid.'

'Oops,' she smiled apologetically. 'Trust me to put my foot in it.'

'No offence taken. You've certainly turned this place around in a short space of time. I hope it does well for you. Do you know the old couple who lived here? What happened to them? Did they sell up?'

'No, Mr Mortimer died earlier this year. I'm sorry, but I'm not sure how well you knew him.'

'Not that well. I'd only been into the old café a few times, when I was younger. What about the woman? Lily, was that her name?'

'Yes, Lily is still the owner. I'd introduce you but she's –'

'Oh, not to worry, I'm sure I'll be calling again on my travels.' He gave her another smile that she noticed reached his eyes. 'Thanks for the cake.'

Kate watched him leave, thrilled when he turned back and smiled at her before he closed the door. Cute ass were the first words that entered her mind. Luckily, there was no one there to see her blush.

Another week passed. Then another. A pleasant July turned into a mediocre August, the weather in the first week being atrocious. It rained solidly for five days, with the sun showing a brief appearance before disappearing again for the weekend. This week had been a little better and the long-term weather forecast promised a glorious end to the month. No one was holding their breath.

Serle wasn't their only regular customer as the business gradually built up. Mistakes were being made, but learned by: not everyone liked dressings on their salads so they made it an optional choice; Chloe soon discovered that she couldn't carry four cups and saucers when she was too idle to get a tray; toast burned if no one kept a watchful eye on it. And although Lucy and Chloe still bickered as if there was an imaginary scoreboard, their comments became less insulting.

Just as Lily thought things were starting to settle into a regular routine, she received the phone call that would send her world into chaos once more.

CHAPTER TWENTY-THREE

It was ten past six in the morning on August sixteenth. Chloe found herself wide-awake and destined to stay that way. She reached up to pull back a curtain, pushed off her duvet and relished the suns rays on her naked body. Even this early in the day, she was hot. Luckily, business was still steady in the coffee shop. Kate had come up with the idea of an ice-cream special; coffee and vanilla scoops drizzled in chocolate sauce. A wafer biscuit added the finishing touch. They'd even put out extra tables and chairs on the forecourt.

The day of reckoning had finally arrived. After two years of hard work, Chloe's exam results were due. She really wanted to pass her A levels with better than average grades, but underneath the worry of failing was the mixed feelings floating around inside her head. Getting those good grades would mean that she'd have to leave Somerley in a matter of weeks, and she wasn't sure if she wanted to. Spending time working here was always meant to be a temporary measure but lately she'd started to think about how she'd feel when it was time to move on. She was having fun, and although the coffee shop didn't give her the huge salary her dad said she could possibly have with a sound education, now that the time was drawing near, she'd started to wonder if she was ready to leave. Though she still texted Manda most days, like they'd predicted, new friends had come along – even if one of them was Lucy. Her local haunts had been replaced by others, so she hadn't missed them. And if she wanted to see her dad, or her brother, she could always jump on the train or get in her car.

She imagined what her dad would say if she mentioned it to him. 'You can't live your life in a two-bit coffee bar, Chloe. What will you do when you tire of it and want to leave? There are no prospects, nothing to work towards. You'll be bored in a few months.'

Would she get bored? Chloe questioned herself as she twirled strands of her hair around her index finger. She had only been working for just over two months. Any work she'd taken could have turned out this much fun, although she very much doubted it. If she'd chosen to work at her dad's shop or the factory, where would she be now? He said he didn't mind if she and Ben did their own thing, but really Chloe knew he wanted one of them to take over. Working for him would have been easy too. She'd have a better car, for starters. Longer lunch breaks and a slightly higher than decent salary.

But it wasn't what *she* wanted. And the more she thought about it, the more she wanted to stay here with Kate and Lily. Chloe felt that she'd be letting them down but she didn't want to let her dad down either. It seemed a no-win situation.

Still, everything could change today. If she hadn't got good grades for her A levels, she'd have to stay here anyway. At least she didn't have long to wait to find out. She got up to take a shower.

'Morning,' Kate welcomed Chloe with a gentle hug of reassurance. 'The big day comes at last. How are you feeling?'

Chloe blew the air out of her cheeks. 'I'm petrified.'

Kate perched herself on a stool and slid a coffee over to her. 'I remember when I had my results. My hands were shaking so much that I couldn't even open the envelope.'

'At least I don't have to do that. My results will go to my home address. But it does mean that either Ben or my dad will see them first. And if it's my dad and I've failed, then I'll be more disappointed that he had to open the envelope to tell me.' Chloe picked up the mug but before it reached her lips, she put it down again with a thud and delved into her apron pocket as her phone began to vibrate.

Kate had opened up and was already preparing the first order of the day for the women at the post office when she disconnected it two minutes later.

'I didn't hear you squeal,' she called over.

'The postman hasn't been yet.' Chloe sighed, her feet dragging across the floor. 'Ben's going to ring me later.'

'Patience, dear,' said Kate. 'Help me with this order and then I'll make you some toast before the rush starts. It might keep those nerves at bay.'

'You've made an impression on a certain friend of mine,' Serle informed Kate when he called in for his usual morning coffee and teacake.

'Oh?' Kate took a quick glance around the busy room. No one waved for her attention so she decided to question him. 'Tell me more.'

'There was a guy I met in here last month. His name is Will.'

'Well, that's an improvement on Laptop Man.' Kate smiled. 'How do you know him?'

'We went to school together and kept in touch for years afterwards. But I reckon it must be a good ten years since I last saw him. He hasn't really changed that much either – still as good-looking as ever, the creep.'

Kate remembered that very well. 'How old is he?'

'He's thirty-nine, the same age as me. We both have the big four-o next year.'

'He doesn't look that old.' She paused. 'I haven't seen him around here in a while, though. Did he come to meet you because he was working in this area?'

'Yes. He wants to know if there is a Mr Kate on the scene now, though. Of course, I told him he'd have to join the queue.'

Kate's hand moved to the open collar of her shirt. 'You might have put him off,' she scolded.

But Serle said exactly what she wanted to hear. 'Oh, I don't think there's a chance of that.'

An hour later, the door to the coffee shop opened and a voice boomed across the room. Kate smiled: she recognised him instantly, even without an introduction.

'I'll have the biggest slice of cake you have and a cup of your finest coffee.'

'Ben!' Chloe came from behind the counter and ran straight into her brother's open arms. 'You said you'd ring me!'

'I thought I'd come in person and surprise you instead.'

'Kate, this is my brother.' Chloe moved to one side, taking hold of his arm.

'I've heard so much about you.' Kate delighted in watching Ben squirm, obviously thinking of how much damage his sister may have done.

'I've only told them the gory details,' Chloe claimed quickly. She frowned as Lucy moved across the room towards them.

'Hi, I'm Lucy,' she gushed, holding on to Ben's hand for far too long. She turned to Chloe. 'You certainly don't take after your brother. He's really good-looking.'

Kate bit her lip to stop herself from giggling. It was laughable how alike Chloe and Lucy were really.

'Lily's in the kitchen,' said Chloe, ignoring her. 'I know she'll want to meet you too.'

Ben stopped Chloe dragging him towards the door by holding up his hand to reveal a white envelope.

'Don't you want to see your results?'

Chloe's heart found her mouth and she gulped. This was it. The moment she'd been dreading for ages, yet anticipating too.

Anxiously, she took the envelope. Her mind played tricks on her as she swore it was burning her fingers. While Kate and Ben started and finished a conversation, with Lucy hanging onto Ben's every word, she put her thumb in and out of the seal at least a dozen times.

A minute later, Kate snatched the envelope from her. 'For goodness' sake, Chloe. *Open it.* We want to know how you've done, even if you don't.'

As Lily came over, Chloe leapt on the opportunity to waste a little more time. 'Lily, this is my brother, Ben.'

'I'm very pleased to meet you,' said Lily.

'Customers, this is my brother, Ben.' Chloe waved an arm around the shop. People at most of the occupied tables nodded a greeting. A couple even raised their cups.

'Well?' questioned Lily.

'She won't open the envelope,' Ben explained with a shake of his head. 'I think she's scared.'

'No, I'm not! Give it here, Kate. I'll open it myself.'

'Now?'

Chloe nodded and the envelope was back in her hands. Without hesitation this time, she ripped it open and pulled out the slip that sealed her fate. She squealed so loud that a young boy and his dog walking past the café stopped in their tracks and turned their heads.

'I've passed!' Chloe jumped up and down on the spot. 'I've passed them all!' Handing the slip to Kate, she hugged her brother again. A round of applause erupted from everyone.

'Well done, you.' Ben twirled her around before placing her back onto the floor. 'What grades did you get?'

'A in Sociology, A in Law,' Kate read aloud. 'And you've got a B in Business Studies.'

'I'm so proud of you,' said Lucy. 'I can't believe you'll be leaving soon.'

Chloe realised the implication and opened her mouth to speak. But Kate's stern look stopped her from erupting.

'Time to celebrate,' said Lily. 'Free cakes all round, I think?'

As relief flooded through her body, Chloe felt light-headed and flung herself backwards onto the length of the nearest settee. Kate hid a smile at the delight of the young man in front of her who plainly had a glimpse of red and white knickers when her short skirt flew up.

'I'm so chuffed,' said Chloe. 'I can't believe I've got a B in Business Studies. That was my worst exam. I finished half an hour before the end of the time limit – I remember discussing it with Callum. Everyone else was still writing. Well, I must have written the right things. I must ring Manda, and Dad.'

She reached for her phone. 'He'll be dying to know too.'

'Congratulations, my dear.' Lily hugged her first before whispering in her ear. 'I, for one, hope you won't be leaving us yet.'

Chloe hugged her back. 'Not if I can help it, Lily.'

'So, what's next?' Ben wanted to know. He and Chloe were sitting on one of the wooden benches in the square, drinking celebratory wine and eating chicken salad baguettes. An elderly gentleman sat reading a newspaper on the bench opposite them and a group of teenagers ambled towards the main road. Chloe had kicked off her shoes and was waggling her bare toes.

'I don't know,' she replied. Her eyes flicked across to the place she'd grown attached to in such a short space of time. 'I love everything about working in the coffee shop. There's a regular crowd of customers that have started to come in, and I can handle my jobs blindfolded now. Even the deafening sound of the steamer exploding every thirty seconds doesn't annoy me anymore.' She picked up her glass and took a sip of wine.

Ben shook his head. 'You can't stay here, Chloe. It's hardly a career, is it?'

'You sound like Dad.' Chloe placed her glass down carefully on the path. 'What if I do want to stay here? He can't force me to go to uni.'

'He'll try. You know he wants what's best for you.'

'But, how does *he* know what I want? Even *I* don't know what I want to do with my life yet.'

'That's precisely why you go to university.' Ben reached across her knees for a paper napkin. 'A degree gives you more options for the future.'

'Not necessarily. There are plenty of graduates on the dole.'

'Not any that I know of.'

'Big brother, I've had enough of the third degree.' Chloe picked up the sandwich box they were sharing and popped her used napkin inside before replacing the lid with a click. 'I've passed three A levels. Let me enjoy my success.'

Ben grinned, screwed his napkin up into a ball and flicked it at her. It hit her full in the face. Laughing as she lobbed it back, he picked up his glass and raised it in the air.

'Here's to my brainy little sister,' he toasted. 'May she make the right decision about her career. To go to university – or not.'

Even from her place at the window seat, Lily could sense the deep love and admiration between the two siblings. She heard

Chloe squeal, then slap her brother lightly on his shoulder before racing around the tree with him hot in pursuit.

She sighed, her heart heavy after hearing the news. Chloe's excellent exam results had come as a shock.

Lily hadn't even thought as far as her youngest member of staff getting good grades and leaving. But now she did, she realised that she didn't want her to go yet. If she did, it would split up a fine team, although it might make her plan easier.

Trust you to get too close already, she scolded herself.

'What time is the taxi arriving?' Chloe asked Lucy as she tottered around on new heels. She, Kate and Lucy were going out to celebrate her exam results.

'I haven't ordered it yet.' Lucy took another sip of her wine, not concerned in the slightest. 'Kate wasn't ready the last time I suggested it.'

But, unbeknown to Chloe, Kate was ready. She was looking through the living room window. Suddenly, she ran across the room, through the hallway and down the stairs like a shoplifter determined not to get caught. She gave Lucy a quick nod as she came into view. Lucy produced her phone from her black clutch bag.

'What the hell's that racket?' Chloe said, as she heard what could only be described as a foghorn coming from the square.

'I'm not sure.' Kate flung open the double doors. 'Let's go and see.'

'Chloe! Surprise! It's me! Chloe!'

Coming clearly into view, Chloe saw a white stretch limousine. Manda was hanging out of the sunroof, flowers in one hand and a bottle in the other.

Chloe waved to her. 'Manda! I'm here!'

The car blocked the street as it drew up level with them. Manda disappeared like a magician's rabbit until a chauffeur all dressed in white opened the rear side door and she jumped out.

'What are you doing here?' Chloe hugged her friend in delight. 'It's been ages since I've seen you. We have a lot of catching up to do.'

'Couldn't let this day go uncelebrated, could I?' Manda grinned. 'And I couldn't celebrate our successes without seeing you.'

Chloe turned to face the others with probing eyes.

'Erm... surprise,' Kate smiled.

'You!' Chloe laughed and proceeded to jump up and down on the spot before hugging her too.

'Come off it, Chloe.' Manda handed her friend first the flowers and then the bottle, which turned out to be champagne. 'You didn't think your dad would let the day pass unnoticed, do you?'

'Oh, but I thought –'

'His idea,' Kate admitted with a shrug of her shoulders. 'He's rung me more times than you this past week to get this sorted.'

'Are you going to get in?' Lily asked, joining them on the forecourt. 'It's rather an exciting car, something I've only ever seen in the newspapers or on the television. Shall I take some photographs now, Lucy?'

'No, madam,' the fine and dandy chauffeur interrupted, tipping his cap. 'I have strict instructions to take you for a ride too, and then bring you back here afterwards before I take the ladies onto their destination.' He waved her forward.

Lily didn't have to be asked twice. Kate locked the coffee shop doors behind her and they all climbed in.

Chloe had never been in a limousine before and was amazed to find out that it had settees either side of the darkened win-

dows, as well as a television, a music centre, a mini-bar and…
twelve bags of cheese and onion crisps!

'They're for me and you,' Manda explained as the chauffeur
started the engine.

'Right, ladies,' he wound down the internal connecting window and pressed hard on his horn. 'Get ready for the ride of
your life!'

Lying in bed later that night, Chloe thought back to the night.
They'd gone to an Indian restaurant for a meal and then called
into a nearby pub, coming out just before midnight, with Kate
laughing, saying that the carriage might turn into a pumpkin if
they left any later.

It had been great to see Manda again, and her dad was amazing to organize the limo for her. And she was happy with her
results after working so hard. Yet part of her was already worrying about leaving all her new friends, and The Coffee Stop so
quickly. This had never been more than a stopgap for her, until
recently.

Did she really want to leave just as it had all begun?

CHAPTER TWENTY-FOUR

Around two thirty, for about an hour every afternoon, was the quietest time in The Coffee Stop. Today, one of the tables was taken by a suited woman in her thirties, busy tapping away on her mobile phone. Another had a slightly teenage, slightly spotty boy with his slightly overweight girlfriend, both of them seemingly hell bent on getting it on right there at the table.

Chloe pointed over to where Lily and Alf were deep in conversation and had been since they'd arrived back from Hedworth forty minutes before. 'Just look at those two sitting over there.'

Kate looked across the room, pleased to see that she was talking about Alf and Lily.

'They'd make a great couple, don't you think?'

'Yes, Alf is such a lovely man. I love how he looks out for Lily.'

'She was lucky to have him around when Bernard died.'

'Hmm,' Kate nodded. 'It's a shame Lily feels that sharing love again would betray Bernard's memory.'

'It was the same with my dad,' Chloe added. 'No one expected him to stay single forever, but even I could tell he felt guilty if he went out on a date.'

Kate was behind the counter settling the bill for the suited woman when Will came in. She looked across at him, trying to catch his eye. Immediately, she felt her stomach squish around as he gave a slight wave before sitting down at table four.

'Will's back,' said Chloe as she walked past. 'I think you should serve him.'

Kate smirked. 'Why, have you gone off him all of a sudden?'

Chloe tried to look insulted but failed. 'Come off it,' she scoffed. 'I never fancied him in the first place. He only has eyes for you.'

'He hasn't been in for weeks!'

'Ooh, counting the days, are we?'

'Oh, away with you,' Kate brushed the comments off and picked up her notepad.

'I'm serious.' Chloe pushed the door into the kitchen. 'Hey, you're blushing.'

Kate put a hand to her cheek as she walked across the room. Chloe was right, which had the added effect of making her blush even more.

'Hi, Will. Long time no see.' Kate hoped she sounded nonchalant.

'Hi. Yes, I've been out of the area for a while. How are you?'

'Good, thanks. You?'

'I'm good, too.'

'Good!' Kate grinned. 'What can I get you?'

'I'll have a regular coffee and a cheese and tomato baguette please. No, actually, could you make that lemonade? It's so warm today.'

'It is, isn't it?' Kate busied herself writing down his order so that she couldn't catch his eye, scared she'd blush even more. 'It's been a good week again so far but they've given out stormy weather for later. How about ice cream to follow?'

'Sure. And, maybe – maybe I could take you out one night?'

Kate looked up as Will gave her that wonderful smile of his. Oh god, what was she going to do now?

All of a sudden, her heart screamed yes, but her head said she wasn't ready yet.

'I'm sorry, I can't,' she told him.

Will's smile faded and he started to fidget in his chair. 'Oh, I… sorry. Just forget I said anything.'

'No, I don't mean… It's just…' Kate paused. What should she say? How could she get him to understand that it was too soon, yet she desperately wanted to go out with him too? 'It's just not perfect timing.'

Will raised his hands. 'Hey, you don't have to explain. But if you do change your mind, you can always –'

Kate had stopped listening, looking over towards Lily and Alf's table. As Lily had got to her feet, all signs of colour drained from her face. She held out her arm to steady herself, lunged forwards towards the chair in front and sat down with a thud.

Alf moved to her first. 'Lily? Are you okay?'

'I think so.' Lily put her hand to her forehead

Kate joined them then. 'Are you –'

'Really, I'm fine,' Lily reiterated.

'But you've gone so pale.'

'It's nothing that a lie down won't cure. I'm sure it'll pass.'

Kate touched Lily's elbow. 'I'll help you upstairs.'

'For goodness' sake,' Lily snapped, getting to her feet unaided. 'I'm not an invalid. I can manage perfectly well by myself.'

'Maybe you can, but I'm still going to help you.'

After she had settled Lily on the settee, Kate came back downstairs. Noticing that Will had left, she let out a sigh. Why hadn't she just said yes? Silly woman.

She cleared a couple of tables and sidled over to the counter with the dishes.

Propped up by the side of the till was a serviette. Will had written his name and phone number on it.

She smiled, popping it into her pocket.

Chloe had been out at the bank when Lily had been taken ill. Kate relayed the tale on her return.

'How is she now?' Chloe said afterwards.

Kate shrugged and then sighed. 'Some of her colour has returned but she still looks pale. I'll take her another drink later. She barely touched the last one.'

'Do you think she's lost weight?'

Kate nodded.

'And Alf says she doesn't want to go to bingo with him.'

'Maybe she doesn't feel like company all of the time.'

'But she sits with us night after night.' Chloe ripped open a bag of pound coins and emptied them into the till. 'Lily and Rosie are permanent fixtures in the living room. Even when there's no one there, more likely than not she waits up for us.'

'She's been through a rough few months when you think about it, though,' Kate reasoned. 'She's lost her husband and she's opened the café again. It must have taken a lot out of her.'

'Maybe you should try and talk to her. If you don't pry too much, she might tell you something.'

But Kate shook her head. 'I've tried twice already. She just changes the subject. I'm not sure what to do.'

'What about having a quiet word with Alf?'

Kate purposely stopped at his table the following afternoon. After much persuasion, Lily had taken a day off to recuperate. Chloe had called on Harry for some magazines and Lily had been banned from entering the shop until tomorrow. Kate had popped in to see her last night but she still hadn't got a good colour about her.

'Do you think Lily looks a little down in the dumps?' Kate asked, passing Alf a piece of sponge cake to enjoy with his coffee.

'It's hard to tell,' Alf replied. 'For the life of me, I've never been able to work her out. She never lets on how she's feeling, especially when she isn't too good. That's always been her problem.'

Kate pulled out a chair and sat down opposite him. 'We're worried about her, Alf.' She flashed him her best convincing smile. 'Maybe you could talk to her?'

'And what makes you think she'll open her heart to me?'

'She's known you longer than us. With Irene away in Australia, you're one of her closest friends.'

Alf raised his bushy eyebrows. 'There's a lot that you don't know about Lily if you're asking me as a close friend. You know she thinks a lot of you girls.'

Kate leaned forward so that table eight wouldn't be able to hear her. 'I didn't mean that kind of a friend.'

Alf's eyes began to twinkle. 'She's not interested in any more than friendship,' he admitted, 'though I have had some fun trying to persuade her otherwise.'

Kate got to her feet as the front door opened and two women rushed in from the rain shower. Then she sat down again.

'Go on, please,' she tried one last time. 'See if you can find out what's bothering her. She won't tell us.'

'Have you tried hard enough?'

'How hard is that?'

'Extremely hard.'

'I've tried a few times, but she changes the subject.'

'Yes, she's good at that.' Pausing to stir his coffee before he spoke again, Alf continued. 'Let me see what I can do.

'Although I can't promise anything,' he warned quickly when he saw Kate's face break into a smile.

CHAPTER TWENTY-FIVE

Another week went by and as September crept in slowly but surely, the clocks due to go back in a few weeks, trade at the coffee shop hadn't slowed. Even though she wouldn't be around if she went to university, Chloe had suggested hot chocolate and marshmallow specials at their last meeting, to start on the first of October. They'd produced flyers to pop on every table to raise a bit of interest.

At the end of her shift that day, Kate thankfully ushered the last two customers out and locked the door behind them. Busy daydreaming as she wiped clean the last two tables, Kate turned as she heard a noise behind her. She knew it wasn't Chloe as she'd just gone upstairs.

Lily's heels clicked slowly across the laminate flooring. Made-up as immaculately as ever, her hair had been freshly set that morning when she'd popped into Hedworth to run some errands. But for all her radiant beauty, she still had a sad look in her eye.

'Lily!' she cried. 'How are you feeling?'

'Much better, thank you.' Lily got to Kate's side.

'Are you sure? You still look –'

'Really, I'm fine now. Are you all on your own?'

'Yes.' Kate knew she was being given the brush off. 'What brings you down so late?'

'I came to see how things are going with Chloe and Lucy.'

'It's got a lot better,' Kate answered. 'And tonight will be a tester for them, I suppose. Can you believe I said I'd go out with the two of them on a Friday night? I must be mad.'

'Sounds like fun. I hope it's going to make things easier for you. I'm well aware that I can't work as much as I used to.'

'But we work for you! We enjoy it and we're a team – well,' Kate grinned, 'most of the time we are.'

Lily leaned on the table for support and Kate drew out a chair for her. Lily sat down before continuing, 'I feel like I'm not doing my share. It's my business and I'm letting you do all the work.'

'Isn't that what you pay us to do?'

Lily smiled. 'Have you decided what to do about Will yet?'

Kate had confided in Lily about her predicament but Lily had talked to her and made her see sense.

Will was the first man to show an interest in Kate since she'd separated from Nick. It would have been hard for her, no matter who it was, but Lily said it was worth letting go every now and then, worth taking a chance. She reached into her apron pocket, her hand resting on the serviette that Will had left for her. She'd been thinking of texting him for the past few days but hadn't plucked up the courage yet.

'Do you know what, Lily? I think I'm going to take a chance and go out with him for a drink. You never know – it might be fun.' She grinned.

'Well, the quicker you finish,' Lily smiled before shooing her away as she got up again, 'the quicker you can go and call him. Hand me that cloth.'

It had taken Kate an age to get ready before the three of them headed for Hedworth and Heroes Wine Bar.

She'd been panicking all night about what the two younger women would be wearing. In the end, she'd chosen the easy way to be cool in dark skinny jeans and a deep orange top that accentuated the tone in her shoulders and upper arms. Still, she felt decidedly old as she watched a girl run along Hedworth High Street, her short, white skirt showing off toned legs, cropped top showing off her waist, blonde hair trailing behind her. The young man she was running towards came forward and twirled her round in his arms, the skirt leaving nothing to the imagination. Embarrassed – or was it envious – she looked ahead of her, the sky revealing a menacing grey cloud between the buildings as they crossed over the road. At least it wasn't raining yet.

'What on earth's that?' Kate pointed down to Lucy's hand, where there was a sliver of leather in her palm. Lucy was as slightly dressed as the girl who had run past them earlier, in a denim miniskirt and ankle boots, her chest squashed into a tiny T-shirt.

'My handbag,' Lucy grinned. 'Do you want to see what's inside it?'

'Is there room for anything?'

Lucy opened a zip at the side of the tiny black purse and pulled out a lipstick. 'My key is in there,' she pointed to another zip 'and my money is in there. What more do I need?'

Kate gave her a blank look. 'Hairbrush, hair spray, blusher and brush. Mobile phone, credit card for emergencies.'

'You bring all that with you on a night out?' Chloe marvelled. 'No wonder you're tired at the end of it, with all that weight to haul around.'

'That's my summer essentials. There's more in winter. Spare stockings, umbrella…'

The thud, thud of the lively up-tempo music meant all dialogue had to be suspended as they went into the venue. Heroes seemed to be as popular as they'd heard. Not a single inch of floor was left uncovered as they pushed their way to the bar.

The drinks flowing freely, half-past eleven came round only too quickly. Kate took hardly any persuading when Chloe suggested going on to a club. Stumbling as they walked to Rembrandts, they tried in vain to keep their hair in some sort of style as the shower that had been forecast turned nasty. Once inside, they flew up two flights of stairs to the first of three dance floors and made their way through the crowds until they found a space.

'This is terrific,' Lucy screamed at Kate over the sound of the music. 'I've really enjoyed myself with you two tonight.'

Kate's face lit up as if she hadn't seen her in ages, rather than the minute or so it had been. 'Hiya, Lucy,' she slurred. 'Where've you been?'

'To the loo.'

'Toodle-do?' Kate laughed.

'Where's Chloe?'

Lucy pointed to her right where Chloe was dancing with a man who could really move around the floor.

Her hair was being tossed provocatively in every direction as she worked her stuff.

'Whoops.' Kate felt herself fall forward again but managed to stay upright. God, she was wasted. She focused on Lucy and, when she could see only one of her, flung an arm around her neck and hugged her fiercely.

'Whose round is it next?'

Lily switched on her bedside lamp, put on her reading glasses and looked at the clock. It only revealed what she already knew since she'd looked at it five minutes earlier. It was twenty to two in the morning.

Even the mug of tea she'd got up to make hadn't settled her.

The girls must be enjoying themselves, she thought, as she punched at her pillows and propped herself up. Kate had told her not to wait up as they'd gone through the door. She could still hear them heading down the stairs, chattering nineteen to the dozen. And then there had been silence.

Aware she wasn't going to get any more sleep until she knew they were back home safe and sound, Lily slid her legs round to the side of the bed and pulled herself up. Not knowing what to do next, she parted the curtains and stood staring out into the street.

Where were they? She opened the window but all she heard was the usual noises of the night.

Reluctantly, she climbed back into bed.

Finally, three quarters of an hour later, they were home. Lily couldn't help but smile as she listened to them trying to keep the noise down.

'Be quiet!' yelled Kate. 'You'll wake Lily.'

'We are being quiet!' Lucy laughed as she missed the top stair and fell onto her knees. 'I'm SO glad I'm staying over though.' She lost the grip on her shoes, now in her hands, and they clattered on every step before they reached the bottom.

Chloe tried to pull her up straight and instead collapsed in a heap of giggles by her side.

'Shush!' cried Kate. 'You'll wake the whole street.'

'Not before you do.' Lucy slowly got to her feet and balanced hazardously at the top of the stairs before Chloe pulled her arm and she flew forward into the wall.

'Ow!'

'Go to bed, you two!' shouted Kate again. 'See you tomorrow.' Her final words as she slammed the bathroom door.

Lily smiled to herself. It seemed so strange but she had almost come to think of the girls as if they were her own family. In just a few months, they had become more than staff – which was good really, considering.

Finally, Lily felt herself relax. They were noisy but they were safe. And pretty soon they'd be in bed.

Then maybe she could get some sleep.

CHAPTER TWENTY-SIX

The next morning, Kate turned over and flinched as she connected with the pain in her head. Gradually, the clock came into focus and as quick as her body would allow, she dragged herself up. She was late for work – very late.

'You look like I feel,' Lucy sympathised when Kate made it downstairs with Rosie in her arms.

'I'm so sorry,' she said. She placed Rosie onto the floor and attached her lead to her collar. 'Give me a few minutes and I'll be back.'

Even the fresh air didn't do anything to alleviate her headache so, with Rosie settled upstairs again, Kate sat with her head in her hands at the counter as Lucy took care of the small queue of takeaway orders. Chloe came out of the kitchen and purposely wafted a bacon butty she'd made for herself under Kate's nose.

'Get that thing away from me,' Kate gagged and turned her head from it. 'I can't face that this morning.'

'In case you hadn't noticed,' Chloe made a huge deal in checking her watch, 'we started well over an hour ago.'

Kate blanched. 'Sorry, I can't take my alcohol like you.'

'It's a good job I didn't come with you then,' Lily laughed as she slid over a glass of water and a packet of aspirins before going back into the kitchen.

'We did go heavy on the drink,' recollected Chloe. 'I told you not to buy that last bottle.'

'Please tell me you mean a bottle of lager.'

'Nope. I mean wine.'

Kate's eyes widened and her hand rose to her mouth. 'I never drank a whole bottle, did I?'

'Not by yourself. You brought it out of Rembrandts in that bloody big handbag of yours and we finished it off on our way home.'

'Ouch. No wonder my head's hurting. I can't believe –' Kate stopped talking as her mobile phone rang out.

'Was that Will?' Chloe asked afterwards.

Kate nodded, annoyed to feel her skin start to burn.

Chloe flew back to Kate's side as soon as it was physically possible. Suddenly her eyes widened, reminding Kate of Ermintrude the colourful cow from the children's television program, *Magic Roundabout*.

'Ohmigod!' she shrieked, before continuing in a whisper as someone walked past to go to the loo, 'you're going out with him, aren't you?'

'Yes. I said I'd meet him for a drink.'

Kate tried to act disinterested but secretly her insides were fizzing and not all of it was to do with her hangover. Before going out the night before, she'd sent Will a text message. He'd replied and, over the course of the evening, they'd started up a conversation.

'About time!' said Chloe. 'I think you'd better have some lessons before you go on your first date in absolutely years and years, though.'

Kate flicked Chloe's leg with a teacloth as she ran past. She followed her into the kitchen. Lily was sitting on a chair making a note of what stock she had left in the pantry.

'You could learn a lot from me,' Chloe went on. 'I happen to be a mistress of the dating profession. I can teach you a thing or two.'

Kate sniggered.

'I am!' insisted Chloe.

'He is a handsome chappie,' Lily added into the conversation. 'Quite sexy, if I'm honest.'

At the mention of sexy, Kate began to imagine what it would be like to feel Will's firm body on top of hers. His brown eyes reading her mind as the tip of his tongue searched around the inside of her mouth before making its way slowly down her body. Blushing again, she chastised herself inwardly. Where had that come from?

'Are you two going to do any work today?' Lucy interrupted in an exaggerated-but-friendly tone. 'There are two tables waiting for orders and Serle's come in with a long list that he hasn't pre-ordered.'

'Yes, sir, right away, sir. I'm coming through, sir.' Kate saluted her disappearing figure and followed her out into the shop. 'Oh dear, Serle, you'll have a long wait now. Didn't I tell you to phone first? We're too hungover to get things right today.'

The following afternoon, Alf had invited Lily for lunch at the Red Lion in Hedworth, their favourite eatery. They were seated in a tiny booth; wooden benches either side were covered in burgundy velvet. Stripey, flocked wallpaper lined most of the walls, almost as chocolate brown as the carpet, and decorative brass horseshoes hung from original beams. Alf and Lily loved it all, including the dark atmosphere and the jukebox that played 45 records that they could sing along to.

They were busy tucking into shepherds pie, chips and vegetables when he started the conversation. Lily had known this was going to be the chosen topic for today. She'd observed the looks going back and forth between him and the staff since her dizzy spell last Friday.

'The girls are concerned about you, Lily,' he said.

'Oh?'

Alf put down his cutlery. 'We're all concerned about you. You don't feel like going out. Half the time I see you, you look exhausted. And you're losing weight.'

Pretending to be more interested in the young baby sitting at the next table rather than catch his eye, Alf's concern was clear when she finally looked up. She didn't like being deceitful, but she smiled to reassure him.

'I'm fine.' She patted his wrinkled hand.

'But they're worried. Can't you talk to them? Put their minds at rest.'

'There's nothing to talk about.'

'They wouldn't be worried about nothing.'

Lily removed her hand from his to catch the barmaid's attention. 'Could I have a glass of water, please?'

'But, Lily –'

'Please don't fuss, Alf,' she stopped him in mid flow. 'Really, I'm fine. Now, have you decided what pudding you're having after you've eaten all that lot? I'm sure you can manage apple pie and custard, my treat.'

Lily picked up the menu, hoping to hide the blush that was spreading rapidly across her cheeks. She didn't like fibbing at the best of times, even if they were only little white lies. And Alf didn't need to know everything, did he?

Although it was now the middle of September and the weather had been bright and cheerful for the past two days, it was decidedly chilly after dark. For her date with Will, Kate decided on something stylish yet casual: boot-cut jeans, white fitted shirt and black ankle boots. She reached for her long lime-green cardigan and draped it over her arm before dashing downstairs.

Moving a vertical slat to one side, she peered out onto the square, relieved to see Will waiting for her.

Thank god she'd had the sense to wear trousers, she thought, taking in the lustrous black pick-up truck. She'd never be able to climb into that thing without flashing her knickers if she'd worn a skirt.

'Hello, Kate.'

Kate turned at the sound of Lily's voice behind her as she came into the room. She noticed her colour was slowly returning but then realised she'd had help from a tub of rouge, and her grey hair had been set in rollers. Unless she'd slipped her shoes on, Lily had even managed to bend and fasten them up herself and she was only limping slightly.

'Hi, how are you feeling?' she asked.

'Oh, I'm much better,' Lily replied. 'I said it was just a bug. Anyway, what are you up to?'

'I'm meeting Will.' Kate felt herself blushing. 'He's waiting outside.'

Lily prised open the blind to take a quick peek.

'Don't let him see you!' cried Kate.

'Oh, he's too busy reading his paper.'

They both peeped through at the same time Will decided to turn his head. Quickly, they stepped back.

'Do you think he saw us?' gasped Kate, nerves all of a flutter.

'No.' Lily's eyes twinkled. 'But why are you so anxious?'

Kate sighed loudly. 'Oh, I don't know. I suppose it's all the emotion of Nick coming back to me.'

'He hurt you a lot, didn't he?'

'I suppose.'

'But you're only going out for a drink with Will.' Lily smiled and touched Kate lightly on her forearm. 'Now, go on, before he changes his mind.'

As soon as he spotted her, Will jumped out of the truck and met Kate halfway across the cobbled forecourt.

'Hello, you,' he said before kissing her gently on the cheek.

Kate smelt the tangy notes of his aftershave and immediately sensed her skin flushing. She'd forgotten how attractive he was close up. Come to bed eyes seemed happy to see her. And that dark, floppy hair was so... adorable? Oops – she was off again. She grinned.

Will threw back his right arm. 'My carriage awaits you.'

The picturesque pub he drove to was tiny for the amount of people milling around in the lounge but Will managed to get served quickly and they took their drinks through to a quieter part of the room at the back of the building. They found a corner to squeeze into and sat down.

'So, how's the new –?'

'Have you missed –?'

Kate and Will smiled at each other. Then neither of them spoke.

'It's lovely to see you again,' Will spoke softly, leaning forward to flick a stray piece of hair away from her cheek.

Kate shivered at the sheer intimacy. 'Likewise,' she replied.

They chatted amiably for a while.

'Are you hungry?' he asked afterwards.

Not for food, Kate thought. She shook her head in response.

'Another drink, then?'

Kate didn't notice the décor as Will walked away. Instead, she focused on the material of his black T-shirt stretched taut across his back and the definition of his firm buttocks, seeming more prominent through his jeans. When he walked back minutes later, struggling to carry two glasses of lager, a small can of salted nuts and a bag of crisps, she realised she'd already missed his company.

'I didn't know which you'd prefer,' Will said, 'so I bought both.' Tearing off the lid, he shook a handful of nuts into her outstretched palm. Not the kind she wanted, she thought, but at least he was willing to share.

For God's sake, she laughed inwardly, *get a grip of yourself. You're acting out a scene from a Mills and Boon novel. In a short while, you'll be panting breathlessly, yearning for his manly lips crushing down onto yours. Bruising them with longing.*

'How long have you known Serle?' Kate asked, for want of something to say.

'Far more years than I care to admit,' said Will. 'I knew him at school but lost touch when we left. But then he became a regular at the gym I used to go to. Future Bodies at the leisure centre – do you know it?'

'Yes, I'm a member.'

'When I lived locally, Serle and I used to go at roughly the same times so it was easy to partner up. Couldn't keep up the weight he pumped though, despite the fact that my battered ego would always try.'

'Where do you live now?'

Will took a sip of his drink. 'Over in Warbury. It's about thirty miles away. I travel around in my job, covering a fifty-mile radius.'

'What is it that you do?'

'I'm a computer engineer. My dad still lives around here though. How about you? Do you have any regrets about moving to Somerley?'

'Not now,' she told him. 'It was strange at first, I must admit, but good now that I've settled in.'

'And it's given me a chance to get to know you.' Will moved towards Kate and lightly kissed the corner of her mouth. 'I have to return home tomorrow but I'm back at the weekend to see my dad. Perhaps I could see you again, maybe on Saturday night?'

Hearing the seduction in his voice was all Kate needed to bring up an image of his firm torso pressing against her breasts. Ramming the nuts into her mouth was the only thing she could do to stop herself from laughing out loud.

For the rest of the evening, Kate attempted to maintain a conversation whilst resisting the urge to pull Will towards her and kiss him. Trying to concentrate was nigh on impossible because she kept being drawn to his lips, then his eyes and back to his lips. There was no mistaking it. She was in lust.

As the night drew to an end and the room emptied around them, Kate could have sworn her heart stopped beating when Will moved his face towards hers. But no, there it was, amplified now as it bumped away. Now the moment had arrived, all those feelings of being twelve years old with first kiss nerves came reeling back as if they'd never gone away.

'I'm glad we've got together at last,' Will whispered. As his hand reached behind her head, urging her to move towards him, Kate had one last chance to gaze into his eyes, his face slightly silhouetted in the light of a lamp behind.

'Me too,' she managed to whisper back before her lips felt the heat of his and she crossed her legs to stop herself exploding. Nick Bradshaw? Sorry… who was that again?

CHAPTER TWENTY-SEVEN

It was a Tuesday evening. Chloe sat at Lily's feet as Kate joined them in the living room. Even though the evening news had only just finished, she was dressed in pink pyjamas. Busy painting her toe nails a fiery-red, she'd already started on the wine.

'Is there anything decent on the television tonight?' Kate asked.

'Oh, you're bored already without darling Will to take you out,' Chloe teased.

At the mention of his name, Kate grinned. She couldn't help herself. She *was* bored without Will. Since their first date, she'd met him several times over the past fortnight.

Chloe didn't have time to reply as her mobile rang out from within the pile of nail varnish bottles surrounding it on the carpet.

'Oh. Hi, Dad. I won't be a minute.' She covered the mouthpiece over with her fingers. 'I'll take this in the hall. Don't want to get moaned at in public.'

'Has she made up her mind about university yet?' Lily questioned Kate when the door closed behind her.

'I think she's too late now.' Kate stretched out her right leg to inspect her toes. Maybe Chloe would do her a pedicure next. 'It's hard for her, I assume. She wants to please her dad, yet I think she wants to stay here.'

'He shouldn't pressurise her.' Lily shook her head. 'She should be able to choose what she wants to do. It's her life. He can't live it for her.'

'I know, but I don't think he'll give in until he has his own way.'

'It won't be the same without Chloe.' Lily moved her legs to the right a touch, striving to get comfortable.

Kate nodded in agreement, looking around the room that had become so familiar. The Coffee Stop was part of her life now. No one from Brentside would believe she'd be happy to chalk up boards and churn out coffee instead of preparing reports for the corporate management team or evaluating the latest pilot scheme they'd put in place.

'I know what you mean,' she said. 'It's only been four months, yet we've become so close. And it's strange, I really enjoyed my job before but now I feel more fulfilled, happier to muck in and get the work done.'

'With Old Mother Hubbard watching over you,' laughed Lily.

'Was your dad asking when you were going to enrol?' Kate asked when Chloe re-joined them.

'Yes.' Chloe sighed, taking her place on the floor again. 'I've told him I'm going to check out courses this week, although I don't see what the rush is.'

'You might lose a place if you don't.'

'Part of me wants to go and enjoy the student way of life,' Chloe replied after some thought, 'even if I do have to work really hard. The other part of me wants to stay here. It's driving me mad.'

'Why don't you take a year out?' suggested Lily. 'One of my friend's granddaughters did. She travelled around parts of Australia before qualifying as a social worker. I'm sure that will keep your dad happy and give you time to think about what you want to do in the future.'

'But won't you have regrets later?' Kate didn't give Chloe time to answer. 'Qualifications gain you extra points.'

'Not necessarily.' Chloe shook her head. 'There'll always be something I can do without a degree.'

'Maybe, but you won't earn megabucks like your brother.'

'Money isn't everything.' Chloe rested her back on the armchair and pulled up her knees. 'I don't want to be stuck in an office atmosphere all day. I like it here.'

'Well, I for one think that's sensible,' said Lily. 'There's no point in doing anything you're not happy about.'

'Thanks, Lily,' said Chloe. 'It's nice to have someone on my side.'

Kate raised a hand. 'You misunderstand me if you think that I want you to go. Of course I want you to stay but it has to be your choice.'

'I *know.*' Chloe had that bothered look on her face again. 'That's what I'm afraid of.'

Once her shift had finished the following evening, Chloe found herself in one of those A to B moods, where she'd got into her car at point A and was driving on autopilot to point B without even realising that she was in control of a vehicle. Her mind kept trawling through last night's conversation. All along, she'd known what she wanted to do. She just had to man up now that she had made a decision.

She manoeuvred her car into a designated visitors' spot and switched off the engine. Looking up at the building in front of her, Chloe's heart began to race.

She made her way through the empty reception area, past the photocopier that loved to chew up her college work, past the faded settee in the waiting area that she'd fallen asleep on many times and on to the end of the corridor. Her stomach flipped and momentarily she felt sick as she caught a glimpse of her dad through the frosted glass. She knew he'd still be here, even so late.

'Chloe!' Graham's face was a fusion of misunderstanding and pleasure at seeing his daughter standing in his office doorway. 'I hadn't expected to see you today.'

Chloe ran towards him and threw herself into his arms.

'What's the matter? Has anything –'

'I'm sorry, Dad,' she sobbed, 'but I have to let you down.' Chloe wiped at her eyes as she tried to explain what she knew he wouldn't understand. 'I can't do it, Dad. I can't go to university yet. I'll do it next year but not this year. I want to stay at the coffee shop with Kate and Lily. I've enjoyed working with them so much and I don't want to leave them. And Lily isn't well. I can't leave her now.'

'You can't stay there!' he said. 'You have to be realistic about these things. It was only a summer job, a bit of fun but now you need to settle down and start studying again.'

Chloe moved across the room and slumped down in a chair. Reluctantly, she took the cotton handkerchief he offered, knowing she had no choice but to hear him out.

Graham sat down at his desk and rubbed his hands over his face before putting one on each arm of the chair. Chloe inspected her nails while she waited for him to speak.

'I thought you were happy to get a better education,' he said finally.

Chloe shook her head and folded her arms. 'No, *you* thought I'd be happy. I'm only doing what you want me to do.'

'That's because I'm older and wiser and know what's best for you.'

'Not necessarily,' she said under her breath. A little too loudly, she realised as she watched the expression on his face darken.

'Do you think I would have got all this,' he swung his right arm out, 'if I hadn't done well at university?'

'Maybe,' she huffed.

'The answer is no. My degree gave me somewhere to start. I know it doesn't help me now but it enabled me to learn the ropes. That's when I set up on my own.'

'I only want to take a year out!'

Graham looked long and hard at his daughter before shaking his head. Chloe turned away from his stare.

'I know you, Chloe,' he said. 'Once you've made up your mind to do something, I won't be able to stop you. I know you won't go to university now, but I'm damned if I'm going to make it easy for you. You've obviously come to get my blessing. Well, I'm not going to give it to you.'

'You make it sound like I'm getting married.'

'You know perfectly well what I mean.'

Holding in the tears on the brink of falling again, Chloe realised there was no point in saying anything else. She stood up abruptly.

'Fine, have it your way. I'll go to university just to make you happy.'

'Oh, please.' Graham sat forward. 'You'll do as you feel fit anyway. But I have to say, I'm extremely disappointed in your attitude. I thought you'd be more of a grown-up about the situation.'

'I am a grown-up!' Chloe retaliated, her cheeks nearing the same shade as her hair. 'So I think it's about time you started to treat me like one, instead of keeping me as your little Chloe. I'm eighteen, Dad, not eight.'

The glass shook as she slammed the door on her departure. Chloe marched back out of the building and got into her car.

She'd driven all the way to her house and was in the kitchen before she allowed herself to cry.

'Kate Bradshaw, will you please concentrate! If you don't watch what you're doing, you're going to lose your footing and fly off the back of the treadmill. You'll be going out with no one this weekend then.'

Kate turned to Lucy who was running on the next machine to her. 'I'm sorry,' she smiled. 'I can't help it. My mind keeps wandering.'

'More likely, you're thinking of where Will's hands may be wandering to,' Lucy smirked. She slowed the machine and began to walk at a fast pace. Kate decided to join her. It would be easier for her to concentrate that way.

Lucy wiped her fringe out of her eyes. 'Why have you got to wait until Saturday? From the look on your face, you're missing him already, and from the amount of texts he's sent you, so is he.'

'He's working back at home for most of this week.'

'So was he staying over when he was visiting the solicitors?'

Kate nodded. 'He used to live in Somerley. He moved to Warbury about ten years ago. When we went out, he stayed over at his dad's. His mum died in summer and he's helping to sort things out.'

Kate had learned all this over the course of her past few dates with Will. Their conversation had been so natural. She'd found him so easy to talk to that she'd told him all about Nick and her pending divorce.

Will hadn't seemed bothered about it, a fact Kate was glad about.

'You've gone off in a dream.'

Kate looked across at Lucy and grinned.

Lucy held up her hand. 'Don't say sorry again, you're driving me mad.' She switched off the machine and turned to get off it.

'Well, I know one thing for sure, Kate Bradshaw,' Lucy interrupted her thoughts. 'This one's more than just a fling.'

'What do you mean?'

Lucy rolled her eyes to the ceiling. 'I'm telling you, he's brought a sparkle to those blue eyes of yours. I think you could be falling for him, already.'

Kate couldn't help but smile. It was true. Even in their early days, she couldn't remember being this smitten with Nick. She had got it bad – and she found that she liked the feeling.

When she felt a little calmer, Chloe made coffee and took it through into the conservatory. In the empty house, she sipped the hot drink while she stood looking out over the garden. The wind tried its best to rip the remaining leaves away from the trees while she wished she was back in Somerley. It was strange, but this room didn't feel like her sanctuary anymore. Damn her dad and his stupid principles. How dare he make her feel like a child!

A few minutes later, the kitchen door opened behind her. Chloe turned to see the only person that could make things worse: Maddy.

'Hi, Chloe,' said Maddy. Along with a smile, she wore a beige delicate-knit jumper above dark trousers. The scarf around her neck was a multi-coloured swirl of silk. 'I was surprised to see your car outside. How are you?'

'Absolutely marvellous,' Chloe replied sarcastically. *Please don't let her stay. Please let her go upstairs and have a shower or something. Then I can leave without having to talk to her.*

All hopes of that were dashed when Maddy took off her jacket and placed it over the back of a kitchen chair. She flicked on the kettle before joining her in the conservatory.

'I suppose Dad's called you,' Chloe accused. She sat down in the leather settee, hurled off her boots and pulled up her feet.

Maddy nodded. 'He only wants what's best for you.'

'So what did you say to him?' Chloe snapped.

'I told him to let you go,' Maddy replied. 'I said it was time that you made your own decisions, your own mistakes and your own rules.'

Chloe frowned as she watched her go back into the kitchen. For a moment then it sounded like Maddy was siding with *her*. That couldn't be right, surely?

Moments later, Maddy sat down in the wicker chair opposite. 'When I was your age, I fell in love with a guy called Martin Shaw.'

Chloe couldn't help but snigger. 'Isn't that one of *The Professionals*?'

Maddy looked surprised.

'I've seen it on digital TV.'

'Oh, right. Well, he wanted me to move away with him and start a new life. All *I* ever wanted to do was open my own clothes shop, eventually design my own label and have a chain of stores.' Maddy looked over at Chloe to see her pulling her face in disinterest, but still listening intently. 'I know, I know.

'Call me naive, but I was only your age at the time. Before I met Martin, I was hell-bent on doing a course in business studies. He persuaded me to move to Newquay with him.'

'So what happened?' Chloe tried, and failed, to act disinterested.

Maddy looked at her with a twinkle in her eyes. 'I got pregnant by the bastard. He didn't want to know. I moved back home and my parents looked after Craig while I worked in a pub.'

Chloe looked surprised but Maddy laughed it off. 'It took me years to get back on my feet again. That's why it's only now that I have a successful business under my belt.'

The penny dropped. Chloe realised she'd been reeled in hook, line and sinker.

'You're going to tell me you went back to college, aren't you,' she snapped again.

'Yes, but for evening classes. It was easier to fit around Craig.' Maddy put down her drink. 'What I'm trying to tell you is that you *can* do both. You want to keep working and Graham, your dad, wants you to keep studying. So go to work during the day and study for one or two nights a week. It's easier to fit in. It might take a bit longer to get where you want to be but you still get there. And trust me, it's much more satisfying.'

All of a sudden, shame flooded through Chloe. Kate had told her to give Maddy a chance but her pig-headed nature hadn't allowed her to back down. She'd had no idea that life had been so tough for Maddy, mainly because she'd never bothered to find out. To her, Maddy was always there as a threat, ready to steal away her dad at the first opportunity. All Maddy had ever done was try to get on with her. But all Chloe had ever done was make life as uncomfortable for her as possible.

Her coffee finished, Maddy stood up and smiled. 'He'll come around,' she said. 'I can't understand why he's being so stubborn. It's not as if you want to give up and go to live in Newquay with someone you hardly know!'

Chloe warily reached for Maddy's hand as she walked past. 'Thanks,' she said softly.

The kitchen door opened again. 'Oh no, it looks like my two favourite women are ganging up on me. It's not fair, two against one!'

Chloe shared a conspiratorial look with Maddy before turning her attention to her dad standing in the doorway. The first thing she noticed wasn't that he'd changed from his work suit into his jeans. It was that he was wearing a smile. The smile, she remembered so well, that told her he wasn't annoyed with her anymore.

'You shouldn't creep up on us like that,' said Maddy. She gave Chloe's hand a squeeze before letting it drop, 'when it's obvious that we're still talking about you.' She kissed him lightly on the cheek before turning back to wink at Chloe.

'I'm not sure that I want you to stay anymore,' Kate said when Chloe had gathered them both in the living room to tell them the news. She moved onto the settee next to her. 'I don't like people who keep changing their minds all the time. The next thing we know *you'll* be off back-packing and leaving us in the lurch.'

'Well, I'm pleased that you're staying,' said Lily, even though she knew Kate was teasing Chloe. 'I'm so glad I'm not losing my, how do you say it, "diva".'

'I'm not a diva!' Chloe cried as Lily smiled at her. 'Well, okay, just a little bit of one. But, stroppy diva or not, you're too attached to me now.'

'Anyway, like I said earlier,' Kate wasn't going to be ignored, 'I'm not sure I want you to stay now.'

Chloe threw her a look of insolence. 'What are you wittering on about, woman?'

Kate winked at Lily. 'Don't tell me you've forgotten about that man you interviewed as Chloe's replacement?'

'Ah, yes,' Lily joined in with the joke. 'You'd better ring him up, Kate. It's a shame, but we have our diva back – I suppose it's a small sacrifice to make.'

Getting ready for her next date with Will, Kate was having a hard time controlling herself. It was weird to think that she'd only known him for a short while, yet as soon as they'd gone out on a date, she had begun to miss him every second he was away. No matter how many phone calls and text messages had flown back and forth between them, it hadn't been enough. Her stomach went all peculiar whenever she thought of their goodnight kisses, the smile spreading wider each time she remembered how he'd teased her with his tongue. Just those few kisses had brought back feelings of lust that had been buried in her sexual archives many years ago. She ached to see him in the flesh.

Flesh, she shuddered with desire. She thought back to how Will had run his tongue across her upper lip before moving in for the kill, remembering the feel of his erection straining against his jeans as they pushed their bodies as close as was possible.

'God, I feel like I've known you for ever; these past few days I've missed you so much,' Will whispered to her as she climbed into his car. 'Come here.' Within seconds, their lips locked and Kate felt as though she'd never left him. What was happening to her?

'I suppose we'd better go from outside the coffee shop,' Will said a few minutes later when they hadn't moved. Reluctantly, he started the engine.

The rest of Kate's night flew by in a mixture of delight and frustration as she and Will went to a restaurant in Hedworth. But it had been too busy for intimacy and they left shortly before eleven. They pulled up back outside Church Square and the kissing started again, tenderly at first, then harder, more forceful and more passionate. Kate had never been a 'back-seat-of-the-car' woman. But she really wanted him, and as her hands moved lower she knew he felt the same.

Suddenly, Will broke away and got out of the vehicle. He ran round to the passenger side and flung open the door.

'Come on,' he grabbed Kate's hand.

'Where are we going?'

He led her along the pathway and pushed her up against the trunk of the oak tree. Kissing her more urgently now, he pressed his body as near to hers as was physically possible. Then his hands were inside her jacket, and then inside her jumper.

Kate wasn't sure if it was the cold night air or his skin connecting with hers that made her struggle to catch her breath. Mirroring his action, she pulled out his shirt and ran her fingers up and down his spine as she explored his mouth. He pressed his hand around her breast and for a moment she thought her feet had left the ground.

His hand moving lower now, Kate followed suit. She reached for his crotch, turned on more as a moan escaped from his lips. Her hand fell on his belt.

Suddenly Will's hand was on hers, pushing it away. 'No! We can't do this.'

We can't?

He pulled back, his eyes never leaving hers. Even in the pale lighting, Kate could see how much his pupils dilated.

'I wished I had my own place up here now. Would you think it was presumptuous of me to book a hotel somewhere and we can go away for the night soon?' he asked.

Kate laughed, somewhat breathlessly. 'Presumptuous is the wrong word. I'd say it was more necessity.'

Will treated her to that smile again. 'I want it to be special rather than hurried, no matter how frustrated you can feel I am.'

'Oh, I would say you're extremely frustrated.' Kate pressed on his erection again, relishing his look of anguish.

'You wouldn't have done it here, would you?'

Kate shook her head. 'No, but it will give me something to fantasise about while I'm at work.'

'Oh, God, Kate,' Will pulled her towards him again. 'I don't think I can wait that long.'

CHAPTER TWENTY-EIGHT

When Chloe had told Kate of her plans to enrol at the local college, Kate had given her a couple of hours off to attend their enrolment day. She'd only been there for a few minutes but already it seemed like she'd never been away from a learning environment. She integrated herself into the hustle and bustle all around her, moving when a deliveryman wheeled a trolley loaded with copier paper past her. There were all kinds of people milling around. Extremely young like herself; extremely old like the lady who announced at the top of her voice that she was enrolling for her second course learning computer studies.

Chloe spotted an open door and made her way towards it.

'First time here?' a man approached her in one stride. She nodded and he pointed to a table in the far corner. 'Help yourself to a prospectus and, if you get stuck, give me a shout.'

Chloe turned to speak to him but already he was a blur. She politely pushed her way over to the corner of the room to a table piled high with booklets. The course she was after started at lunchtime and went on until nine. Once she'd flicked through the pages and found what she was looking for, she made her way back down the corridor. Not looking where she was going, she collided with a man.

'Oh, I'm sorry,' she apologized as her prospectus flew out of her hands.

'Here, let me.'

He bent down to retrieve it, giving her a bird's eye view. Dressed casually in jeans and a checked shirt, it was hard to put an age to him. By the amount of laughter lines visible, and a few grey hairs appearing here and there, as he stood up again, she realised he was a lot older than he looked. And tall too which, as well as suiting her, went great with his toned physique. He indulged her with a smile while he handed everything back.

Jeez, he was hot!

'Thanks,' she murmured and looked away in embarrassment as his eyes bore into hers.

'No problem. It's so busy in here, isn't it?'

'Yes. Can you tell me where room 41b is?'

'I don't know. It's my first time here too.'

'Oh, sorry! I thought you were one of the lecturers here.'

'No, I'm going to be a mature student.' He grinned. 'An old fart, you might say. I've been made redundant so decided to come back to college to learn something new. Start my own business up while I have the opportunity.'

'Oh.' Chloe nodded. 'That's good.'

'I'm Jack, by the way.'

'Chloe.' She smiled.

'Are you going to do a course?'

'Yes, business studies, I think.'

'Great.' He smiled too. 'So, come and find me – we can grab a coffee, if you like?'

'Oh, I'll make sure I do just that,' Chloe whispered as he walked off. She watched him continue down the corridor.

It was a few seconds before she realised that someone else was speaking to her.

'Have you chosen anything yet?'

Chloe turned to see a young woman, she guessed around her age, maybe a little older. She had a round face, short blonde hair and her front teeth were uneven as she smiled nervously. She loosened her scarf before she sat down beside her.

'I've decided to do business studies,' she added, the panic clear in her voice. 'I hope I'll be good enough.'

'I'm doing that too,' said Chloe.

'Do you think it will be hard?'

'Probably, but I suppose I'll do nothing for the first six months and then everything for the last few. I always leave revising to the last panicking minute. I'm Chloe, by the way,' she added with a smile, realising she might have made another friend already.

'I'm Fran.'

Chloe scanned the corridor but Jack was nowhere to be seen. She turned back to Fran. 'Shall we go and enrol?'

Lily straightened up, wincing as a pain ran up the length of her spine. She knew she shouldn't have sat in the armchair for so long with Rosie but she'd been so engrossed in watching Gene Kelly dancing on and off the kerb in a rerun of *Singing in the Rain*.

'Are you all right?' Kate asked, looking up from the magazine she was reading to see that Lily had gone pale again.

'I'm fine.' Lily forced a smile. 'It's my arthritis playing up. My doctor says it's better in the summer when it's warmer, but I can't tell the difference at any time of the year.' She moved herself around in the chair and lifted her feet onto her footstool.

'You sit there and rest.' Kate put down her sandwich. 'I'll get you a cold drink.'

'No, please finish off your lunch. I'll be fine once my tablets start to take effect.'

'It's okay, it won't take a minute.'

Lily laid back her head, realising she'd overdone things again. She was worried that she had been feeling so ill for over a week now. Things were happening too fast. It could mean only one thing – something she didn't want to come to terms with yet.

But she was too exhausted to think about what to do next.

When Kate returned with her drink a few minutes later, she was asleep.

'Hello, you,' Kate greeted Will with a huge grin as he came through the front door into the coffee shop an hour later. She kissed him lightly on the cheek. 'I didn't know you were in town today.'

'It's only a whirlwind visit, I'm afraid.' Will handed her a brochure. 'I've picked out a hotel in Manchester, wondered what you'd think.'

Kate took the brochure from him.

'It's on page seventeen. How's Lily, by the way?'

'She's still a little under the weather. We've banned her from the shop, but if I know Lily, she'll be back downstairs soon.'

Will gave a half smile before pointing to the brochure. 'What do you think?'

Kate eyed the photographs with glee. The hotel looked fabulous. Four-poster beds, eight acres of gardens, indoor heated pool and Jacuzzi.

She kissed him again. 'I can't wait.'

He pulled her closer. 'No, neither can I.'

'Yuck,' said Chloe, walking past. 'Put him down.'

'Don't want to,' said Kate. 'Have you time for a coffee?' she asked him.

'No, I've got to go. I'm late for my next appointment already. I'll call you soon. Bye, Chloe.'

Minutes later, Chloe noticed that Will had forgotten his file. Seeing the hotel brochure peeping out of it, she pulled it out.

Wow, she sighed, wishing she might be that special to a man one day. The place looked amazing. She stared closer at the photograph and imagined herself sitting in the grand hall, in front of a roaring log fire with someone who loved her deeply.

As she closed the file again and went to put it behind the counter, a few pieces of paper slipped out and onto the floor. Chloe bent to retrieve them. As well as the hotel brochure there was a letter. Curiosity getting the better of her, she unfolded it to see more. She frowned. What the –

'God, I'm sure I'd forget my head if it wasn't attached to my shoulders.'

Chloe jumped as she saw Will walking back across the room. Hastily, she shoved the letter inside the file and gave it to him.

'I was just going to let Kate know,' she replied.

'Thanks, but I need the brochure so that I can book the room.' His eyes rested upon hers as he rubbed his hand back and forth across his chin.

Chloe felt the colour in her cheeks rising as Will continued to stare. Then just as quickly, his eyes began to twinkle and he grinned.

'Don't tell her but I'm going to book champagne and arrange for us to have dinner in the room.'

Chloe began to breathe normally as she watched him go again. She wished she'd had a little longer to look. But, every time she thought about what she had seen, she came to the same conclusion. And it wasn't good.

After a fitful sleep, Chloe was up early the next morning, still wondering what to do for the best. She couldn't believe that Will had tricked Kate. He'd tricked them all, really.

Should she say something to her or let him explain himself?

But just then, she heard Kate coming out of her room and then walking across the landing. Hearing the bathroom door open and shut shortly afterwards, Chloe dashed into her bedroom. Her eyes roamed around until she found what she was looking for. She grabbed Kate's mobile phone and, with a quick glance over her shoulder, flicked through the contacts list. Finding the number she was after, she wrote it down quickly, put back the phone and without anyone seeing her ran back to her room.

Once she'd heard Kate go downstairs, she sent a text message. As she had predicted, her mobile began to ring straight afterwards.

'You got my message then.'

'Who is this?'

'It's Chloe. Who else do you think would know your little secret?'

Silence.

'I am right, aren't I?' she broke into it.

'Yes, but it's not what it –'

'My God, Will, you piece of lowlife. You sly, conniving, evil… how could you do that to Kate? She's my friend. She's going to be destroyed when she finds out.'

'If I could just explain!'

'I don't think it's me you should be explaining to.'

'I know that, but –'

'Look, I'm no good at keeping secrets. And this is one that I don't want to keep from Kate. So, either you tell her tonight, before you plan on seducing her at the weekend, or else I will.'

'Chloe! I can't just –'

'Tonight, Will. If she doesn't know by tomorrow morning, I *will* tell her.'

Chloe snapped her phone shut before he could answer.

Later that morning, still worried about Lily, Kate slipped into Lily's bedroom but, finding her asleep, left her a glass of orange juice on the bedside cabinet before tiptoeing out of the room and going back downstairs.

'How is she doing?' Lucy asked after taking an order from an elderly couple that had just walked in.

'Okay, I think,' Kate replied, 'although you never can tell with Lily.'

Lucy reached for a saucer and clattered a cup onto it. 'I could do more hours, if it helps.'

'You've already been covering when Chloe is at college.'

'So?' Lucy moved behind Kate and popped a chocolate muffin onto a plate. 'Before I started to work here I used to sit at home all day, waiting for Karl to come in, moaning when he was late. Now, I don't know, it sounds stupid saying this, but I feel like I belong, like I've got a routine to my life. And Chloe and I are getting on better now, so it's much more fun.'

'What did go on between you two?' Kate was curious to know as she tidied up the counter.

'Nothing really.' Lucy's cheeks began to burn. 'I suppose I was jealous of her. She's so full of life. But since that night in Rembrandts, we've got to know each other better. I really like her now. I don't know why I didn't give her a chance in the first place. I'm a bit like that, though. It's insecurity, I think. I have a terrible time with Karl because I think he's too good for me.'

'I'm just glad that you worked things out.'

'Well, I think working here has made me realise that I don't need to have everyone's undivided attention. People like me for *me*. I don't have to impress anyone by dressing in the latest designer gear, or going to the best holiday resort or going on about where I live. I'm just lucky, that's all.'

'Oh, give over with the soppiness,' Kate smiled.

Lucy gnawed at her bottom lip. 'I'm sorry if I caused you any problems.'

Kate laughed. 'Lucy, you didn't give me problems, you gave me nightmares! Still, if you're up for it, I'll sort out a new rota.'

'Great. So are you looking forward to your night of passion in the fancy hotel this weekend?'

Kate grinned. 'I most certainly am. But I can't believe how nervous I feel.'

'Oh, don't be.' Lucy slid the order onto a tray and picked it up. 'It'll be exciting... and so romantic. There's nothing better than being treated to a dirty weekend. I hope you've treated yourself to some new underwear too?'

Kate nodded, thinking of the chocolate brown and cream lacy set that was packed in her overnight bag ready for the occasion.

'Where's he taking you tonight?'

'We're just going for a drink, in a pub nearby. Quite a nice surprise, actually. I didn't think he was down this way today.'

Kate made her way over to the window where Chloe was standing staring out of it.

'What's up, Chloe?' she asked. 'You've been in a day dream all day.'

Chloe flinched. The last thing she wanted was to slip up about Will. So she said the first thing that came into her head.

'Do you think a man of forty-three is too old for me?'

Kate raised her eyebrows in surprise. 'I would say so, yes.'

'Forty-three isn't that old.'

'It is when you're barely eighteen.'

Chloe turned to look out of the window again.

'Have you met someone?' Kate probed.

Chloe nodded, thinking back to her first encounter with Jack. Seeing him again in the college canteen on the first week had made the start of the new term even more exciting for her.

'Have you been dating him?' Kate cut short her daydream.

'Oh, I've only seen him around college during breaks,' Chloe fibbed. She'd actually been seeing Jack for two weeks but hadn't dared tell anyone. She wanted to get to know him a little better first. What was the point in everyone freaking out about the age gap until she was certain that the relationship would develop?

'A man of forty-three surely must have been married before?' asked Kate.

Chloe averted her eyes. She knew what would come next.

'So he's divorced?'

Chloe nodded.

'Are you sure of that?'

'Yes, he told me. And why should the age gap be a problem? I'm a mature eighteen-year-old. I can handle myself.'

'That's what an *immature* eighteen-year-old would think,' Kate replied.

'But what else *is* there to think?' Chloe continued. 'I like him a lot, he likes me a lot and neither of us wants to settle down.'

'If you want my honest opinion,' said Kate, 'he's too old for you. There are a lot of prejudiced people out there, me included, I'm afraid, who are going to want you to fail because you're not conforming. It's up to you to prove them wrong, to make sure he doesn't use you as a trophy to show off on his arm and then discard you when he's had enough.'

'He won't have time for any of that,' Chloe grinned, determined not to let Kate's doubts influence her. 'He'll be too busy keeping an eye on me!'

As Kate went to serve a lady who had just come in out of the rain, Chloe sighed inwardly. Even if she had shared something that she'd wanted to keep to herself for now, at least she hadn't given away any of her thoughts about Will. She hoped he'd be man enough to tell Kate the truth – just so that she didn't have to.

At eight thirty, Kate sat in a booth waiting for Will who was getting their drinks at the bar. Being a cold and windy night, the room was fairly empty. But that wasn't the only thing that was chilly. Will had been so quiet since he'd picked her up. There had been no usual happy-to-see-you embrace when she'd got into his truck. Instead, he'd started the engine and driven off. It was as if he wanted to get here as soon as possible.

'Did you get salt and vinegar flavour?' Kate asked when he finally joined her. Will handed her a bag of crisps followed by a glass of wine. 'I know you men are terrible at remembering the little things.'

Will's expression remained unchanged. Kate noticed him swallow as he sat down across from her. She frowned, looking into his eyes but they didn't hold any clues.

Then he began to speak. 'Kate, there's something I need to tell you.'

'Please don't tell me that you're married and have three children. I'm not going to share you,' she joked, hoping to lighten the ominous atmosphere that had descended over them.

'What is it?' she added into the uncomfortable silence that followed. '*Are* you married?'

'No.' Will gnawed on his bottom lip. 'But you're still going to hate me.'

Kate stared at him with genuine concern when he looked back again. 'Why don't you let me be the judge of that?' she replied.

Will cleared his throat. 'Do you remember when you first opened The Coffee Stop and I was back and forth at the solicitors a few doors away?'

Kate nodded, recalling how she used to look forward to his visits.

He paused for a moment before speaking. 'I was there to buy up the land at the back of Church Square.'

'But I thought you were a computer engineer.'

Will shook his head. 'I'm a property developer. I've had plans drawn up to knock everything down and build a new shopping centre.'

Kate gasped. In a split second, she had worked out everything.

'And The Coffee Stop doesn't feature in those plans, does it?' she asked quietly.

CHAPTER TWENTY-NINE

'I'm sorry,' said Will. 'This isn't exactly the sort of thing I can spring on you. I was going to tell you this weekend.'

'Was that before or after you'd slept with me?'

Will flinched. 'When I put the bid in for the land, the coffee shop wasn't open. It didn't feature as part of the original plans so I thought I'd scope it out to see if it had potential.'

Kate stood up and slung her handbag over her shoulder. 'If you wanted to find out more, you could have asked Lily. There was absolutely no need to string me along, making me think that you liked me.'

'But I do! It's just that –'

'You tricked me!'

'I never meant –' Will slid out of the booth as Kate moved across the floor. He reached for her hand when he caught up with her, but she snatched it away.

'How could you?' she asked, feeling the tears welling in her eyes.

'Under any other circumstances, I'd be happy to let you into every secret of mine. But it's like,' Will raised his hands in the air, narrowly missing a bar man with a full tray of glasses, 'all the times I've watched a film and the guy loses the girl because he falls for her after some stupid bet he's taken up. I knew you'd react like –'

'Like what exactly?'

'Like this.'

Somewhere, through all the confusion and chaos, Kate started to understand what he was trying to say.

No, she wouldn't have been happy whenever he'd chosen to reveal his identity. But that didn't let him off the hook.

'All that time I thought you were coming in to see the coffee shop, you were sizing up the joint, weren't you? Seeing whether to feature it in your new development or…' she paused. 'You are going to keep it going, aren't you?'

'I –'

Kate held up her hand to silence him. 'Do you know what, Will? I've heard enough.'

'Wait!' he shouted after her. 'You've got it all wrong.'

She wasn't sure if the noise she could hear was her heart beating loudly or her heels clicking on the flooring as she walked off.

In the middle of the room Will twirled Kate around to face him. 'I didn't mean to hurt you,' he said.

'Why didn't you tell me who you really were?' she demanded.

'The timing wasn't right. It *never* would have been right. Can't you see?'

'So what was tonight all about? And this weekend away? Is that it, now your little secret is out? You could have done all that without involving me.'

'Precisely!' Will relaxed his shoulders, only now aware of people turning to stare. He lowered his voice before continuing. 'The only reason I'm with you is because I want to be. But I thought that, if I left it any longer, it would seem worse when I eventually told you. Look, I've messed up but if Chloe hadn't found out, I would have told you this weekend. I'm sorry. Please come and –'

'Wait!' Kate held up her hand. 'You're telling me that Chloe knew as well?'

Will sighed. 'Yes, though I don't know how. She said that if I didn't tell you tonight, then she would.'

Kate gasped. 'You've discussed it with her?'

'Not in so many words. I spoke to her on the phone. She –'

Kate couldn't believe what she was hearing. One minute she was looking forward to a weekend away with a man who she thought cared about her. The next she was staring at a liar, a cheat, a man who had used her to get insider knowledge about how well the coffee shop was doing. How could everything go so wrong in such a short space of time?

'So I'm the last one to know?' she whispered.

Will frowned. 'Please, come and sit down again,' he begged. 'Let me try to explain.'

Kate shook her head. 'Not now. I need some time alone. I'm going to call a taxi.'

Chloe sat in her pyjamas, her left leg hooked over the arm of the settee. She tried to concentrate on her magazine but all she could think about was Kate. Would Will tell Kate what he planned to do or would he bottle out? She knew if he hadn't told her that she would go through with her threat. There was no way she was going to let him lead Kate on. But she had thought Will was a decent guy until she'd seen the letter.

And he certainly thought a lot of Kate now. Chloe could see that from the way his eyes lit up whenever he saw her. No, she'd been right to give him a chance to explain first. And either way, she'd be there for Kate.

An hour later, the door flew open and Kate walked in. She threw Chloe a look of pure evil before sitting down next to Lily on the settee.

'You're back early,' stated Lily. 'It's only half past nine.'

'Bad period pains,' Kate fibbed, at the same time glaring at Chloe. Then she got to her feet again.

'Drinks anyone?'

'I'll help,' said Chloe and followed her out of the room.

'How could you?' Kate said as soon as the door closed behind them.

'He told you then.' Chloe gulped. 'I can explain.'

'Yes, please do. Please tell me how you found out, how you contacted him to let him know without telling me. How you've ruined my weekend away and any plans I had for the future.'

Chloe's mouth gaped open. 'I... I'm sorry. I wanted to tell you but I couldn't find the words. And it *was* all Will's fault. I thought I should give him the chance to explain first.'

'But *you* knew and didn't tell me. You decided, in your wisdom, that *he* should tell me so that you didn't have to.'

'No, I –'

Kate ignored the tears welling in Chloe's eyes. 'You made me look a complete fool. At least if I had known, I could have gone prepared.'

'I'm sorry.'

'Sorry! Is that all you can say? How do you think I felt? He took me out on the false pretence that he fancied me and all the time he wanted to find out about the coffee shop.'

'Did he say that?' said Chloe.

'No,' admitted Kate. 'But he must have done. As soon as we sat down in the pub, he confessed everything. How did you find out?'

'When Will called yesterday with the hotel brochure, he left behind his file. As I put it behind the counter, a letter fell out. I only had time to have a quick look because he came back. I didn't think it was my place to tell you.'

Suddenly Kate realised that not only had Will deceived her, but Chloe had too. And she trusted her far more.

'You should have told me,' she said.

'After all you've been through with Nick, I didn't know *how* to tell you. You have to believe me!'

'I don't know who to believe. Can't you understand that?'

'What are you going to do?'

Kate needed time to think things through. 'I'm not sure. He did seem sincere when he saw how upset I was.'

'Was that before or after he tried to get into your knickers?'

Kate gave Chloe a warning look.

'Well, the guy's a creep,' she continued. 'He should have come clean from the beginning. If it –'

'There you go again. You always try to blame other people. It's never you, is it?' Kate moved away but turned back. 'This is your fault as much as his, and don't you forget it. I feel pretty sick about the whole episode without you rubbing my nose in it.'

Kate stormed off to bed but once there, she couldn't sleep. How the hell had she got herself into this mess? She wished she'd never met Will. He'd used her to get information about The Coffee Stop. And even if he had no interest in her, she had fallen for his games – hook, line and sinker. She felt such a fool.

She was still lying awake when her phone vibrated on the bedside table, just before midnight. She fumbled for it in the dark.

'Kate, it's me. Please don't hang up. I can't stop thinking about what's happened. I'm so sorry I hurt you.'

Lying on her side, Kate pulled her knees up into the foetal position. She tried not to sniff and give him a clue that she'd been crying.

'You used me,' she said.

'I never meant to.'

'Maybe not, but that doesn't change anything.'

There was a long pause.

'Look, I know I've done this all wrong but do you think we could talk in the morning? Please?'

'I – I don't know,' she said. Then she switched off the phone.

For the next hour, Kate watched the luminous fingers on her alarm clock travel once around its face.

Her mind wouldn't settle and she kept running over things.

Will was an idiot.

But he was the sweet kind of idiot.

What did he take her for, thinking he could use her like that?

But he had been sorry about it afterwards. Probably hadn't even realised how hurtful he'd been.

What about the plans to develop Church Square? What would happen to The Coffee Stop? Did the plans even include The Coffee Stop?

But then again, he'd said the plans were drawn up before The Coffee Stop had opened. So maybe the plans were going to change?

Maybe there was a slight chance that he actually did fancy her? His actions seemed real as she thought back to their last date. Then there was the incident under the oak tree and the weekend they'd been planning.

'Oh, go to sleep, you idiot!' she whispered aloud, squeezing her eyes tightly shut.

CHAPTER THIRTY

Chloe threw a critical eye over her reflection before twirling around to check her black lace-topped hold-up stockings hadn't snagged while she wasn't looking. Her hair was pinned up tightly into a chignon, a few wispy strands hanging down. Bronze and yellow toned shades of make-up accentuated her eyes, her skin enhanced with fake tan. The dress she'd chosen to wear was black and had a flirty skirt that fell just above her knee, a neckline that swooped down to reveal just the right amount of cleavage and was backless apart from a thick lace panel down the length of its middle. Chloe always thought she looked sophisticated whenever she wore it, yet she felt she needed a second opinion to help alleviate her nerves. She needed the encouragement to put a smile on her lips.

But she wasn't about to get it from Kate. It was three days since the fiasco with Will, and Kate was being polite and talking when spoken to – otherwise their working day would be impossible – but there was none of their old conversations, none of the giggles and good times. Even Lucy had been dragged into it. Kate was hardly speaking to her either.

There was so much Chloe wanted to share with Kate. How she felt about Jack, for starters. But, really, she wanted to tell her she'd had the best sex in her life the night before.

Chloe had been so nervous when she'd slept with Jack, her excitement completely overshadowed by self-doubt. Jack was forty-three. She was eighteen. Jack would have had many lovers. She had been with three boys and two of them had been merely fumbles. Jack had an ex-wife. She had an ex-seventeen-year-old boyfriend. Sexually, she knew he'd be able to show her all sorts of things. She wouldn't be able to show him anything.

A vague flush of colour tinged her cheeks as she remembered what they'd done together. It had all been too much for her when he'd removed his clothes and she'd froze, but he'd been so gentle and she'd gradually relaxed. It had been an amazing experience; the older man was definitely more experienced. She couldn't wait to see him again.

Hearing a horn and hoping it was her taxi arriving, Chloe forced herself to put all thoughts of Kate on hold. Tonight Jack was taking her out to dinner at Leonard's restaurant. The gesture had proved to Chloe that he wanted more from their relationship.

He was already there when she arrived at the restaurant fifteen minutes later. He was dressed in the obligatory jacket and collar, pale blue shirt and navy checked tie. So used to seeing him in jeans, Chloe felt her heart flutter.

She walked across the plush reception area, feeling a little unsteady but it was nothing to do with the heels she was wearing.

'You look lovely.' Jack kissed her lightly on her cheek and took her coat as she shrugged it off. 'Would you like a glass of wine?'

Feeling like a five-year-old child at a rich uncle's house, Chloe perched on one of six cream settees placed around the room. Leonard's had a reputation for being the best place to be seen in Hedworth, and it was everything she had thought it would be. The wall in front of her had thick, wooden doors that she presumed must lead to the dining area. To her right, floor-to-ceiling windows overlooking the extensive grounds and car park were dressed in taupe drapes, similar to the colour of the carpet.

About fifteen people were waiting to go through to eat, including a group of seven sitting next to her. They were making lots of noise, the soft background music barely audible through peals of good-natured laughter.

'What time are we eating?' Chloe asked Jack when he joined her again.

He checked his watch. 'Not for half an hour or so.'

Before she knew it, the huge oval clock chimed eight times, and they were shown to a table at the back of the restaurant. Jack pulled out a chair and Chloe sat down, taking the menu held out for her.

By the time their main course had been eaten, she had begun to relax. The good-natured ambience radiating from the rowdy seven sitting two tables away found its way to their table too, the wine Chloe had drunk beginning to take affect.

Jack reached for her hand and gave it a squeeze. 'Would you like to come back to my place afterwards? I rather fancy having you as my desert.'

Chloe giggled. 'I don't think I have anything better to do.'

'Why, you cheeky little minx. I'll have –'

'Dad?'

Chloe looked up to see a young woman walking towards them. Dark hair streaked with caramel and honey highlights, a short spiky fringe framed eyes that seemed a little dangerous. Dressed from head to toe in clothes Chloe made a guess would cost at least three months of her own salary, the woman immediately made her feel inadequate in her little black dress, not to mention young.

'Oh, for fuck's sake.' Jack put down his cutlery and got to his feet.

'*Dad?*' A rush of despair shrouded Chloe's bare shoulders. Jack had told her that he had a daughter who was twenty-three and a son, twenty-one. Please, no. Don't let it be her.

'What the hell is going on?' the woman spoke as she reached their table.

'Charlotte!' cried Jack. 'I didn't expect to see you here.'

'Evidently not. So, I repeat – what the hell is going on?'

Chloe looked at Jack as she caught the angry look in the woman's eye, but he didn't look her way.

'Nothing is going on,' said Jack. 'I'm just out for a meal with a friend.'

A friend, thought Chloe. 'I –'

'A friend?' Charlotte interrupted. 'I would say she was young enough to be your daughter but then as *I'm* your daughter, it seems a little silly.' She turned to Chloe next. 'And just what the hell is your game?' she whispered loudly. 'You're making him look a fool!'

'I don't think this has anything –' Chloe started.

'He's far too old for you.' She leaned her knuckles on the table. 'I can't believe you'd even consider such a relationship. Just what is it you're after? A father figure? Experience? Money? Because if you think you're going to use him as a sugar daddy, then you're very much mistaken.'

'That's enough, Charlotte.' Jack touched her arm but she brushed it away.

'I can speak for myself,' said Chloe, taken aback by her accusations. 'I happen to come from a very wealthy background,' she spoke out in her defence, knowing a little white lie wouldn't go amiss. Her dad wasn't *that* rich. 'If all I wanted was money, I'd have asked my own father.'

'Oh, don't play the innocent with me.' Charlotte's eyes bore into hers. 'What else could you possibly be interested in, apart from that?'

'There are a lot of things –'

'Does Mum know about this?' Charlotte cut in again, turning her fury onto Jack.

'This has nothing to do with your mother.'

'What does she mean?' Chloe gasped. 'What the hell is going on, Jack? Are you still married?'

'Of course he's still married.'

'We're separated.' Jack's glance at Chloe was pitiful.

'He's stringing you along, love. This isn't the first time he's had an affair with a teenager. My mother left him when she found him in bed with someone else your age.'

'Charlotte!'

'What? Don't tell me you've grown a fucking conscience.'

A few diners in their vicinity paused to wonder if they had actually heard her swear. Charlotte's eyes flicked around in embarrassment. She lowered her voice before adding, 'She's practically the same age as me.' She looked at Chloe again. 'That is, unless she's lied about that. I bet *her* sort will do anything to get a man with money.'

Chloe lowered her eyes.

'How old are you?'

'I'm twenty-five,' she lied.

Chloe hadn't wanted to tell Jack her proper age in case it had put him off. Now she was wondering why the hell she *had* lied about it. She knew it would backfire at some stage.

'Right,' said Charlotte. 'And my hair's purple with red stripes. Tell me the truth.'

'It's none of your business anyway, and I am telling the –'

'That's enough!' said Jack. Most of the diners had now stopped to stare over in voyeuristic interest.

Chloe stood up and threw her napkin across the table. 'I don't know what's gone on in the past but is what we're doing now so terrible?' She looked from Charlotte to Jack and then back again. 'We've only been out a few times. I'm not planning on marrying him.'

Jack closed his eyes and pinched the bridge of his nose.

Charlotte snorted. '*Marrying* him?' she cried. 'Listen, honey. There is absolutely no chance of you *ever* doing that.'

Chloe stayed headstrong, although she could feel herself crumbling inside. 'That's up to Jack.'

'You're damned right it is. He must be losing his mind to –'

'To what? To *sleep* with me?'

Jack's jaw dropping only angered Chloe more. She glared at Charlotte as she stood tall, ready to fight back. 'I'm not trying to trap him, if that's what you think.'

'You'd better not try it.'

Charlotte stared back and a battle of wills began.

'Sit down, Chloe,' said Jack. 'Causing a scene will only make things worse.'

'I'm not the one causing a scene!'

'No, you just happen to be the one who is making my dad look silly – surely you can see that? He's forty-three and –'

'How many times do I have to tell you that I am not too YOUNG?'

The noise in the room decreased at the sound of Chloe's raised voice. Standing up made the rest of the diners aware of where the action was taking place. Even the party of seven came to an abrupt halt. Again, Chloe looked at Jack, but it was no use.

In frustration, she stormed out of the restaurant.

Kate sat in her bedroom. Tears poured down her face. God, how could she have fallen for someone like Will? After all she'd been through with Nick, she shouldn't have given her heart to another man so freely.

She wasn't a bad person. Surely she deserved another chance?

Since she'd seen him, Will had sent a few texts each day but so far she'd ignored them. Luckily, he'd only been into the coffee shop once, and she'd hidden in the kitchen until he had gone. He'd had the manners to stay away since then.

There was a knock on the door. 'Kate, can I come in?' Lily pushed the bedroom door open tentatively.

Kate brushed away her tears but knew Lily would see them.

'Chloe told me what happened between you and Will,' said Lily.

Kate looked up.

'She didn't betray your confidence. I just badgered her into telling me. I couldn't understand what was going on between you and her, nor why you were so quiet and I didn't like to ask at first. But this has been going on for days.'

Unable to speak, Kate burst into tears.

Lily rushed to her side quickly and held her close. 'It doesn't have to be like this.' She rubbed Kate's shoulder as she cried. 'You only need to think things through.'

'I'm all out of thinking, Lily.'

'Then let me do some for you.' Lily pulled away and cupped Kate's face in her hands. I know he's been silly, and I can understand why he kept the details from you, but he really cares for you, anyone can see that. He's a fool, but I think you should give him another a chance. For you.'

Kate tried to shake her head. 'I can't.'

'Yes, you can. You have to remember how you felt before you found out who he was. Your eyes used to sparkle whenever his name was mentioned. Your smile was tenfold when you came home after a date. He's made you feel complete again.'

'But he was going to knock down The Coffee Stop.'

'Was he really? I've known all about Taylor Constructions for some time. Why do you suppose I decided to open up again?'

Kate frowned.

'I was distraught when I heard what was being planned. So I thought, what could an old woman of sixty-nine – yes I'm sixty-nine, don't look so shocked – do to stop that? The only thing I could think of was to open up the café again, hope to make it a success and maybe, just maybe, it could be incorporated in the corner of the proposed new shopping precinct. But then you and Chloe came along and it turned into much more than a café.'

'But he used me to see how well it was doing!'

'No, he didn't – and secretly I think you know that, don't you?'

Kate looked at Lily, to see her eyes full of compassion.

'Please take the time to listen to an old woman's wise words. Don't waste what chances come along in love. Because you'll only regret it later, when you realise what could have been.'

'But aren't you mad at him too?'

'Not really. I think Will has been silly not telling you who he was but I think that's his only mistake. You should talk to him before you write him off completely.'

Kate smiled a little then. 'I'm so glad to have met you, Lily Mortimer,' she said.

Lily pulled her into her arms once more. 'I'm so glad to have met you, too, Kate Bradshaw.'

'Oh, and Lily? Have you been getting Botox injections? You don't look anywhere near sixty-nine.'

Despite joking with Lily, once she left the room, Kate's tears fell again. It was one thing for Lily to suggest patching things up with Will. But how was she going to mend a broken heart?

Back at Leonard's Restaurant, Chloe sat in the middle of the same settee she'd been sitting in two hours earlier, the leg draped over her knee swinging violently. Her eyes flitted across to the wooden doors before back to the clock again. She'd been there for over ten minutes and still there was no sign of Jack. But she wasn't going to go without seeing him.

If he's not here by the time the second hand reaches twelve, I'll go home on my own, she fumed.

If he's not here by the time it reaches six.

Three minutes later, Chloe stood up, smoothed down her dress and walked over to the cloakroom. She was putting on her coat by the time he came through. Jack held out one sleeve for her and she slid in her arm.

'What kept you?' she whispered loudly. 'I've been waiting for ages.'

'I've been waiting for a taxi.'

'You could have waited with me.'

Jack grabbed her elbow and marched outside. He held open the door of the taxi. Chloe slid along the seat.

'27 Martin Avenue please,' he muttered. 'It's just off Raymond Street, left at the roundabout before the bypass.'

27 Martin Avenue had been a whole new experience for Chloe, in every sense of the word. For starters, she'd never dated a man who owned his own place. Not that it was much to look at yet. Jack had only recently moved to the two-bed townhouse and was yet to call it his own. The living room had anaglypta-papered walls, painted puce pink. A blue-grey carpet with specks of pink the exact same colour of the walls covered the whole floor area, apart from where it was dominated by a brick fireplace. For the first time, Chloe noticed how depressing it must be to come home to. Maybe it wasn't too bad what he'd said. He was separated from his wife after all. Divorce was the logical next step. She decided to cut him some slack.

Jack poured himself a drink before sprawling glumly on the settee.

Chloe took off her coat and laid it over the back of the armchair before moving to sit next to him.

'Try not to let them get to you,' she soothed.

'No one's getting to me.' Jack tossed back his drink and went to get another.

Chloe crept up behind him and kissed his neck lightly. Lost in the moment, Jack pushed back his head, so she chanced putting her arms around his waist. But then his shoulders dropped, he knocked away her hands and turned slowly to face her.

'Oh, not *you* as well,' her voice rose in distress. 'You're as bad as all the rest. I've had Kate and Lucy warning me about trophy girlfriends. And now this. Everyone thinks we're going to fail. We might as well give up now.'

Jack lowered his gaze. 'That's not a bad idea.'

Chloe swallowed. For a moment as she stood there in the silence of the room, she had an awful feeling he was about to finish things.

'What do you mean?'

'Charlotte and her brother, Matt, mean the world to me. My separation was hard on them, even though they're adults themselves now. But just seeing Charlotte, more or less the same age as you, made me realise how wrong this is.'

Chloe started to relax again. This was just a case of nerves, she was sure of it. She knew she should have gone back to the table before Charlotte stuck her nose in. Now she'd have to try twice as hard to convince him.

'I'm sure they'll get used to us.'

'There is no us! Charlotte's right. It won't work.'

'I –'

'The right decision is to end this. Right now, before it becomes even more painful. I was flattered. I'm sorry. You *are* too young. It will never work.'

'But that's pathetic. You're giving up because of a few years between us?'

There was a pause before he spoke again.

'How old are you, really?'

Chloe gulped. The question, along with his acidic pitch, completely threw her.

'I've already told you. I'm… I'm twenty-five,' she lied.

'What's your date of birth?'

'I'm… I…'

'Not quick enough. It should roll off your tongue.'

Chloe bit her bottom lip. 'I'm eighteen.' She watched as the blood drained from his face in horror.

'Jesus Christ! You're barely a child!'

'I'm old enough to love someone!'

'No, no, no!' Jack put down his glass and stepped backwards.

'It's true! I've been in love with you from the moment I met you.' Chloe's hand went to her chest.

'No!' He sounded wretched.

'*That's* why I know this will work. So what if people think we can't make it. We can say we told them so when we're old and grey.'

Jack recoiled slightly at the reality of her words. 'Chloe, when you're old and grey, I'll be decaying in my grave.' He went to get another drink but settled for the bottle.

'I'll still fancy you.'

'You *are* so innocent.' The Jack she knew treated her to a half-cocked smile. 'I need to call you a taxi.'

'I can stay here, if you like.'

Jack spun round on his heel. 'Look, it's *over*. Can't you see that?'

Chloe's bottom lip trembled. Finally, it started to sink in that he *actually* meant what he said. Bile rose in her throat and she swallowed hard, trying to comprehend what was happening.

'You can't mean that!' she sobbed, flying across the room into his arms. 'We… we made love the other night!'

'We shouldn't have.' Jack's fingers traced her tears. 'It has to end. I'm so sorry.'

Chloe batted his hand away.

Jack sighed. 'I'll get my phone.'

As soon as he left the room, Chloe's face crumpled. She grabbed her coat and ran down the hallway.

Grappling with the door handle, she cried out in exasperation as she heard him shout her name. She wrenched the front door wide and ran out into the street. The biting wind nearly took her breath away, but she didn't stop until she got home. Only then did she realise how stupid she'd been. It was twenty minutes to midnight and she'd run through the dark, and mostly deserted, streets on her own. Anything could have happened to her.

Struggling to see where to put the key in the door as the tears poured down her face, at last it opened and Chloe rushed upstairs, collapsing in Lily's favourite armchair.

CHAPTER THIRTY-ONE

'Chloe came home really upset after seeing Jack,' Kate told Lucy as she flicked the sign to open after letting her into the building.

Lucy stopped in her tracks. 'What happened?'

'I think it's over between them.'

'Ouch. How is she?'

'Devastated, poor thing. She looks awful.'

Kate made them coffee as she relayed what she'd been able to extricate from Chloe earlier that morning. Even though they hadn't been on friendly terms for a few days, she couldn't let that stop her when Lily had told her what had gone on the night before. Lily had found Chloe crying in the living room but hadn't been able to get much sense out of her because she'd been so upset. Kate had tried to console her this morning but Chloe had still been teary so she'd told her to stay in her room for a while.

'I said he was too old,' Lucy sighed, her head moving from side to side.

'Whatever you do,' Kate pointed a bossy finger at her, 'don't say that to her.'

'She can't be that upset, surely? She's only been seeing him a matter of weeks, if that.'

Kate's eyebrows shot up. 'Can you remember being dumped when you were eighteen?'

'I'm only twenty-five. Of course I remember. I cried for weeks when my first proper boyfriend called it a day after eight months.'

'It does hurt when it's over,' stated Kate.

'Yes, but it's usually after six months, or a year, even.'

'Who are we to judge how quickly she's fallen for him? And imagine how it feels when everyone's been telling you that it will never work.'

'I suppose so,' relented Lucy.

They finished their coffee in silence while both women thought more about the situation – even if it isn't love, at eighteen you really think it is.

Was it just a tiff, Kate wondered? Although from what Lily had been able to tell her, it seemed pretty serious stuff. Annoyed for being too wrapped up in herself, she realised she should have been there for Chloe. Still, whatever the outcome, she knew they'd both be there for her.

'She must be going through hell,' she broke into their silence, reaching for a polystyrene cup as she spotted Serle walking across the square.

'I know,' Lucy agreed. 'We'll look after her, poor kid.'

'Whatever we do,' warned Kate again. 'We mustn't mention the kid word either.'

Later that evening, Kate held two mugs of hot chocolate in one hand as she stood in front of Chloe's bedroom door. She knew Chloe would probably want to be alone with her thoughts, but she knocked softly anyway.

Chloe sat on top of her bed in her pyjamas and dressing gown with her back against the wall, her arms wrapped around her knees.

'How are you feeling?' Kate asked.

'Like I've been dumped,' Chloe replied.

Kate sat down on the bed beside her. 'I wish I could help you.'

Chloe wished that too. 'Did you feel like this when Nick left you?'

'Yes,' said Kate.

'I'm so sorry about what happened with Will. I didn't know what to do for the best.'

'I know. I'm sorry I overreacted too. I don't know what I would have done in the same position. But it wasn't down to you, it was down to Will.' She held her arms out for a hug. 'You will get over Jack, you know.'

Chloe hugged her back. 'I feel so stupid,' she said. 'I've made such a fool of myself.'

Kate shook her head. 'I think you've been very grown up about the situation.'

Chloe frowned. 'What do you mean?'

'Well, you could have acted like an immature eighteen-year-old and screamed and shouted at him. You could have gone around to his house and damaged his belongings. You could have done all that, and much more. But, instead you handled it like a grown up.'

'Kate,' Chloe smiled through her tears, 'I think you might have taken over my agony aunt position.'

Kate smiled too. 'Although maybe I should be taking my own advice. I could have been more grown-up about things lately. I'm sorry too. I should have been there for you and I wasn't.'

'You tried to warn me off before when I mentioned Jack's age.'

Kate paused for a moment. 'But it was wrong that you felt you couldn't tell me about him the morning after. I thought we had a special bond and –'

'We do have a special bond! That's probably why I didn't tell you. I just wanted it all to work out right. But it didn't.'

Kate hugged her again when she saw fresh tears forming. 'Bloody men,' she said softly as she stroked the top of Chloe's head.

As Chloe's hurt changed to humiliation, at first she'd thought it better that she missed her lectures for a couple of weeks, until she was able to cope with seeing Jack again. But a few days later, she was determined that he wasn't going to stop her from attending college. Besides, she wanted to get things over and done with. Sooner would be the adult thing to do.

She arrived just in time for her first lecture so that she didn't have to see him during the lunch break.

Unable to explain her feelings to Fran, at their dinner break she bought a sandwich from the canteen and made sure that Jack saw her in the queue before heading for her car. She knew he'd come after her.

As he drew near, she popped up the passenger door lock and he got into the car beside her.

'I wanted to see you,' he said, 'to explain things a little better.'

Chloe shifted her gaze. Now that she'd got this far, she couldn't bear to see his face so close to hers.

She longed to touch him yet at the same time she knew she wanted to slap him.

'I'm sorry,' Jack continued. 'I put my feelings first. I knew you were too young when I met you, but you blew me away with your innocence. You were everything I wanted to be – young, free, exciting. You made me come alive for the first time in months. But I didn't understand how I was messing around with *your* feelings.'

Chloe stared ahead, unsure what to say. The rehearsed speech had gone. The hurtful things she was going to say, just to make herself feel better. What was it that she was going to call him? Oh, yes, an unfeeling bastard with a bitch of a daughter.

'I should have thought of you –'

'You should.'

'– and what this would do to you.'

'I trusted you.'

Jack nodded. 'I never meant to hurt you.'

'Oh, like you never meant to fuck me? What was I, Jack? A playmate who you could use for a few nights and discard until an older model came along that took your fancy?'

Jack's expression was grim. 'Ouch, you sound so grown up.'

'That's rich, coming from you.'

'I should never have said that you were a child.'

'No,' Chloe's words were so soft they were barely audible. 'You really shouldn't have.'

'But you should never have said you were twenty-five.'

'You should never have said you were divorced, either, but it doesn't make it quits.'

Once Jack had gone, Chloe sat in her car. Tears poured down her face at her embarrassment, but a small part of her realised that what he had done by finishing things was for the best. She'd had to do a lot of growing up since coming to Somerley but this had tested her to her limits. Luckily, he'd shown his true colours before she had been really hurt. She didn't need a man like him.

She sighed loudly. She'd wanted to be too grown up, hadn't she? And by doing so, she'd been used rather than had fun. She couldn't let this get under her skin and spoil things. She had to chalk it up to experience, no matter how painful.

Jack wasn't worth it, of that much she was sure.

Lily woke later with a jolt, to find she'd fallen asleep in the armchair again. Even before she'd pulled herself up straight, she knew her back would be aching. That would mean another day of painkillers and smelly muscle rubs. She groaned loudly.

Still dark outside, the clock read ten to three. Rosie caught her eye as she dramatically turned around in a circle before flopping back down again in exactly the same place.

Perhaps she ought to head back to her own bed, she surmised. She had a long day ahead of her tomorrow – no, today, she corrected herself. She couldn't put things off. Time wasn't on her side any longer.

Lily still felt nervous about telling the girls. No matter how she looked at it, it was going to be tough.

The guilt trip she'd taken over the past few days was enormous. The telephone call from Dr Warren asking her to come in and see her straightaway had always been expected but, once she'd visited the surgery, she hadn't intended on having to bring forward the date of everything by so much. Did she have the right to inflict her pain on two women whom she had known for so little time? Surely she was expecting too much from them now?

She'd cook them a meal. Prepare their favourite food and have a bit of a laugh with them first. Then she'd tell them.

CHAPTER THIRTY-TWO

Once she had got over the shock of the news, the next morning Lily asked Kate and Chloe if they could spend that night in with her.

She went downstairs at the end of the day and, on the stroke of five thirty, she shooed Kate and Chloe out of the kitchen

'Isn't there anything we can do to help?' Kate wanted to know as she locked up for the night. The vertical blinds whooshed across the windows of the coffee shop, hiding the view of the stormy night.

Outside, the rain coursed rowdily down the windows. For once, she was glad to stay in.

'No.' Lily gently pushed her out of the door that led upstairs. 'Leave me be. Come back at seven, I'll be ready then.'

Once they were gone, Lily pulled out a chair at the kitchen table and began. First on the menu was a prawn cocktail starter, a simple choice but a firm favourite of Chloe's. This would be followed by spaghetti bolognaise with slices of garlic bread, easily Kate's most loved dish. Dessert would be Angel Heaven, originally concocted by Lily, but loved by them all. Ice cream, cake, a little fresh cream, all layered together with different flavoured sauces and sprinkled with flakes of chocolate. Perfect.

At ten to seven, Lily popped two more strong painkillers from their wrapping. Feeling queasy now, she didn't want either Kate or Chloe to spot her discomfort. But they noticed immediately.

'Lily, you look dreadful,' stated Chloe.

Lily smiled up at her. 'I look that welcoming?'

'Why don't you go and sit down?' said Kate. She led her through to the front. 'We can finish off in here.'

'That would be good,' Lily nodded. She flinched when her legs bent, her knees almost buckling as she took her weight whilst trying to sit down in the chair.

'Is that better?'

Lily faked a smile and nodded again as she tried to compose herself. She had to be strong and get through the meal without them sensing that anything was wrong.

'I can still remember the first time that you tried to make a cappuccino,' Kate said to Chloe as she made them coffee to finish off the meal.

Chloe hid her face in her hands. 'Oh, I know. Trust me to put the milk in the wrong place. And then there was Alex and Tom to deal with. Tom was a sweetie but, with all his cheap compliments, Alex needed locking up for sexual harassment.'

From behind the counter, Kate sighed as she remembered back to the earlier days. 'Oh, I do miss those two, even now.'

'And,' shouted Chloe excitedly, as the rain poured down the bay window, 'remember when we were working outside and that summer storm came over?'

'I remember!' Kate laughed as she joined them again. 'I nearly went down the street with the menu board, the wind was so strong. Then two of the chairs and a table blew over and slid across the cobbles!'

'But ten minutes later,' Chloe recalled, 'the storm passed and the sun came out again. It was as if nothing had happened.'

'Well, apart from the state of our hair.'

Kate pointedly looked at Lily as Chloe giggled. She reached across for Chloe's hand. 'It's good to hear us laughing again, Chloe.'

'Kate, Chloe,' said Lily. 'I – I need to tell you something.'

'What is it, Lily?' Kate asked, suddenly starting to feel uneasy.

Lily looked up again, tears in her eyes. 'I had a phone call, late yesterday afternoon. It was the results of some tests that I'd had, just over a week ago.'

'Tests?' Chloe frowned. 'What tests? You never mentioned anything.'

Lily went quiet.

'Lily?' Kate questioned.

'I…' Lily stuttered. 'I had cancer a few years ago. I managed to fight it that time but… it's come back again.'

'How long –' Chloe started.

Kate threw her a look that said 'not yet' so Chloe moved around to Lily's side of the table and pulled a chair near.

'Five years ago, I had an operation to remove a growth from my stomach but now it's returned,' said Lily. 'Earlier this year, I was given two years to live – it's the reason I opened the coffee shop, because I didn't want to be alone – but it's spread rapidly over the past few months. That, plus my angina and arthritis, and the odd cold here and there, has made me weak and irritable – as I know you've both noticed.'

'Why didn't you tell us sooner?'

'I'd only just met you. I had no right to burden you with this. But I'd already been to the hospital. When I started to vomit and lose weight, I knew the cancer had returned.

'I felt such a fraud,' Lily went on, her voice breaking with emotion, 'lying to you, but I couldn't tell you where I was going. But then I had the phone call yesterday.'

'How long, Lily?' said Kate, knowing that was the only unanswered question between them now. 'And, please be honest with us.'

Lily glanced up.

Kate wrapped supple hands around Lily's aged ones.

'A matter of weeks, if that,' said Lily.

'No!' said Chloe.

'It's true,' whispered Lily.

'But that could mean days!' Chloe looked directly at Kate for confirmation. 'Couldn't it? It could mean days!'

Lily attempted to comfort her with a smile. 'I'm not ready to go yet, child.'

'What can we do?' Kate found her voice, if a little shaky.

'You can't die!' Chloe blurted out between sobs. 'We've only just got to know you. What will we do without you?'

'Chloe, we have to think of Lily,' Kate said gently. 'We need to find out how we can help.'

'But it's *so* unfair. I don't want her to die.'

'Sometimes life doesn't work out as planned, but my time on earth has been good,' Lily tried to appease her. 'I was married to a wonderful man and have so many fond memories of him. And, as morbid as it seems, I believe in God and the afterlife. I'll be with Bernard soon.'

'How can you talk like that?' Chloe sobbed.

Lily pushed herself up and walked, painfully and slowly, towards the kitchen.

Kate stopped her long before she reached the door and placed an arm around her shoulders. 'We'll look after you,' she wept.

Chloe ran across to join them. 'Lily, we *can* do it… if you want us to.'

Lily burst into tears again.

No one moved. No one spoke. They stood together. Three women united in the still of the room. Silent except for the cries of grief, the tears of unhappiness.

'I can't stand for much longer,' Lily spoke finally.

Kate and Chloe moved away.

'I'm going to lie down. Do you think you could load up the dishwasher? I'm sorry that I have to leave it to you.'

Kate wiped her tear-stained face with the back of her hand. Trust Lily to think of them.

'Of course we can,' she told her. 'Shall we help you to your room?'

'No, thank you. I can manage the stairs for now.'

'We're both here for you,' Chloe called after her. She sat back down at the table, rubbed her eyes and looked across at Kate. 'Do you know how to care for someone who's dying?'

'No.' Kate leaned heavily against the counter. 'But we can't let Lily see that. We've got to be strong. It's not going to be easy, but whatever we feel it's going to be much harder for her. She's going to be the one in pain.'

Chloe's face screwed up again. 'Don't talk like that. She's not going to die yet.'

'Chloe,' Kate used a forceful tone to stop her hysteria, 'she's going to die soon. It doesn't matter if it's next week or next month. She's going to die soon.'

Kate's tears began to fall long before she got into bed. Although she hadn't known Lily for long, already she'd become so attached. Not only to her, but to Chloe, and to Lucy. They were like an extended family.

They had their ups and downs, just like families did, but they had been there for each other. Lily was right.

They were a good team. And now it was all going to end.

What would happen to them? Kate knew she was being selfish thinking about herself after what Lily had just told them, but she'd be homeless, she'd be jobless, and she'd lose two good friends. She wouldn't go back home. She'd have to stay in Somerley.

And what about the coffee shop? Perhaps Lily would sell it to someone else before she died. Maybe Will would get his way after all, she fumed, before thinking that was wrong to assume. Lily obviously thought a lot of her and Chloe to tell them that she was dying. Maybe she'd want them to be secure, have a job after she'd gone. The coffee shop had re-opened in Bernard's memory, so surely Lily would want it to stay the same?

Kate would pick her moment and talk to Chloe about it. But right now, maybe for at least another few weeks, it wouldn't be fair.

Chloe had fallen asleep as soon as her head hit the pillow. It was in the early hours of the morning when she jerked awake. Ever since she'd first stepped through the creaky doors, she'd loved everything about the coffee shop. Here in Somerley, she'd formed friendships with Kate and Lily, and Lucy eventually.

She'd looked to them when she'd needed advice. She'd teased them, laughed with them, cried with them.

She enjoyed living with Kate and Lily, talking about their problems and enjoying girlie conversations, but now she was scared it was going to end. If Lily was right, she could be gone in two, maybe three weeks.

She might not even last that long.

Chloe realised that she needed to be strong. Being the baby of the bunch, they'd expect her to sulk and cry. But she wouldn't do that. She'd cry on her own at night if she had to. She'd show them that she could be strong, she owed them both that much. But then again, maybe she was tougher than she thought. Perhaps losing her mum at such an early age had taught her resilience.

Why was life so unfair? Couldn't they all have had just another year together? Already Lily had started to deteriorate. Without her make-up, her skin was so pale. She looked like she was wearing hand-me-down clothes, two sizes too big. Chloe couldn't even take a photograph of her now. She wanted to remember Lily how she had been: a kind woman who'd help anyone in trouble; a fair woman who wasn't afraid to speak her mind when things needed to be said; a loving woman for the way she'd taken them into her home.

Yes, that's how Chloe wanted to remember Lily. Not like she was now, a frail old lady without the energy to enjoy what life she had left.

Lying in her bedroom, Lily closed her eyes to stop the steady flow of tears. In her heart of hearts, she knew she'd been right to tell them. She was sure that Kate and Chloe would be there for her now. It would be like having her own daughters beside her, something that she'd always longed for.

One thing was certain, though. She must contact her solicitor, Mr Stead, first thing in the morning and finish off her funeral arrangements. She needed to do it quickly in case her body let her down.

She had to be prepared to be in great pain during her last days. She needed to get everything possible sorted while she was still able to do so. She didn't want to be any burden to Kate and Chloe.

But there was only so much time left.

CHAPTER THIRTY-THREE

The rain came down as Lily watched the wind playing with the leaves, tossing them around like clothes in a washing machine. Inside, she felt safe and warm. The forecast on the radio had promised snow before the week was out. She wondered if she would see it.

It was the beginning of December and, although not long to the big day, Lily knew she wouldn't see another Christmas. Since her meeting with Dr Warren, weight had dropped off her as she was having trouble keeping down any food, and she felt exhausted all the time.

Out of the corner of her eye, she could see the flickering fairy lights on the tree that Kate and Chloe had set up especially for her. 'You can be festive while we're working,' Kate had commented as the two of them stood dressing it. They'd even found some of Lily's old decorations to hang, mixing her bedraggled red and blue baubles with their new glitzy golds and silvers. Lily had thought it such a treat.

Kate had switched the gas fire on during her last inspection. Lily felt like a queen the way they made a fuss over her. It was more than she could have hoped for.

Her legs began to complain about the amount of time she'd been standing, so she forced herself to sit back down. The single chime from the clock announced that it was lunchtime. Everyone would be busy downstairs, she thought. Maybe she'd have time to have a nap before they came to fuss over her again.

So much had happened to her over the past few weeks that she'd hardly had time to stop and think. But now, as her body was slowing down, it gave Lily the opportunity to realise how lucky she'd been. Lucky to have been blessed with a long and, for the most of it, healthy life; to have known such a wonderful man, even though the relationship had been far from perfect at times; lucky to have had the café and a good home. Although she and Bernard had never been rich, they had enjoyed a modest standard of living.

And Lily had been fortunate to find two young ladies who had given her so much joy during her last few months. It had been fun opening the coffee shop again, even though it had been hard work. Leaving so soon, however, had not been part of the plan.

Still awake when Will knocked on the door an hour later, Lily beckoned him in.

'Thank you for coming to see me. Did you get in without being accosted?' she asked.

'Well, I don't have a knife in my back.' Will gave her a shy smile. 'I'm not Kate's favourite man, despite my intentions to keep the coffee shop open.'

'So that is your plan, then?'

'Yes.' Will nodded. 'It's a credit to you how quickly you pulled it together.'

'How *we* pulled it together,' Lily corrected. 'If it weren't for Kate and Chloe, I'm not sure it would have been so successful.'

Will nodded. 'Before I knocked the building down, I wanted to see if it could be incorporated. The plans were about to be changed.'

'Why didn't you come clean with Kate?'

'Because she was right.' Will shrugged. 'I did originally come in to scope the building and business. I just hadn't intended falling for her at the same time.'

His words made Lily smile widely.

'The shop means a lot to me, but I know it's all about business and money nowadays. So it's nice to hear that you have a heart. Anyway, sit down, please. I want to talk to you some more.'

Will took off his coat, placed it over the back of the settee and sat down. Lily waited for him to settle before she began.

'I'd like you to sort things out with Kate,' she told him.

Will sat back with a sigh. 'I've tried ringing, texting, emailing. I even called in for coffee once but she's not talking to me. She's professional but nothing else. I missed my chance.'

Lily shook her head. 'Nonsense. She's hurting, that's all. If you give her time, she'll come around.'

'I really did like her,' he admitted. 'A lot actually.'

'Then *wait* for her,' Lily encouraged. 'That's all I ask.'

'I thought Lily might like these.' Serle managed to catch Chloe before they locked up the coffee shop for the night. He held out a small bunch of flowers.

'Thanks.' Chloe took them from him.

'You know, I'm useless at this sort of thing.' He stood with his baseball cap in his hand as he bowed his head. 'I thought –'

Quickly, Chloe gave the flowers back to him before running from the room in tears.

'I'll take them.' Kate came hurrying over.

'I didn't mean to upset anyone,' said Serle, obviously upset that he had.

'She's not coping at the moment,' Kate explained. 'People keep asking how Lily is all the time. If it's not a regular who knows the situation, it's someone who hasn't seen her for a while and is genuinely asking after her welfare.' She looked beyond Serle, to where Christmas cards hung over string arches. 'There are so many greetings of goodwill arriving every day. We've hardly got anywhere left to put them. Her friend, Irene, is coming back from Australia soon but I'm not sure she'll make it in time. Poor Alf sits at his table every afternoon, looking dejected, staring wistfully into space. There are reminders everywhere. We never seem to be able to switch off.'

Serle tipped his head to one side. 'How is she today?'

'She's had a rough night. I went in to her in the early hours, but you know Lily. She told me to go back to sleep. She's still got all her faculties, thank goodness, but she's getting weaker every day. There's a twenty-four-hour shift of nurses coming in from tomorrow morning. That will be a relief. I know I wouldn't be able to cope without them.'

'Will Chloe be okay?'

Kate nodded slightly. 'We'll get each other through it but I'm going to keep an eye on her. She hasn't been to college for a couple of weeks. I think she's finding it hard to concentrate. It's a tough course, even without this kind of distraction.'

Serle took off his beanie hat and placed it on the counter. 'Take it easy, Kate. You don't have to worry for everyone.'

'But I feel like I have to be Mrs Smiley all the time.' Kate's lower lip began to tremble. 'It's hard to be bright and cheerful to customers when all I can think about is Lily.'

'Life goes on. She would understand.'

Yes, Kate thought, and Lily would understand that she was trying to keep busy, even if all she could think about, selfishly at times, was what would happen to her and Chloe.

Alf gently tapped on the living room door before pushing it open. Lily sat in the armchair by the window.

Roughly half a dozen pillows propped her up and a patchwork quilt, made many years ago, covered her legs. Her eyes were now deep and dark hollows, saggy jowls hung down her cheeks. Her skin had turned a sickly shade of grey, her lips a slight tinge of blue. And, much to his dismay, her beautiful hair had hardly a curl.

As he moved quietly towards her, Alf was certain she didn't know he was there and he hadn't the heart to wake her. Looking down at the woman he'd loved for as long as he could remember, he didn't feel sad.

Although he knew she'd been keeping quiet for a long time about the pain she was suffering, he would miss her terribly. She'd been a reliable friend to share problems with. Loved and admired by everyone who had the pleasure of knowing her.

He sat down on the settee but half an hour later, Lily was still sleeping. He thought back to the conversation they'd had just the day before, when he'd taken coffee upstairs with her. 'I want you and Irene to help the girls with my funeral,' she'd told him. 'They're going to be upset when it happens and I'm sure they'd like you to help. I've arranged most of it already and it's all paid for but I'd like you to oversee things.'

Despite his earlier misgivings, Alf was certain that Kate and Chloe were capable of looking after everything. Lily would have nothing to worry about. But he had agreed to help, all the same.

He wiped a tear from his cheek. He was going to miss her so much; more than he could ever disclose to anyone. Quietly, he got up and left the room, closing the door behind him. Lily was a tough old boot. He knew she wouldn't leave without saying goodbye.

Kate had been anxious but pleased when Will rung again to suggest they meet, maybe go for a walk that weekend. Despite him leaving her messages after their argument, she hadn't heard from him in a week, and she hadn't wanted to be the first one to make a move.

After a lot of small talk, they'd arranged a time for Sunday afternoon. Gut feeling and her own eyes told Kate this was the last weekend that Lily would be around. Every hour, Lily seemed to decline before them. Now that the nursing team had arrived and were at her side constantly, Kate felt that she could relax a little, knowing that everything was in hand. It was good to get some fresh air.

Rosie seemed oblivious to the gale force wind and the grey threatening sky as she ran ahead of them in the park. The atmosphere between Kate and Will wasn't icy as such, yet it felt like there was much to be said and neither of them knew how to begin.

'It must be great to be a dog,' said Kate, falling into stride nervously beside Will. 'The only important thing in Rosie's life is time. What time is she having her next feed, what time is she going for a walk?'

'When was the last time she had a pee?' Will joked. 'Can she hold it until her next pit stop?'

They followed the path around the outskirts of the small lake, the wind battling with the branches on the trees. Kate caught her breath as a gust almost knocked her off her feet and she wondered if the reason why there weren't too many people in the park that afternoon had something to do with the atrocious weather.

More likely was the fact that there were less than two weeks to go before Christmas and most people would be shopping. Kate hadn't even begun to think about the holiday season – how could she, with Lily's death hanging over her like the stormy clouds above?

'I wish we could do something to help ease Lily's pain,' she spoke moments later.

'There's nothing you can do,' Will said calmly, 'except be there.'

'But that's what I'm frightened of, Lily dying when I *am* there; that I'm going to go to pieces at the crucial moment.' Her eyes filled with tears. 'I don't know if I'm strong enough.'

'I wish I could find the right words to say, but I can't. All I can talk about is my own experience, my own feelings. Death affects everyone in different ways. No one can predict how they'll react until they lose someone close and, even then, it depends on who that person is and how the relationship has been while they were alive.'

Kate nodded slightly. 'Were you with your mum when she died?'

'Yes, it was tough, but I needed to be there. When she was dying, I thought I wouldn't be able to cope too. Seeing her in so much pain was awful. But the doctor assured us that she was comfortable.'

'Did she look any different?' Kate felt ashamed but she was scared of seeing Lily's dead body. She found it hard to believe that undertakers dressed them in their best clothes and made up their faces.

'Half an hour before she died, they asked Dad and me to leave the room so that they could wash and change her.' Will swallowed. 'When we went back in, Mum was tucked in under clean sheets, wearing fresh nightwear and they'd brushed her hair. I'll never forget that. The fact that she died a few minutes later didn't deter them from making her look nice for us… and for her.

'She died in her sleep,' Will continued after a pause while he gazed across the lake, his eyes glistening now. 'I remember noticing how blue her hands were. I held on to one and my dad held the other. She took a few final breaths and then... nothing.'

Kate touched him lightly on his arm. 'I'm sorry.'

Will sniffed. 'What for? It was one of the best moments in my life, one that I'll never forget. Morbid I know, but it was such a personal time.'

'How's your dad doing?' Kate took Rosie's lead out of her coat pocket as she noticed a black Labrador in the distance.

'He's good,' he told her. 'I don't get to see him too often. But I'm thinking of moving nearer to him again.'

Kate felt a flush of warmth ripple through her body and decided to take Lily's advice.

'Does that mean you'll be around to take me out on the odd occasion, now that you don't have to use me anymore?' she teased, blowing away strands of hair stuck to her lipstick.

'Maybe.' Will treated Kate to that wonderful smile of his. With a huge sigh of relief, he pulled her into his arms and planted a kiss on the tip of her nose.

CHAPTER THIRTY-FOUR

When Kate opened the seventeenth day of Rosie's advent calendar and flicked the square of chocolate to her, it had been over a week since Lily had set foot in the coffee shop, in fact, since she'd been downstairs at all. Every time she saw her fragile figure, Kate had the overwhelming urge to hug her, to squeeze her, but she didn't dare for fear of hurting her. Lily had always been small, but there was hardly anything left of her now.

Kate sat down on the chair they'd put beside Lily's bed. Although the room was hot, she could feel the cold right through to her bones. She hugged herself to get warm, all the time thinking about death, about the time when Lily would say goodbye instead of goodnight.

Lily stirred in her sleep and moved her head slightly. 'Kate?' she whispered. 'Kate, will you look after everything for me?'

Kate moved closer. 'Yes, of course.'

Lily managed to open her eyes a little and slowly brought her hand up to touch Kate's cheek. Kate blinked away more tears. It shocked her to feel the touch – as cold as hers, but for a very different reason.

'I don't want you to worry… when the time comes… for me to leave you…'

Kate wanted to push Lily but was afraid it would do her more harm than good. 'I'll be fine,' she lied, nodding vehemently.

When Lily closed her eyes again, Kate wondered if that would be the last time she'd hear her speak.

She wondered if she'd even last out the day.

But Lily did manage to last out the day, and the following night too, although she hadn't opened her eyes since Lucy had kissed her goodbye just after midnight. Dr Warren, Lily's GP, had said she would, in all probability, go peacefully in her sleep. The oxygen cylinder that she was attached to was helping her to breathe and, no matter how much Kate wanted her to talk, they were to leave her to rest.

Now, just after three a.m., Chloe was asleep, wrapped up in her quilt and lying on Lily's ottoman at the foot of her bed. Even curled up in a ball, her knees overhung. Kate looked towards the door as Tracey, the nurse on the night shift, brought in two mugs of tea.

She sipped at her drink while she thought of how it was just over seven months since she'd arrived at Somerley. Back then, she'd thought she was grown-up at thirty-two, but really she was as immature and vulnerable as that nine-year-old child on the day that her father had walked out. Kate hadn't realised how insecure it had made her. Nick was forever moaning about it during every argument, but she'd thought it was said in the heat of the moment. How could she be insecure? She was married, managed to run a home and pay the bills without falling into masses of debt and she held down a responsible job.

But, now she'd had time to get away from the situation and cope with day to day life on her own, she'd realised how dependent she'd become on Nick, how she'd let him control her. Not in a direct way – he never told her what to wear and she had money if she ever wanted to buy anything – but because she was scared of being without him. The failed relationship with her father had made her understand that she'd never felt safe unless she was with a man of her own.

Although she hadn't realised it at the time and had looked at the move as a chance to get away from Nick, coming to Somerley had been the best thing that she could have done. It had taught her that she *could* live without a man, that she *was* capable of doing so, and that when she did eventually settle down again – maybe even with Will – she would be an equal. Lily had given her the strength to get through any situation; Kate admired what she had done in the face of death when she'd lost her husband, her soul mate.

Kate gently picked up Lily's hand and held it in her own. She wanted her to respond, to say, 'for goodness' sake, child, stop trying to squeeze the life out of me.' But she knew there was no hope of that.

They'd closed the coffee shop today as a mark of respect. Kate couldn't believe they would never share another breakfast meeting downstairs. She'd miss the way Lily always had to have a cup of tea before she'd discuss anything. She'd miss the way their boss was always present, mostly listening, but letting them make their own mistakes, guiding them if they went off course. A professional chairperson, as they all called her. And she was about to leave them.

Tomorrow they would think about the future. For now, Kate's time and thoughts belonged with Lily.

Even though her mind was just about working, Lily couldn't remember when she had last found the strength to open her eyes. Every breath that she took felt like her chest was going to explode and she had some sort of straps across her face, irritating her skin. Her body must be drugged, for she felt no pain – just overwhelming exhaustion.

For one last time, she wanted to look at her girls. Finding Kate and Chloe to help her after Bernard's death had been a godsend and she couldn't believe her time with them was fading fast. She knew they'd cope without her. They thought they weren't strong enough, but she knew better.

She felt someone wipe a cloth across her forehead and relished the dampness on her flushed skin. She was hot, yet cold, frightened, and yet peaceful. It felt surreal; she wanted to die, but she didn't want to leave them yet.

Still, Bernard would be waiting for her.

With all the strength she had left, Lily willed her eyes to work. The light stung as she turned her head but she couldn't lift a hand quick enough to shield them. Instead, she lay until she could see and thanked the Lord that it was night, and that the room was dimly lit by the lamp at her side.

Straight ahead, she could just make out a person wearing a pale blue top and dark trousers. At the bottom of the bed, she saw Chloe, her neck hanging at an awkward angle. Lily would remember her as a porcelain doll – beautiful, fair-skinned, with enchanting eyes.

Another push and she turned her head slightly to catch sight of Kate. Lily would remember her as a fine piece of collectible china – delicate, irreplaceable and precious.

She didn't want to leave them but she knew it wouldn't be long now. And at least her plan had worked.

One lone tear trickled down her face as she mouthed her goodbyes.

It was three hours later when Chloe awoke. She sat up, pulled down her legs and stretched her arms above her head. Lily didn't look as though she'd moved all night. It was strange to think that only the day before she'd squeezed Chloe's hand and managed a weak smile. Now she looked as if there was no energy left inside her. Perhaps there wasn't.

The sound of the doorbell in the distance broke into her thoughts.

Kate woke up with a start. 'What time is it?' she looked across the room.

'Half past six. I think the nurses are doing a switch. Shall we go into the living room until they've finished?'

An hour later, Chloe knocked quietly on Lily's bedroom door. 'Can I come in?' she asked the nurse as she stood on the threshold.

The nurse nodded. 'Yes, you can have a few minutes with her, if you like.'

Chloe gasped as she drew level with Lily. Her colour had paled significantly. Even attached to the oxygen cylinder, her breathing had rapidly deteriorated. She reminded her of an old engine running out of steam.

Fighting her feelings, she took Lily's hand in her own. 'I don't want to go without saying goodbye but I don't want to be here when… when… oh, Lily, I'm going to miss you so much. I want you to know that I've been really happy since I came to Somerley. I love working here. I love Kate and Lucy. And I love you. Why do you have to go so soon? I've only just got to know you. Please don't leave us yet.'

She tried to calm her tears, even though she couldn't help thinking that Lily had already gone. Could Lily hear what she was saying or was there only a body left in the bed? Had her soul gone to Heaven already?

'Say hello to my mum for me,' Chloe whispered, giving Lily's cold hand one last squeeze. 'Tell her that I miss her so much. Tell her that I've been a good girl. Tell her… tell her…'

Chloe broke down again and placed her head on the bed. 'Why did this have to happen now?'

With less than a week to go until Christmas Day, Lily sensed that Bernard was waiting for her. She pawed at the oxygen mask until it came away effortlessly and her eyes opened with ease. He stood at the bottom of the bed, looking every bit as handsome as she remembered in his black suit. Lily couldn't remember him looking so well for a good while.

Without difficulty, she found that she could sit up. She reached out to him and he came to her side.

Sitting on the edge of her bed, he leaned forward to gently touch her face. Lily felt her heart melt. It was so good to see him at last.

Bernard's face broke out into a smile and as he pulled her into his arms, Lily closed her eyes for the very last time.

CHAPTER THIRTY-FIVE

Dear Kate and Chloe,

It doesn't seem right for me to give you individual letters because I care about you equally. When I first met you, I had an idea. A plan, you might say. Call me stupid, if you please. I mean, how many women would want to start again after working hard all their lives? Surely I should have been slowing down? Because you see, I knew I was dying.

I knew I didn't have long to live when Bernard died and I didn't want to die alone. I chose you two because you each seemed to have a little of me in you. Kate, you are strong, yet sensitive. Someone I could rely on at all times. Chloe, well, you filled me with youth and hope that everything would go my way.

There wasn't a day that passed when I didn't think of Bernard and how different things might have been. But then I wouldn't have met you two. You both gave my failing hope such a boost and showered me with love and affection. You helped me through my darkest months. I was alone for a time after his death and I hated it. Every day, I would walk into that desolate cafe and think of better times. I very nearly sold it all. But you made it work for me. Therefore, it gives me great pleasure to hand The Coffee Stop over to you both.

My plan was to find someone to share my last days with. Once I'd found someone that I could trust, who had the interests of my business at heart, I felt that I could die in peace. I didn't want to leave everything I'd worked hard towards to someone who wouldn't care. I also wanted to leave something of myself behind in a new establishment. I know it sounds like a strange idea but my initial proposal was to choose one person from three. Luckily for me, I never found a third person – because I could never have chosen between the two of you.

Kate, I want you to know that I have seen a confident woman appear over the past few months and she is a wonderful person. You accepted a challenge and you have helped to make The Coffee Stop such a huge success. I'm very grateful for your help and support, even through your heartache. True love and happiness will find you again. Maybe even with a certain Mr Taylor?

Chloe, I know you will be hurting. You're bound to be after coping with your mother's death at such an early age, the memories are sure to come flooding back. I only hope it isn't too painful. Forgive me if it is.

Keep up the studying and don't you worry about Jack. He can't be right for you if he can hurt you like that. Life's too short, Chloe. Find yourself a young man and live a little first.

And if it doesn't work out, you always have the luxury of tomorrow.

Now, first things first. Before the funeral, I want you two to concentrate on getting into the Christmas spirit. I know you won't feel like looking forward to the New

Year but it'll help take your mind off things. And don't be afraid to look in the bottom of my wardrobe.

I'm sure you'll find that Santa has come early to the coffee shop.

Just a finishing note to tell you that my solicitor, Mr Stead, will be expecting your call. It will only be an informal meeting, there's nothing for you to worry about.

Take care for now. I will always be close, even though you can't see me. Just pretend I am in the next room, watching over you.

Please don't grieve for me because part of me will always be there with you. We had a special bond, in such a short time. I love you like you were my own daughters.

Thank you for making me happy.

God bless,
Lily

Kate walked the few streets to the park in a daze, praying that she wouldn't bump into anyone she knew.

She'd brought along Rosie for comfort but the dog wanted to play. The park almost deserted, she let her off the lead. It was only three o' clock in the afternoon, but already the dark was starting to obscure her view.

At the entrance to the play area, she pulled her collar close for further protection against the bitter wind and sat down on a swing. She swayed to and fro as she thought of Lily. At eleven thirty-three that morning, she had finally found peace. Chloe had fallen into Kate's arms and they'd cried together for a while.

It would have been wonderful to have known Lily for longer. Things would be strange without her there to watch over them, but Kate knew that no matter what the future held, she and Chloe would stick together.

Their family unit would just be one less.

Would she find true love and happiness with Will, she wondered, smiling through fresh tears as she recalled Lily's written words. Two nights ago, knowing his dad would be out, Will had taken her to his family home. They'd sat on the settee, with the glow of the woodburner their only light. It had felt right to slip onto the carpet and make love with the curtains closed to the world. It had been slow and tender. She'd cried afterwards, for Lily; for their loss, for her pain. As Will had wrapped his arms around her, she'd realised that they might have something special – no one can profess to know what the future holds, but Kate knew once she'd felt something similar with Nick and hadn't appreciated it. This time she wouldn't make the same mistakes.

Dragging her foot in the sand as she swayed in the wind, she looked up towards the darkening sky. Kate had trouble believing in the afterlife, but if there was such a thing she knew they'd be together. Bernard would be with Lily now.

It was meant to be.

Chloe sat huddled in Lily's favourite armchair, the letter in her lap. Lily was right about what she'd written. Memories of her mum had come flooding back, but those weren't crowding her mind right now.

Chloe was overwhelmed by the loss of Lily.

She didn't have to think hard to understand why she had loved her so much. The things that she'd done for her were vast and varied. She'd listened to her endless wittering on about anything and everything, teased her about Kate being more popular with the men after the diva had passed on *her* tricks of the trade, watched *Buffy the Vampire Slayer* without complaining.

She remembered how a cup of tea would go further than an apology, how Lily would always stick up for Kate when she was in the right and try to show her things from a different perspective. Chloe knew she was right about Jack too. In the back of her mind, she'd always known that there was too much of an age gap between them, but she'd just wanted to be with an older man. It had been a tough lesson to learn but she was getting over the humiliation now. She was going to slow down and grow old in her own time – Kate said she'd be knocking *off* years to make herself feel better soon.

But the main thing that Chloe had become conscious of was that, sometime during the past few months, she had grown up. Her childish tantrums and bitchy comments had slowly disappeared. She'd learned to accept Maddy's relationship with her dad. She'd made Lucy's life hell for a while, until she'd realised she'd got her completely wrong, and she'd found a special friendship, an everlasting union of sisterly strength with Kate.

And, all at once, she realised that she wouldn't have done any of that without Lily giving her the opportunity to work at the coffee shop.

Chloe blew her nose loudly. It was going to be so tough without Lily.

CHAPTER THIRTY-SIX

As 'Do They Know It's Christmas' played in the background of the coffee shop, Kate held onto her head with a grimace.

'I can't believe we drank so much last night,' she said quietly.

Chloe winced as the sudden movement of her head caused a pain to shoot through it. 'I can't believe I have a hangover. I'm eighteen – this isn't supposed to happen.'

Yesterday, after a morning of phone calls to everyone who needed to be informed of Lily's death, Kate and Chloe spent a reflective afternoon together. Lucy came around at five thirty and Will arrived at seven.

Between them, they drank lots. Some of them cried, all of them laughed. Lucy finally left at eleven thirty and Kate slept with Will's body snuggled around hers. He'd left earlier that morning, promising to return as soon as possible.

'It was good therapy, though.' Kate clunked the Alka-Seltzer into a glass of water and watched it fizz.

Quickly, she knocked it back, banged down the glass and shuddered.

'I still can't take it in that the coffee shop is ours.'

'I've often wondered what the advert meant when it read "excellent prospects for the right people." What prospects are there, working in a small coffee shop?' said Kate. 'There's hardly a lot of scope for promotion. It was her *plan* that she was referring to.'

'But she doesn't really know us that well. What about leaving everything to Irene? Or Alf, even?'

'Lily wanted her legacy, for want of a better word, to go on, I suppose. I think I admire her for that, too. We know it wasn't easy for her.'

Chloe smiled. 'She really did love us like we were her own daughters, didn't she?'

'She did. And it means that we don't have to go our separate ways. I wouldn't have liked that.'

'Me neither,' came back Chloe's immediate answer.

Kate stood up with a sigh. 'I need another coffee.'

Chloe stared out onto Church Square, the square that had just become her permanent home. Only now was it beginning to sink in that she was going to be a partner in a very successful coffee shop. Before her very eyes, she could see another shop, and another. When Kate joined her with fresh drinks, she had moved onto franchises and there were at least fifty shops all over England.

'Do you fancy coming home with me for Christmas, Kate?' she asked. 'You'd be more than welcome. I know it'll be hard for you to keep up, but you can have a sleep in the afternoons before we go out on the razz.'

Kate raised her eyebrows in mock horror before grinning. 'It's good of you to ask, but I think I might fancy my chances with a certain man I'm fond of.'

Chloe nodded. She really wanted to share the holiday with Kate, especially after she'd lost Lily, but who was she to spoil her happiness? Kate really deserved it. And she was looking forward to spending some time with her own family. This would be the first Christmas that she and Maddy would feel better about.

'Don't suppose I mind so much, then,' she replied as the music changed to Wham's 'Last Christmas'.

'At least one of us needs to let the New Year in with a bang.' She picked up her drink and raised her cup in a toast. 'Here's to you, Lily Mortimer. I know you're listening, because you're only in the kitchen.'

Kate smiled. 'When she says she's in the next room, it doesn't mean the kitchen.'

'It's the next room at the moment.'

'You're absolutely right!' Kate too picked up her mug and raised it in the air. 'Here's to Lily... and to us.

'And here's to The Coffee Stop.'

A LETTER FROM THE AUTHOR

Ever since I can remember, I've been a meddler of words. Born and raised in Stoke-on-Trent, Staffordshire, I used the city as a backdrop for my first novel, TAUNTING THE DEAD, and it went on to be a Kindle #1 bestseller. I couldn't believe my eyes when it became the overall number 8 UK Kindle bestselling books of 2012.

Since then, my writing has come under a few different headings - grit-lit, sexy crime, whydunnit, police procedural, emotional thriller to name a few. I like writing about fear and emotion – the cause and effect of crime – what makes a character do something. Working as a housing officer for eight years gave me the background to create a fictional estate full of good and bad characters.

But I'm a romantic at heart and have always wanted to write about characters that are not necessarily involved in the darker side of life. Coffee, cakes and friends are three of my favourite things, hence writing under the name of Marcie Steele too. I can often be found sitting in my favourite coffee shop, sipping a cappuccino and eating a chocolate chip cookie, either catching up with friends or writing on my laptop.

If you'd like to be kept up to date with news of my latest releases, you can sign up to my email list at this link:

www.bookouture.com/marcie-steele

Mel Sherratt (Marcie) x
Keep in touch!

www.facebook.com/MarcieSteeleauthor
www.twitter.com/marcie_steele

MARCIE STEELE BOOKS

Stirred With Love

That's What Friends are For

MEL SHERRATT BOOKS

Somewhere to Hide

Behind a Closed Door

Fighting for Survival

Written in the Scars

Taunting the Dead

Follow the Leader

Only the Brave

Watching over You

Lightning Source UK Ltd.
Milton Keynes UK
UKOW05f0805080117
291602UK00017B/392/P